THE PARADISE GARDEN

Also available from Headline Liaison

The Journal by James Allen
Sleepless Nights by Tom Crewe & Amber Wells

The Paradise Garden

Aurelia Clifford

HEADLINE
Liaison

Copyright © 1995 Aurelia Clifford

The right of Aurelia Clifford to be identified as the Author of
the Work has been asserted by her in accordance with
the Copyright, Designs and Patents Act 1988.

First published in 1995
by HEADLINE BOOK PUBLISHING

A HEADLINE LIAISON paperback

10 9 8 7 6 5 4 3 2

All rights reserved. No part of this publication may be
reproduced, stored in a retrieval system, or transmitted,
in any form or by any means without the prior written
permission of the publisher, nor be otherwise circulated
in any form of binding or cover other than that in which
it is published and without a similar condition being
imposed on the subsequent purchaser.

ISBN 0 7472 5069 3

Typeset by Avon Dataset Ltd., Bidford-on-Avon, B50 4JH

Printed and bound in Great Britain by
Cox & Wyman Ltd, Reading, Berks

HEADLINE BOOK PUBLISHING
A division of Hodder Headline PLC
338 Euston Road,
London NW1 3BH

The Paradise Garden

Prologue

The Morgan two-seater was weaving slightly as it rounded the last of the hairpin bends and emerged onto the high moors. Dave Bracewell knew he wasn't drunk – he hadn't touched a drop – but it was hard to concentrate on the road with Stacey's fingers resting on his thigh.

He could feel her heat soaking into him through his trouser-leg, and his pulse was racing so hard and so fast that he was sure she must be able to hear the sloosh and thump of blood pumping through his overheated body.

It was still early spring here on the moors, hardly what you'd call tropical, but it could have been forty below and neither of them would have noticed. Dave loosened his tie but the lump in his throat wouldn't go away.

He glanced across at Stacey, her long brown hair streaming out behind her in the slipstream. Her full lips smiled at him, candy-pink with lip gloss, and her fingers tightened about the taut muscles of his thigh. He almost groaned out loud with frustration as her fingertips crept just a fraction closer to the throbbing heaviness of his manhood.

'Having a good birthday?' She had to raise her voice to be heard above the roar of the engine, but it still had a soft, sweet quality, almost a purr.

'All the better for being with you,' he said, grinning and changing up into fourth, letting the car have its head, speeding along the moorland road between banks of heather and bracken.

'I've got a present for you.' Her fingers edged a little higher up his thigh. 'Do you want to know what it is?'

He knew what it was. They both did. This was their third time out together and neither of them were in this for the conversation. Sooner or later they were going to have sex – the hot, wet, ferocious sex they had been working up to for weeks. During lunch Stacey had dropped every hint in the book that today she was going to give him something really special. She'd made that much pretty obvious. The hunger radiating out of her was almost frightening. Dave moistened his dry lips with the tip of his tongue.

'You bet I do.' His left hand strayed from the steering wheel and stroked her knee, left bare by the bum-hugging skirt she had worn specially to show off her long, slim legs.

'If you stop the car I'll show you.' Slowly and deliberately, Stacey unbuttoned her jacket. Trying hard to keep one eye on the road, Dave watched her in the rear-view mirror, his mouth dry and his senses reeling.

Underneath the jacket she wore no bra – in fact she was completely naked. Her breasts were small and juicy. As the cold air hit the flesh of her large, flat nipples, the pink aureoles tensed and hardened, puckering into long and succulent teats which simply begged to be sucked and bitten. It was more than a man could stand.

'Oh my God, Stacey . . .' He swerved momentarily, profoundly thankful that there was no traffic coming in the other direction. 'Any more tricks like that and you'll have us off the road.'

Untroubled, Stacey pushed her hair back, lounging back

in her seat so that her jacket fell open and her breasts pointed heavenward, the crisp March air playing on them with its lewd fingertips. She liked Dave, liked hearing him talk about his favourite games, his secret fantasies. He was nothing like her husband, James, who seemed almost to have forgotten her existence. Long before he'd asked her, she'd made up her mind to have an affair with Dave. A red-hot, passionate, wicked affair in which nothing would be forbidden.

It was common knowledge that sexual relationships between teachers at the exclusive Whitby Academy were sternly discouraged – particularly when one of the teachers was married to the Headmaster's son. But Stacey didn't care. She wanted Dave and she was going to have him.

'Don't you like my breasts?' she pouted in mock disappointment.

'Like them!'

Dave gave up trying to drive and brought the car to a halt in a convenient layby, the engine turning over like a growling tiger, hungry for prey. He looked down at his hands and saw that they were trembling. How did Stacey manage to do this to him?

With her long hair and small breasts, she was so petite and innocent-looking, you'd never think she was a teacher. Dressed like that, she looked more like one of his sixteen-year-old pupils. The thought made his cock rear in his pants and he remembered the fantasy he'd once told Stacey about. The fantasy in which she was a naughty schoolgirl in his class . . .

'Why don't you touch them then?' Stacey ran her hands over her breasts, rubbing her nipples with her open palms in slow, circular movements. She adored the sense of power it gave her, knowing that Dave Bracewell was getting a hard-on just watching. In her fantasy, she could almost believe that he really was her teacher and she was seducing him. 'They're getting cold.'

'Don't you think you should cover up? Someone might see.' It was broad daylight and even up here, on the moorland road, someone might well drive past and catch them in the act. And with what he had in mind, he definitely didn't want to be spotted.

'I want you to touch me,' she insisted, taking hold of Dave's hands and placing them on her breasts. Instinctively his fingers closed about the small, firm globes, weighing and caressing them, feeling her warmth beneath the wind-chilled skin. She giggled. 'I want you to do more than that . . .'

'I want you too,' he assured her. 'Believe me, Stacey, you don't know how much.' His mind was working quickly. He wanted her just as much as she wanted him but, on the other hand, he didn't feel inclined to get them both arrested for indecency. 'But I don't think this is the right place, do you? I mean, the car's only a two-seater, there really isn't room.'

'Where then?' Stacey thought it best not to mention that she'd had sex in a lot less room than this. She smiled at him, a smile that was at once innocent and knowing. Her soft brown eyes were looking right into his. 'Where then, *sir*?'

He felt a shiver of excitement run right through him. Oh, how it turned him on to see her playing the naughty schoolgirl in that short, short skirt . . .

He ran the possibilities through his mind. They could go

to one of the local hotels – no, that was much too risky, they'd be sure to be recognised. And his rooms at the Academy were out of the question. He glanced at the road map and something clicked in his head. Of course! Why hadn't he thought of it before?

'I know where.' His face broke into a smile as he remembered the place was only a ten-minute drive away. He put the car into gear.

'Where?' Reluctantly Stacey did up the bottom two buttons of her jacket as the Morgan accelerated back onto the highway.

'It's this place called Highmoor House. It's been empty for ages.' He omitted to mention that he'd once taken one of Stacey's predecessors there and they'd had fantastic sex in the grounds. Mind you, it had been summer then and the place hadn't been empty quite so long. It was probably like a jungle by now. 'Just leave everything to me.'

Stacey lay back on the Morgan's all-leather upholstery and let her mini-skirt ride up a little higher on her thigh. She was wearing black hold-up stockings, ones with lacy tops and seams up the back – she'd chosen them specially with Dave in mind and, to judge from the expression on his face, he wholeheartedly approved.

A biker appeared over the horizon and rode level with them for a second or two before overtaking and roaring off into the distance. Stacey hoped he'd enjoyed the quick flash of breasts and thigh she'd treated him to as he passed by. There was such sensual desire inside her today, she wanted to share it with everybody. She wanted to screw the whole, wide world.

Passing through the village of Highmoor, they turned onto

a bumpy track and followed the line of a curving, crumbling wall, dripping with ivy and moss. Somewhere in the far distance, almost entirely hidden by overgrown trees, loomed the dark shape of a house.

'That it?'

Dave nodded, let go of the wheel for a moment and gave Stacey's thigh a really good squeeze. There were three deliciously bare inches of creamy-white flesh between stocking-top and groin and he longed to run his tongue all over them, inching his way with desperate slowness towards the gusset of Stacey's panties.

'You're sure you want to . . . ?'

She pulled his face down and crushed her soft mouth against his, pushing her tongue between his lips. She tasted sweet and spicy, like cinnamon.

'Of course I'm sure.'

Dave turned off the ignition and opened the car door.

'We'll leave the car here then.'

Stacey got out and wriggled her skirt down over her thighs. Each movement made her pert breasts wobble inside her half-open jacket, driving Dave crazy – as she knew it would.

Highmoor House stood behind a screen of tangled oak and beech, its once-splendid Elizabethan architecture sadly neglected and its grounds so riotously overgrown that it was hard to tell where they stopped and the scrubby moorland began.

'Can we get into the house?'

'We don't need to. I know a place.'

He set off and she followed him, her high heels sinking a little way into the soft ground as he pushed his way through tangles of bramble and bracken.

'Dave . . . !' she protested, ensnaring her skirt on a spike of dog-rose.

He turned round with a wink and a grin.

'This is it.'

'What is?'

'This bit of wall here. We can get into the grounds this way.'

'What? You want me to *climb over a wall*? In this skirt?' Stacey didn't know whether to be angry or amused at Dave's audacity. 'You have to be out of your mind, David Bracewell!'

'Come here, that's right . . . put your foot there . . .' He put his hands on Stacey's hips and hoisted her up with his arrogantly strong arms. She scrabbled for a handhold on the rough stone wall and suddenly found herself sitting on the top. Dave clambered up beside her, jumped down onto the other side and lifted her down into a dense tangle of vegetation.

'Bit of a shambles,' commented Stacey disparagingly, stepping gingerly over brambles so as to avoid laddering her stockings. This wasn't quite what she'd expected but, then again, it was an adventure and Stacey McGovern liked adventures.

'Don't worry, trust me, it'll be great. Here, let me give you a hand.' Dave stretched out his hand and smoothed it over the firm dome of Stacey's rump. My, but he wanted her. Wanted her so much that the marble-hard shaft of his prick was straining painfully against the inside of his trousers.

Pushing through a jumble of interlacing branches, they

stumbled through overgrown pathways until at last they reached a small stone building, beside a crumbling wall of reddish brick. Bracewell heaved a sigh of relief. It was still here and if it was open to the elements on one side at least it still had its roof. It was cosy and dry. It was just what they needed.

Stacey stood and surveyed it, her head on one side.

'What is it?'

'It's . . . oh, I don't know. A sort of summerhouse.' Dave's hand explored the generous curve of Stacey's backside. He could feel her quivering at his touch, smell the tang of sweat mingling with her heavy, musky perfume.

'It's quite pretty I suppose,' she conceded, looking at the ornate tracery of the stonework, half-hidden by the encroaching ivy and columbine.

'They say lovers used to meet here once,' said Dave, taking Stacey by the waist and pulling her towards him. 'Hundreds of years ago.' She gasped at the joyous arrogance of his swollen dick, hard and throbbing against her belly as he embraced her, darting kisses on her face and neck and bare throat. 'They came here if they wanted to be sure nobody would see them.'

His hands roamed over her body, exploring it as he had never quite dared before. On their previous assignations there had always been other people around, people who might see and report back to other people who might not understand.

Stacey responded to him with a passion stronger than either of them had anticipated. This secret, forgotten place seemed to embody a sensuality all its own, a secret excitement which worked its way into your body and filled your mind with the wickedest, the most arousing thoughts.

'I promised I'd give you a special present for your birthday,' she whispered. 'I hope you like it, *sir*.'

She took her hands from Bracewell's waist for a moment, and unbuttoned her jacket, this time sliding it down over her arms and letting it fall with a light swish onto the stone floor of the summerhouse. Her lover's hands trembled as they touched the ivory-white perfection of her bare shoulders and back, the creamy, pink-tipped globes which quivered at his caresses.

Bracewell gave a little gasp of pleasure and surprise as he felt Stacey's fingers unbuttoning his shirt, peeling it open and exploring the bare skin beneath.

'You're a bad girl, Stacey McGovern,' he murmured as her fingers explored his belt buckle, his trouser buttons, his zipper. 'I shall probably have to teach you a lesson.'

'Oh yes, sir. I'm a very bad girl,' purred Stacey, her nipples iron-hard with desire as she stripped this new and exciting lover. She adored seeing her lovers naked for the first time, experiencing the unique excitement as each inch of bare flesh came into view, exploring it with fingers and tongue.

'Oh, Stacey. Have you any idea how much I've wanted you? I wondered if we would ever . . .'

Stacey smiled and kissed his throat as her fingers caressed him.

'But I always knew we would.'

Stacey's hand slipped inside his trousers and the feeling was so ecstatically good that he was half-afraid he might come in her hand. And that would be the end of the world because Dave wanted to come in so many other places – in the warm cavern of Stacey's mouth, in her tight wet haven or spurting his desire across the firm, juicy hillocks of her breasts.

'Oh Stacey, you'd better not. I might . . .'

'Don't you like it? Don't I turn you on?'

Anticipating Dave's answer, she tightened her grip about his shaft and began manipulating him, very gently, very slowly. She knew exactly what she was doing, driving him to the point of madness but always reining in his exuberant desire a fraction of a second before the point of no return.

'You're a witch.'

His frenzied fingers tore at the button on her skirt, at last succeeded in unfastening it, then he slid down the zipper with a quiet hiss. It was the only sound to break the silence, save the song of a solitary chaffinch and the soft harmony of their breathing.

Stacey's skirt fell to the ground and, without even looking down, she stepped out of it. Dave's eyes devoured her, taking in the flat white belly, the slender thighs, the tiny triangle of black lace which covered her pubis, the material so thin and diaphanous that he could clearly make out the swollen labia beneath.

She was shaven. A shiver of delight made him close his eyes for a moment, the excitement almost too much to bear. This wonderful, shameless hussy had shaved herself for him. She must have guessed how much it turned him on to glimpse the rose-pink frill of a woman's inner sex pouting through the outer labia like an insolent tongue.

Stacey sat down on the stone bench which ran along the inside of the summerhouse. Strangely enough, although outside the air held a wintry chill, here in the summerhouse

PARADISE GARDEN

it was balmy and warm. As if to confirm this false spring there were tiny, jewel-bright flowers blossoming on the tendrils of foliage which had pushed their way up through the walls and floor of the old stone building, reclaiming it for nature.

Even the stone bench felt warm beneath her bare thighs and buttocks. She smiled at Bracewell, parting her thighs provocatively so that the triangle of lace was pulled taut across her sex.

'Oh, Stacey...' whispered Dave hoarsely. His mind was spinning, the only coherent thought left to him the drive to possess this gloriously insolent nymphet, this girl-woman whose so-innocent obscenity was driving him to distraction. His cock felt huge, immensely swollen, hard as an iron bar in Stacey's knowing hand. Instinctively he answered her gentle caresses with thrusts of his pelvis, unable to resist the urge to bring himself off and spurt all over her bare belly.

But Stacey too had desires, desires far stronger than the vague sexual itch which had first made her want to seduce Dave Bracewell. Then, it had seemed just one more challenge, to bed the handsome, dark-haired maths master she had lusted after ever since he had come to the Academy. But now she was here with him, practically naked, in this hidden and profoundly sensual place, she felt astonishingly different. The drive inside her was as hot as a raging furnace, as insistent as the need to breathe. Would this hunger inside her belly ever be stilled?

As Dave watched, she released his prick from her encircling caress and began toying with her own body, the fingers of her left hand pinching and kneading her nipple

Aurelia Clifford

whilst with her right hand she massaged herself through the gossamer-thin lace which veiled her sex so imperfectly, so arousingly.

Dave could see everything, *everything* as she rubbed herself. As her fingers moved away from her clit he saw how hard and distended it was, like a tiny penis sliding in and out of its pink sheath. He marvelled at the moisture dripping out of her, soaking the gusset of her panties, a testament to her excitement. Her breathing was low and shallow and rapid, her lips curving into a smile of triumph as she brought herself closer and closer to orgasm.

'Watch me,' she whispered.

'Let me . . . let me take you,' pleaded Bracewell. 'I need you, Stacey, I need you so much.'

'Watch me. Look, *sir*, I'm touching myself. Do you like to touch yourself?' Her smile was both wicked and angelic, the smile of an innocent schoolgirl who knows instinctively what to do.

'Oh, Stacey, please don't do this. You're driving me crazy.'

'I'm masturbating, sir. That's the proper word for it, isn't it? Do boys masturbate?' She rubbed a little harder. 'Yes, of course they do, don't they, sir? I watched them in the changing-rooms once, rubbing and sucking each other's stiff pricks until they spurted all this lovely creamy-white stuff. I wonder what it tastes like . . .'

It was Stacey who began gasping now, hardly able to continue playing the game as the desperate pleasure within her mounted and Dave could do nothing but watch her, as helpless as a teenage virgin in a peepshow.

'Do you like to masturbate, sir? You can do it now if you like. Or would you like me to suck your dick?'

Oh God, thought Dave, his cock aching for release. *You know damn well, Stacey McGovern. You know damn well how mad I am to have those candy-pink lips around the tip of my dick...*

'Oh, oh, oh!'

Stacey's eyes widened and suddenly there was wetness everywhere on her fingers, soaking her gusset, forming a damp smear on the grey stone beneath her as her body tensed and twitched and her pussy poured forth its well-spring of honey-sweet juice.

He seized hold of her and wrenched down her panties, the wet fabric giving off the most erotic scent, the irresistible perfume of an adolescent girl's sexuality. He knew he had to taste that sexuality.

Bending between her open thighs, he pressed his face close to the soft wetness of her sex. The nectar of her orgasm was still oozing out from between the swollen outer labia and the inner lips were coral-pink with pleasure.

Stacey threw her head back as he kissed her, his greedy tongue darting like a serpent's into the inner sanctum of her haven. She was tight, she knew she was, as tight as any virgin despite all the men she had seduced, and the feeling of her lover's tongue entering her was every bit as pleasurable as having some young stud's dick inside her.

No, better – better by far; for whilst Dave's tongue was scything in and out of her, his fingers were toying with the delicate flesh of her sex, teasing her inner labia, running the very tips of fingernails lightly over and over the secret folds, tormenting her to screaming point by almost – but never quite – touching the hypersensitive head of her swollen clitoris.

'Please, please!' Now it was her turn to beg. She so wanted him to lick and stroke her to another orgasm.

But her lover wanted to make their pleasure last, to make it go on and on and never stop. And here, in this secret place, it felt as though that dream might almost come true.

'Now. Please, now. Oh sir, don't be cruel to me. Lick my clit, please lick my clit . . .'

Even the terrible torment of frustration felt wonderful. Stacey had never enjoyed sex as much as this before; she was more accustomed to the hard thrust, the brutal pleasure of a swiftly stolen orgasm. This was purest torture, but the sort of torture that felt so good you wanted it to go on and on forever. Her hands slid up to her breasts and she began rubbing and pinching her nipples. Almost immediately, she felt a warm ooze welling up out of her eager womanhood.

There would be time for the rest later, time for anything and everything they desired. Time to have his dick thrusting into her mouth, filling her warm, wet womanhood, pressing tightly between her breasts. Yes, time for everything . . .

As Stacey lay back on the stone bench, thighs parted wide to admit her lover's eager tongue, she half noticed a leafy tendril curling prettily about her wrist, the petals of its blossoms a deep magenta against the pink-white flush of her skin.

Strange how she had not noticed it before. It seemed to wind itself about her, its touch like a soft and sensual kiss. Strange how the air felt so warm, so deliciously welcoming in the old summerhouse.

It was almost as if it didn't want them to leave.

Christopher Maudsley pushed open the door and stepped

into the public bar of the Black Lion, grateful for its warm, cosy fug after the chill of the evening.

The landlord looked up from washing glasses and gave him a nod of recognition.

'Nah then, Chris.'

'Whisky please, Jed. Make that a double, it's bloody perishing out there.'

The landlord filled a glass from the optic and slid it across the polished bar-counter.

'Been out on a bit of business, then?'

Maudsley nodded, rummaging in his pocket for change.

'I've been up to the old house.'

An old man sitting at the other end of the bar looked up in surprise.

'Highmoor House? You've not been up there then, 'ave you?'

'Had to, George. The owners are putting it on the market.'

'What – again?' The landlord went back to polishing glasses.

'They want our firm to handle the sale this time,' explained Maudsley, ignoring the barman's quizzical look. 'So I had to drive over there, nail up a few boards, go through the inventory.'

'Rather you than me,' observed the regular.

'Well, who'd have thought it?' observed the landlord, holding up a pint glass and peering at it as though it might offer him the answer to all the riddles of the universe. 'Five years empty, an' the last people hardly stayed there five minutes. It's turning into an eyesore, is that place. You'd think they'd just give up an' knock it down.'

'Best thing for it,' agreed George. 'You seen the paper?'

he added, shoving across a copy of the *Yorkshire Evening Press*. 'I see them two teachers from Whitby Academy's still missing.'

'Probably run off for a dirty weekend,' suggested Maudsley. 'They'll be in for a pasting when they do turn up, mind.'

'*If* they turn up,' commented George with a certain macabre satisfaction. He folded up the paper and thrust it into his overcoat pocket. 'If you ask me, there's something mighty peculiar going on – that's ten people disappeared in thirty-five years. An' then there's all them stories . . .'

'He's off again,' sighed the landlord. 'Here, George, get this pint down you an' shut up. It's no wonder the tourists don't come here any more. Chris, he fair puts 'em off talkin' like that.'

George accepted his free pint and took a sip.

'Well, I don't care what you say,' he retorted. 'There's somethin' not right round here, an' anyone who buys Highmoor House wants their 'ead examining.'

Chapter 1

'Melissa?'

Melissa Montagu looked up from her computer terminal to see her boss, Dan Greenway, standing in the doorway to his office.

'What is it, Dan?'

'That was the Sales and Marketing Director on the phone. The Lord High Executioner himself. He wants you up in his office right away.'

Puzzled, but relieved to get a break from entering columns of sales figures into her computer, Melissa logged off and stood up, stretching to release the tightness from her aching shoulders. She picked up her jacket and slipped it on.

'I wonder what he wants now.'

Greenway laughed.

'You know darn well what he wants, Melissa. You've won Rep of the Month two months in succession – what's the betting you're about to make it a hat-trick? He's probably grooming you for higher things.'

'Don't talk rubbish, Dan!' She giggled in embarrassment. 'Chance would be a fine thing.'

Melissa made her way to the lift. At twenty-eight, she had most of the things she'd always said she wanted – a fast-track career, a sexy partner, a half-decent lifestyle and plenty of friends. She wasn't bad-looking either, she knew that. Squash and running had given her an enviably well-toned body and with her deep-blue eyes, full breasts and abundant, corn-blonde hair, she could have hooked just about any man she'd wanted at Jupiter Products – *if* she'd wanted. But she already had the man she wanted. She had Rhys.

So why did she feel so restless? What could she possibly want that she didn't already have? What challenges could you set yourself when you'd achieved all you'd planned to achieve?

Well, maybe there was one thing she hankered after. There was the Regional Sales Manager's job, which was shortly to fall vacant. She could do that job with her eyes closed, she knew she could. But would she be given the chance?

As the lift slid slowly up to the sixteenth floor, she wondered what the Sales and Marketing Director wanted to see her about this time. Over the last few weeks he'd called her to his office on several occasions – sometimes, it seemed, for little more than an inconsequential chat. Maybe, just maybe, Dan was right and he wanted to talk to her about the vacancy. Her heart beat a little faster.

Before getting out of the lift she smoothed down her skirt and checked her hair in the mirror. It certainly wouldn't do to turn up looking dishevelled, bad morning or not. Peter Galliano's office was at the end of the corridor, in a long line of directors' suites. If you made it up to the sixteenth floor, you knew you really had made it. Melissa wondered if she would ever manage to get an office up here – and if that was what she really wanted anyway . . .

She knocked on the door and walked in. In the outer office Galliano's PA was busy printing out a report. Ice-cool Candice Soulbury never looked anything less than immaculate. She switched on one of her professional smiles as Melissa entered the office.

'Ah, Ms Montagu. Mr Galliano is waiting for you, I'll just show you in.'

She sashayed across to the door leading to the Sales Director's private office, knocked and – without waiting for a response – opened it.

'Ms Montagu to see you, Mr Galliano.'

'Thank you, Candice. Do come in, Melissa.'

The PA left and Melissa heard the heavy wooden door click shut behind her. Peter Galliano was standing by the picture window, his back towards her, gazing out over London.

'You . . . you wanted to see me, Mr Galliano?'

He half turned and smiled. He was a tremendously good-looking man, thought Melissa, with his light-olive skin and wavy blue-black hair. And those grey eyes seemed to see right into your heart, unlocking your deepest and darkest secrets. To her surprise, she felt herself shiver pleasurably at his smile.

'Please, Melissa, you must call me Peter. I insist.' He turned back towards the window. 'Come over here and look at this, Melissa.'

Puzzled, she walked across to where Galliano was standing. The warm, musky aroma of his aftershave was as soft and sweet as a caress, as intoxicating as a fine wine.

'Isn't it magnificent, Melissa?'

Following Galliano's gaze, she looked down over London, the City stretched out below them and the fat, silvery-brown snake of the Thames slithering between tall buildings on its way to the sea.

'Yes, Mr Galli . . . Peter.'

She froze in astonishment as he took hold of her hand and raised it to his lips, planting the briefest of kisses upon it – so brief that it was all over and he had let go of her hand before she had even had a chance to protest. Had it really happened or was her mind playing tricks on her?

'You are aware, of course, that Jupiter Products is only part of a much larger, multinational corporation.' Without waiting for her reply he continued talking. 'In fact, Jupiter Holdings International owns almost one third of the land and buildings in the City of London.' His grey eyes gleamed with satisfaction.

'That's . . . remarkable,' observed Melissa, unsure where all this was leading.

'Indeed. And each sale you close, Melissa, brings us nearer to owning the whole of the City. Think of that! A single corporation controlling one of the world's greatest financial centres.' He turned away from the window and Melissa found herself looking directly into his eyes. 'I have been much impressed by your recent achievements, Melissa.'

'Thank you.'

'Very pleased indeed. Sales Associate of the Month twice in succession and you are almost certain to win the annual award. You have a great future ahead of you, Melissa. In fact, you might well aspire to becoming Regional Sales Manager at Jupiter Products, if . . .'

'If what?'

'Please sit down, Melissa. May I pour you a drink?'

She glanced at her watch.

'Well, that's very kind, but it's rather early. I don't generally . . .'

PARADISE GARDEN

'But you'll share a drink with me, won't you, Melissa? You'll break the rules just this once?'

'I . . . yes, thank you, I'll have a cognac. Just a very small one though.'

Galliano poured a generous measure into a glass and handed it to her, then sat down – not in his favourite armchair but beside her on the long, black leather sofa which filled one side of his office. He was only inches away from her now and Melissa almost imagined that she could feel a pulsating heat emanating from him, threatening to burn her up. Part of her was telling her to get up and move somewhere else but the rest of her wanted to move closer . . .

'The thing is, Melissa.' Galliano took a small sip of his drink then placed it carefully on the glass-topped table. 'Success isn't just about talent, it's about attitude. If you want to get on in this company, you really must learn to relax more, understand that business moves along so much more smoothly when we know how to give and take.'

Melissa returned his gaze, half suspicious, half excited. More excited than she wanted to admit, even to herself. There was something in Galliano's pale grey eyes, something so deeply and irresistibly sexual, that she found herself smiling back at him, even crossing her legs so that her long, dark wrapover skirt fell open in soft folds, baring her leg to the thigh.

'Really?' She heard herself saying. 'I'm not quite sure I understand. Perhaps you could explain.'

Galliano's arm snaked around the back of her shoulders and she felt his hand on her hair, smoothing and stroking it as though she were some exotic pet.

'I want to see you get on, Melissa, really I do. No-one is

more interested in your success than I am.' Galliano paused. 'I could get you that Regional Sales Manager's job, you know. I'm on the up in Jupiter International – I have great influence in this company. But you have to help me to help you. You have to help me get to know you better, do you understand?' His fingers teased the sensitive skin at the nape of her neck, brushing lightly over the tiny blonde hairs, making her shiver with guilty pleasure.

She shouldn't be doing this, shouldn't be sitting here next to Galliano, letting him caress her, listening to him telling her how he could help her get on if only she was nicer to him. For God's sake, there were laws about this sort of thing! She really didn't have to take any of this ... but oh, how good it felt to have his caresses on her skin.

What was happening to her? Melissa felt so turned on, so hungry for Galliano's touch that she scarcely recognised herself. Lately, she and Rhys had been working such long hours that they had hardly seen each other, let alone had time for anything other than the briefest of sexual encounters. Maybe that was the problem. Maybe she'd been too long starved of the tender sensuality her body craved and it was rebelling against her reason, leading her into a dangerous game from which even now it might be too late to escape.

She forced herself to turn her head and look into Galliano's eyes again.

'No,' she heard herself say. 'I don't understand. Could you explain a little more clearly?'

'I can do better than that,' Galliano replied. 'I can show you.'

His embrace was so sudden, so savage that she made no move to resist him. His lips crushed themselves against hers, his hands shaking as they moved over the front of her blouse, sliding up underneath the silky white fabric to explore the full mounds of her breasts, tempting as ripe fruit within the lacy underwired cups.

In her heart of hearts, in the sensual depths of her soul, she had been yearning for him to kiss her, to touch her, to make her body sing with desire. She wanted this, oh, how she wanted it! His kiss possessed her and she answered it with real passion, hardly able to catch her breath for the raging hunger within her. And she wanted *him*, too, understanding for the first time how much she had hidden and suppressed her hunger for this infinitely desirable man over the long weeks when she had been without her lover.

As he knelt over her, Galliano's skilful fingers slipped underneath her and unfastened the catch of her bra. It felt like the most wonderful liberation in the whole world as her breasts tumbled free, heavy and succulent. Unfastening her blouse, he bent to kiss her nipples, his tongue and teeth and lips erecting them into hard pink crests of unstoppable desire.

Melissa no longer cared whether or not she ought to be doing this. She didn't even care that someone might come into the Sales Director's office at any moment and discover her sprawled half-naked across Galliano's soft leather sofa, whilst he licked and sucked her breasts. All she cared about was the burning tide of desire inside her, a tide which she knew could not now be stemmed except by the power of Galliano's knowing caresses.

He pulled away, his lips wet like the lips of a child drunk with its mother's milk. He was breathing heavily.

'I want you to touch me,' he whispered. It was half-plea, half-command. And he took hold of Melissa's hand and guided it to the swollen hardness distending the front of his suit pants.

That first touch, even through the thick worsted of Galliano's Italian-cut pants, was electric. Melissa was no blushing virgin, she had had other lovers before Rhys. But the touch of Galliano's hot, hard manhood made her feel like a shy sixteen-year-old again, taking her first lessons in lust from the school music-master.

'Unzip me. I want to feel your fingers on my bare flesh,' Galliano told her, bending to plant kisses on Melissa's throat and breasts. His kisses burned with a forbidden fire.

She did not even think to refuse him. Why should she? She was no longer doing what Galliano wanted but what she wanted. Clumsy in her excitement, she struggled to unfasten Galliano's belt, then felt for the tag of his zipper and slid it down.

Underneath he was wearing a tight black pouch whose shiny fabric made his cock look even bigger than it was. And it was big. Melissa felt a familiar, warm wetness inundating the gusset of her panties as she thought of how such a beautiful cock might feel inside her, how it might taste on her tongue.

Even before she peeled down the pouch, she could smell his desire, the tang of his excitement. And as she pulled away the shiny black fabric she saw that the purple plum of his glans was already oozing a slippery-wet tribute to her, diamond-bright drops of sex-fluid trickling from its circumcised tip.

Galliano's eyes half-closed and he gave a low moan as she fastened her fingers about his shaft.

'Yes . . . oh yes . . .' he murmured and the trickle of sex-juice became a little river, the clear fluid running down all over Melissa's fingers. 'You know all my desires and I know yours, my little vixen.'

'You have such a beautiful penis.' Melissa found that her fear, her anger, her inhibitions – all seemed suddenly irrelevant, giving way to an overwhelming, joyful need to fuck and be fucked.

'Tell me,' whispered Galliano. 'Tell me . . .'

'Such a beautiful dick.' The word did not embarrass her in the slightest. It was the right word for the way she felt. She wanted to talk dirty, find new words to describe the way she felt, the way excitement was making her clitoris throb and her vulva pulse with secret, lonely need.

'Now, Melissa, tell me . . . what you want me to do with it.'

'I want you to fuck me. I want you to screw me, shaft me, take me, give it to me . . .' She'd never really talked this way with Rhys, neither of them had ever really been quite daring enough. Maybe they should . . .

Galliano smiled and pinched Melissa's nipples, so hard that the sudden discomfort made her sex-muscles convulse with unexpected pleasure.

'I won't disappoint you, *carissima*,' he promised her. 'I'm going to give you the fucking of your life.'

As Melissa gently stroked his erect shaft, she noticed how the loose seed-purse which held his balls grew taut, the flesh wrinkling and tightening about the ripe fruits of his testicles, readying themselves to spurt their creamy-white tribute. She slipped her left hand under his balls and felt their shape and weight, delighting in the juicy promise that lay within.

Propping himself up on his hands, Galliano eased himself forward over her body, so that the tip of his manhood was only a fraction away from Melissa's glossy lips.

'Go on, Melissa. Take it, you know how much you want to. Take it inside your mouth, see how good it tastes.'

She needed no persuading. The scent of Galliano's manhood was so seductive, the feel of it between her fingers so exciting that she had no power to resist the desire to lap at the glossy lubricating fluid which anointed it.

Putting out her tongue, she let the tip play over the dome of Galliano's glans, rejoicing in the sensations which filled her, her lips and tongue skating over the slippery fluid. It tasted salty-sweet, and with each lick she wanted more. Galliano groaned with need as she wriggled her pointed tongue-tip into the eye of his dick.

'Oh yes. Do it to me, Melissa. Whatever you do, don't stop.'

Parting her lips a little more, she took the bulbous tip of Galliano's penis into her mouth. She closed her lips about the slippery purple flesh, sucking and nibbling at it, listening with growing arousal to the way his breathing quickened. He would not be able to hold out much longer against such wicked kisses.

Hungry beyond belief for her, Galliano suddenly thrust between her lips, forcing first half, then the full length of his dick into the warm, wet, welcoming cavern of her mouth.

Startled, Melissa resisted for a moment as the thick, hard flesh almost choked her, then her excitement took over. Instinctively she began to suck on Galliano's penis, moving her head so that her lips moved back and forth along the smooth shaft, lubricating it with its own fluid and with a thin film of saliva.

Galliano responded with answering thrusts, forcing his dick into her with such enthusiasm that its tip pressed against the back of her throat. She gagged momentarily, but he held her head, whispering to her softly as he fucked her mouth: '*Cara mia, cara mia*, you are so beautiful when you suck on my dick. Suck on it, *bellissima*, drink it all down . . .'

The tide of his semen filled her throat with a series of hard, thick spurts, the sheer quantity of his seed so great that she could not swallow all of it no matter how eagerly she tried. Little trickles escaped from her lips and as Galliano withdrew from her mouth he bent to lick them away.

'I adore the taste of your desire,' he smiled. And his fingers traced the smooth lines of her face, the curve of her neck where his kisses still burned. 'And still you arouse me. Still I want you . . .'

Melissa murmured her inarticulate pleasure as Galliano slid down her body, planting kisses on cheeks and eyes and throat and breasts and belly. Each one seemed to detonate a tiny, explosive charge of sexual energy deep within her, inflaming her desire still further, making her mad with hunger for him.

He unfastened her skirt and slid it down over her hips, revealing the white cotton panties beneath. They were soaked through with the juices of her need and he chuckled to himself as he ran a questing finger over the wet gusset veiling the deep furrow between her thighs.

'Do you want me, Melissa?'

'Want you . . .' She was so transported with desire that she could do no more than repeat his words.

'Do you want me to make love to you, to pleasure you as you have never been pleasured before?'

This time she did not reply but kissed him passionately, forcing her tongue into his mouth, sharing with him the salty-smooth taste of his ejaculate.

Not even pausing to remove Melissa's panties, Galliano slid his index finger underneath the gusset, pushing it to one side. As he did so, he released the sweet aroma of Melissa's sex, a heady cocktail of bath oil, mingled with the spicy oozings of her desire.

His finger pushed into her in a single, swift movement, meeting no resistance, for her womanhood was dripping with welcoming moisture. Her sex-muscles tensed and untensed in a series of delicious spasms as he thrust gently in and out of her, readying her for the full force of his desire.

With the ball of his thumb he smeared a little of Melissa's secretions over the exposed head of her swollen clitoris. At his touch she gave a small, sharp cry and her whole body tensed, poised on the very brink of an orgasm she wanted to keep at bay for just a little while longer. One more incautious caress and he would have taken her too far to hold back.

Withdrawing his finger, he pushed his penis between her legs, his balls still aching with need for her. He had waited a long time for this. With one smooth sabre-thrust he was inside her, Melissa raising her backside to meet him and her eyes wide open as she clutched at him, pulling him deeper and deeper into her.

They moved together smoothly, somehow managing to control the urge to thrust harder and harder, faster and faster. Melissa's whole body was on the very edge of ecstasy, creeping in infinitesimal steps nearer to the point of no return.

She could feel the iron-hard root of Galliano's penis grinding against her pubis, making the hood of her clitoris slide back and forth, alternately hiding and exposing its head.

The tip of his prick was pushing hard against the neck of her womb, making her feel as if he was pleasuring not just her whole body but her whole soul.

Suddenly there was no more question of holding back, there was only complete abandonment – the moment when the glittering summit was reached and the whole world seemed to be tumbling and fragmenting through many-coloured lights. Melissa heard her voice, very far away, sobbing, 'Yes, yes, yes . . .' but it was like hearing someone else. The only recognisable reality was the pleasure, crashing and fizzing and bubbling through her, making her sex-muscles clench and unclench in never-ending spasms of pure ecstasy.

When she opened her eyes, Galliano had withdrawn from her and was standing by the sofa, zipping up his flies. As she sat up, head clearing, he smiled and handed her her skirt.

'I knew you'd see things my way, Melissa.'

She dressed in silence, slowly working through the realisation of what she had done. Had she really done that? Had she really had passionate, intensely exciting sex with Peter Galliano? Had she? She felt the warm trickle of honey-sweet fluid at the top of her thigh and knew that she had.

It had been good. She didn't regret it . . . well, not really. At least, not yet. What she did regret was the smug expression on Peter Galliano's face.

'See it your way?' she enquired coolly, opening her handbag and running a comb through her tousled mane of blonde hair.

'You keep on being nice to me, Melissa, and I'll make sure you progress in your career. Just let me . . . get to know you some more, and you'll have that Regional Sales Manager's job too. Then – well, who knows? The sky's the limit for you, Melissa. With me to help you . . .'

He moved to kiss her but she stepped away, closing her handbag with a neat click.

'Thanks for the . . . entertainment,' she said, giving him the coolest smile she could muster in the turmoil of confused thoughts and emotions. 'But you can keep your help.'

'What?'

Galliano's handsome face registered incomprehension, his jaw dropping open. This really didn't make sense. First she played hard to get for months on end, pretending she hadn't even noticed how much he wanted her. Then, all of a sudden, she dropped the façade and gave him what he – no, what they both – craved. And now, just as suddenly, she was freezing him out.

'It was your dick I wanted, Peter,' said Melissa. 'Not your so-called "help". Thanks for the offer, but I'll make my own way in my career.'

Galliano's look of astonishment turned into a sneer.

'Well, you needn't think you'll get that job without my influence,' he retorted.

'I didn't want it anyway,' replied Melissa, hardly believing what she heard herself saying as the light of realisation snapped on in her brain. 'I was thinking about putting in for a transfer to another region – and you've just made up my mind for me.'

Rhys Montagu walked slowly up the path towards the front

door of forty-three, Laburnum Walk. An ordinary house, in an ordinary London street – on a very extraordinary day.

He hesitated before he slid his key into the lock. What the hell was he going to say to Melissa? All the way home on the Tube he'd been trying to work something out, but his mind was still an empty screen. True, Melissa knew he hadn't been happy with his work for a while but up till now he hadn't let on just how unhappy he really was.

There was that stupid fling he'd had with Tina, the Senior Sub-Editor – that had been one humungously big mistake, even if it had amounted to little more than a drunken fumble after a late night on the newsdesk. He couldn't even figure out why he'd bothered doing it. It was Melissa who turned him on; Melissa he had wet dreams about when he hardly saw her for days on end; Melissa he'd been thinking about even as he lay, heaving and groaning, on top of the Senior Sub.

Then there was all this trouble with the Editor. Colin Gray had never liked Rhys from day one and now, with a major company reorganisation, he'd got his coveted chance to stick the knife in. Colin's ultimatum had been quite clear: accept a pay cut and edit the women's page, or clear your desk and get out.

Rhys had chosen to get out. But how was he going to break the news to Melissa?

Sitting in the kitchen, Melissa stared at the letter again. Surely that couldn't be right. Could it?

She got up to take a bottle of white wine out of the fridge, and glanced at the clock. Seven-thirty, Rhys should be home any minute. There'd be some talking to do tonight and no mistake.

It had been the weirdest day, all things considered. *Really* weird. Had she really done that with Peter Galliano? Yes, of course she had, it was no good trying to pretend it was some sort of erotic daydream. And had she really enjoyed it that much?

She had *revelled* in it. Every explicit second of it. Oh, there'd been no emotional involvement, nothing lasting or deep. She had just given herself up to half an hour of pure sex, as if she had reached an unbearable level of sexual tension and had to release it on someone, *anyone*. Even Peter Galliano.

Funny how that erotic episode seemed to have recharged her sexual batteries, made her realise how much she desired Rhys more than any other man in the world. All she wanted to do was welcome him home, take him to bed and show him that he was the only one for her. What they needed was to forget about stress and work for a while and just concentrate on indulging their sexual fantasies, bringing the excitement back into their lives.

But first there'd be some hard talking to do, thought Melissa to herself as she uncorked the wine and poured herself a glass. She glanced across at the letter, lying white and innocent on the kitchen table, and had to read it a third time to convince herself that she wasn't going mad.

What on earth was Rhys going to say when she told him she'd put in for a transfer to a different sales region? And as for the letter . . . Well, if that didn't bring excitement into their lives, she didn't know what would.

Chapter 2

'A legacy!' Jim Kerrigan looked at Rhys and Melissa over the top of his beer glass. 'You lucky sods!'

'How much?' enquired Jim's lover, Maia. Maia was an elegant fashion-model-turned-computer-analyst with the sort of long, golden legs that men drool over and women would kill for. 'Or am I not supposed to ask?'

'Well...' began Rhys, uncertainly. They hadn't told anyone about this so far and it felt almost indecent.

'A... er... few hundred thousand,' cut in Melissa, spooning mayonnaise onto a slice of cold smoked chicken.

Jim whistled.

'Not *bad*. What happened – some rich uncle peg out, did he?'

Melissa tossed her head. Jim liked Melissa when she did that. It made her wavy golden locks gleam in the candlelight and, much as he lusted after Maia, his dick would keep reminding him that he'd never had the pleasure of Melissa's full-breasted, firm body. Yet.

'Apparently some great-aunt of my mother's died when she was a baby and left her some money,' explained Melissa. 'It went into a trust fund and everyone forgot about it when Mum died.'

'It's been sitting there for all this time, gathering interest – and the solicitors have only just tracked Melissa down,' added Rhys.

'Several hundred thousand, eh?' commented Maia, folding a piece of lettuce on her fork and popping it into her perfectly formed mouth. 'Sounds like my kind of mix-up!'

'Ah, but what are you going to *do* with all this unexpected dosh?' demanded Jim.

'We're not sure yet.' Rhys drained his wine glass and set it down on the white damask tablecloth. 'Though to be honest, it couldn't have come at a better time – our finances have taken a bit of a nose-dive. I've just chucked my job in.'

'Bloody hell.' Jim regarded Rhys with new-found respect. 'That must have taken guts.'

'Stupidity, more like,' replied Rhys. 'The Editor wanted me to take a pay-cut and edit the women's page and ...'

'And his pride was hurt,' cut in Melissa with a grin. It was odd how much better she and Rhys were getting on since they had had that talk ... and a whole, blissful night of lovemaking, accompanied by the bottle of champagne they'd been saving for a special occasion. It was almost like discovering each other's bodies all over again, tasting with a newfound excitement the pleasure which they and only they could give each other.

'Hark who's talking!' commented Rhys good-humouredly. He nodded towards Melissa. 'Guess who's turned down the chance of a big fat promotion and put in for a transfer to the back of beyond!'

'I'm only thinking about it,' said Melissa defensively. 'As a last resort. The Sales Director's being a bit ... you know ... insistent just now.'

Maia returned her look with a smile and a raised eyebrow.

'Insistent? Oh, you mean *horny*, darling?'

Melissa turned pink and spluttered as she choked on a mouthful of wine.

'I suppose you could say that,' she admitted. She wondered if she ought to have told Rhys just how insistent Peter Galliano had been that afternoon in his office. But maybe some things were better left unsaid. And, once they were away from this place, she'd never have to work with Peter Galliano again.

Maia laid her knife and fork neatly together on her plate and pushed it away.

'Melissa darling, there's no need to be embarrassed,' Maia said. 'If the Sales Director wants to screw you and you want to screw him, why not go for it?'

'But I didn't say I *did* want him,' Melissa protested.

'Is he good-looking? Powerful?'

'Well . . . yes.'

'Then you want to screw him, Melissa. What normal woman wouldn't?'

Melissa felt quite shocked by Maia's directness, but then, Maia Kerrigan had always believed in saying exactly what she thought.

'You'd do that? You'd go to bed with your boss to get a better job?'

Maia and Jim exchanged amused glances.

'Not to get a better job,' replied Maia. 'Just because I wanted to.'

'We think sexual freedom's tremendously important,' remarked Jim. 'Don't you?' He was looking straight at Melissa, making her feel deeply uncomfortable.

'Yes, I suppose,' began Melissa, not sure where this was leading.

'What – you mean screwing around?' enquired Rhys, marginally less reticent. 'Well, I won't say I haven't been tempted, Jim, I mean I'm only human . . .'

Maia leant over the table, her low-cut dress clinging to her body like a second skin. She knows how to make the most of that body, thought Melissa enviously. And what a body! Just look at the way she shows off her breasts, the way the neckline of her dress just skims her nipples. And, look, her nipples are so huge and stiff. You can tell she really has the hots for Rhys . . .

Melissa experienced a most peculiar feeling: a mixture of jealousy and excitement. There was something immensely titillating about watching one of your best friends flirting with your husband. She found herself fantasising about what it would be like to watch them together, Maia's golden flesh naked and glistening with sweat as she sat astride Rhys's long, hard cock.

'You may call it screwing around,' said Maia in her husky, seductive voice. 'We like to call it exploring the parameters of our sexual identity.' The way she said it, it sounded not corny but arousing. As she spoke, her eyes lighted not on Rhys but on Melissa, and she ran the tip of her tongue slowly and deliberately over her painted lips.

Jim cut in, slipping his arm round Maia's waist and sliding his fingers upwards to fondle her breast.

'We're not possessive,' he said. 'We don't believe one human being can own another's sexuality – we understand each other's needs.'

'Which are?' Melissa could already guess what they might be but the secret excitement inside her was growing and somehow she just wanted to hear Jim say it.

PARADISE GARDEN

'Which are, to explore *every* dimension of our sexuality. Sexual desire is just an appetite, Melissa – is it so wrong to satisfy it? We take as many lovers as we need to satisfy our physical desires. There's no messy emotional involvement, you understand – just pure physical pleasure.' He stroked Maia's breast and her nipple seemed to become even harder, more protuberant, pushing impatiently against the inside of her dress. 'Pleasure is a wonderful thing to share with someone, don't you agree?'

'Yes, now what could possibly be wrong with that, Rhys darling?' Maia kissed the tip of her index finger and placed it on his lips and Rhys could feel his cock stirring appreciatively inside his pants.

He looked from Maia to Jim and back again. He couldn't quite believe what he was hearing. Oh, Maia and Jim had always seemed a slightly unconventional pairing – the beautiful, intelligent, aloof ex-model and the rough-round-the-edges marine engineer – but he'd never suspected that they had such a fascinating sex-life. Who could resist knowing more?

'So . . . er . . . how exactly . . . ?' Rhys could have cursed himself for his awkwardness. If Jim and Maia weren't embarrassed to talk about their sexual adventures, why should he be?

Jim laughed.

'You mean, how do we get to meet all these sexual partners?'

Melissa hung on Jim's words, but it was Maia her eyes kept drifting back to. There was something in Maia's expression, the way she kept looking at Melissa and smiling, the way she licked drops of red wine off her crimson-painted lips . . .

'Yeah, something like that,' conceded Rhys.

'Anywhere,' said Maia. 'You'd be surprised, you can meet someone you want to fuck in the most unlikely places.' Her eyes flicked away from Rhys and lingered for a brief second on Melissa. 'Even at dinner parties.'

'We have friends in North London who organise sex parties,' Jim continued. 'Very discreet they are, you never get any trouble. We go about once a month and I can honestly say we haven't been disappointed yet.'

'You meet such open-minded people there,' added Maia. 'Singles, couples, straights, bisexuals, leather dykes, C/P freaks . . . anyone who wants good sex and no strings attached. It's a chance to try something new, have a sexual adventure or two, play games you'd never think of playing at home . . .'

'You have sex with complete strangers?' Melissa was thinking of that half-hour of mad, mindless frenzy she had spent with Peter Galliano, that half-hour when absolutely nothing in the world had mattered so much as sexual gratification.

Maia shrugged.

'Of course. Strangers, friends, lovers – they're just words. What does it matter? You don't have to know a man's name to enjoy sucking his dick.'

Jim took a business card out of his inside pocket and scrawled a telephone number across the back.

'Give Rosie a call,' he said. 'You look like you could use an adventure or two.'

Rhys picked up the card and stared at it.

'You mean . . . come to one of these parties?'

Maia laughed.

'We won't eat you. Not unless you want us to . . .'

Melissa looked at the card. She was surprised at how tempted she felt. Her mind was full of pictures: a suburban drawing-room, the curtains closed and the lights down low. Cheap art prints on the walls and a Habitat lamp on the coffee table.

She imagined semi-naked couples dancing to soft, sexy music, their hands slowly undressing each other. Others, their bodies entwined on the floor, hips bucking, mouths licking and sucking and biting. A naked girl standing with her back against the wallpaper, thighs wide apart as a fat cock slid into the depths of her sex. Another, lying on her back, masturbating a dick with each hand whilst a man lay between her thighs, lapping like a kitten at the white cream spilling from her sex.

A girl who looked just like her . . .

She stood up, pushing back her chair.

'I'll just clear these away and make us some coffee.'

As she began stacking the plates Maia got to her feet too. 'I'll help,' she volunteered.

'There's no need, really.'

Maia's hazel eyes sought her out, her bobbed chestnut hair glossy in the candlelight.

'Let me help.'

The two women went off into the kitchen, leaving Rhys and Jim drinking in the dining-room. Melissa put the plates into the sink, checked the coffee machine and switched it on. Maia followed her in, closing the door quietly behind her.

'Did I embarrass you?'

'N-no. No, of course not,' Melissa lied. Although it wasn't

quite a lie because she hadn't only been embarrassed. She'd been excited too. A lot more excited than she was prepared to admit to Maia Kerrigan.

'Oh, Melissa, I *did* embarrass you, I'm sorry.' Maia laid her hand on Melissa's bare shoulder. 'It's just that . . . well, you were saying only the other week that your sex life wasn't quite as exciting as it might be, and I thought you might appreciate a little adventure.'

Melissa took four cups and saucers out of the kitchen cupboard and arranged them on the table.

'It was just one of those things, a bad patch. Rhys was working all hours and I was missing having him in bed with me. I guess I was just feeling . . . sexually frustrated.'

'I know.' Maia took hold of Melissa's hand and made her look into her eyes. 'It's not natural for a woman only to have one partner. I know how you feel, Melissa. I know what you *need*.'

She placed a kiss on Melissa's cheek.

'Tell me you don't feel it too, Melissa. Tell me you don't want it.'

Melissa froze, hostage to a million conflicting thoughts and feelings.

'I don't quite understand what you mean.'

'Of course you do, Melissa. You're just trying to repress it. Let it out, express yourself, admit that what you really need is more sex, bigger and better sex, new partners to spice up your life.' Her fingers caressed the ripe swell of Melissa's breast above the low-cut neckline of her evening gown. 'And new ways of making love . . .'

'No, really, Maia, I . . .'

Maia silenced her by kissing her full on the mouth, her

hands stroking and embracing Melissa whilst her lips possessed her. It seemed forever until she drew away, leaving Melissa gasping, ashamed of her own excitement.

'What you really need is me.'

Melissa tried to draw away but Maia followed her.

'Don't deny it. I know you want me. I saw the way you were looking at me all through dinner.' She took hold of Melissa by the shoulder and spun her round, her back to the work-surface. 'For God's sake, Melissa, don't be a child. I suppose you think it'll turn you into some crop-haired lesbian, just because you want to get it on with another woman.'

'I'm not, I . . . Look Maia, you mustn't. Someone might come in. Jim might . . .'

Maia ran her hands over Melissa's full breasts and the nipples, already tingling with excitement, responded by raising and puckering themselves into hard crests beneath the stretchy black Lycra. Maia rolled them between finger and thumb.

'Jim won't mind, Melissa, you know he won't. And really, it's no good telling me you don't want me. *These* say you do.'

Melissa let out a low whimper of desire. It was true, she wished it weren't, but it was true. She leant back against the work surface and closed her eyes, feeling Maia's burning caresses through the thin fabric of her dress.

'All sex is good,' purred Maia. '*All* sex. You shouldn't deprive yourself of anything that turns you on. Let me show you how to liberate your sexuality, Melissa.'

Maia slid her hands down Melissa's flanks and down onto her thighs, then gradually began ruching up the tight skirt of her dress, easing it up fold by fold, millimetre by millimetre, baring Melissa's thighs.

'If you want me to stop, I'll stop. But you have to tell me, Melissa. If you don't tell me, I shall just go on giving you more and more pleasure. And I *am* giving you pleasure, aren't I?'

Melissa's black skirt slipped a little higher, baring suspender-clad thighs and a pair of red silk panties: panties that Rhys had given her as a surprise present only the previous day. Panties that were just made for taking off . . .

Maia's fingers toyed with the bare flesh above Melissa's stocking-tops, then moved higher, towards the apex of her sex.

'Wet panties,' she whispered. 'Oh, darling Melissa, you've wet your little red panties and it's all for me.'

As if to complete her body's betrayal of her reason, Melissa felt a tide of warm liquid gushing out of her as Maia's fingers probed and petted the soft, moist flesh between her thighs.

'Come for me, baby. Come. If you're really good and come all over my fingers, I'll let you lick out my pussy.'

She couldn't, she couldn't . . . but she wanted to. For the second time in as many weeks, Melissa found herself giving in to desires she hadn't even realised she had. But Maia's touch was so gentle and unerring, seeking out with sweet relentlessness the very heart of her sex and caressing, caressing, caressing her towards the summit of a pleasure to which she dared not surrender.

Yet how could she resist? Already her belly ached with the delicious anticipation of orgasm, her vulval muscles almost imperceptibly tensing and untensing, the mouth of

PARADISE GARDEN

her sex opening and closing like the mouth of some greedy sea-creature.

Eyes closed, pulse racing, breasts tingling with lustful excitement, Melissa was on the very point of surrender to the lascivious impulses that were taking her over. This felt so good – wicked but so, so good.

'I'll take you to one of my parties, Melissa. You'll love it. So many beautiful women wanting to suck your clitoris . . .'

And then the reality came home to her. It wasn't Maia's fingers she wanted between her thighs, not Maia's kisses on her breasts, her labia, her clit. It wasn't the desire for Maia that was filling her with this excitement, this need. It was the desire for Rhys. It was Rhys she wanted to fuck, Rhys she wanted to lick come from her pussy.

With a huge effort of will, she pushed Maia away.

'What . . . ?' Maia's eyes widened in astonishment.

'I'm sorry, Maia.'

'What's the matter, Melissa? I thought . . .'

Melissa pulled down her skirt with trembling fingers, rearranged her hair, tried to ignore the pulsing, burning hunger still raging between her thighs.

'It was nice of you, Maia. Really kind. It's just not what I want.'

Melissa was sitting on the edge of the bed, still dressed, when Rhys came into the bedroom.

'I thought they'd never go,' he remarked, taking off his tie and flinging it over the back of a chair. He stripped off his shirt and pants, and Melissa thought how good he looked. Rhys really looked after his body, kept it taut and fit without being muscle-bound. And she loved the natural light golden sheen that his skin always had, even in the winter. It was as though he carried his own personal supply of sunshine around with him.

He stripped off his silk boxers and stepped out of them. Even after three years together, Melissa had to admit that nature had been kind to Rhys. A thick, uncircumcised penis hung above a tangle of dark-brown hairs, which adorned the heavy seed-sacs hanging between his thighs. Melissa wondered how she could possibly have been interested in Maia – or Peter Galliano for that matter – when she had Rhys to fulfil her every sensual need.

'I still can't quite believe what Maia did,' remarked Melissa, slowly taking the pins from her hair.

'Here, let me do that. It's so sexy when all that golden hair comes tumbling down over your shoulders.' Rhys caressed the nape of Melissa's neck and planted a row of tiny kisses on it. 'What exactly *did* she do? You looked like a startled rabbit when you came out of that kitchen.'

'I told you – she made a pass at me.'

'Did she now . . . ?' Rhys pulled out the last hairpin and felt an appreciative frisson as he watched the long golden rope of Melissa's hair slowly uncoil and tumble into glossy waves about her shoulders. 'Well, all I can say is, I don't blame her. You're the sexiest thing I've seen in a long time, Melissa Montagu.'

Melissa received his kiss with enthusiasm, but drew back, teasing.

'As sexy as Maia?'

Rhys chuckled. Yes, Maia Kerrigan certainly was one

sexy woman but he only had to think about Melissa and he got an erection. 'Ten times more sexy.' He kissed her again, and felt for the tag of the zip-fastener which ran down the back of her dress. 'No, make that a hundred.'

He slid down the zipper and smoothed his hand down Melissa's bare back. No bra. That in itself was a massive turn-on. All he had to do was pull down the front of her dress and her big breasts, firm yet soft, would fall like ripe mangoes into his eager hands. He forced himself to wait. Make it last. Make both of them wait until they couldn't stand it any longer. Then, and only then, would they fuck.

'Melissa . . .' He stroked her back, running his finger down to the sexy little hollow where her lower back met the deep crease between her buttocks. Beautiful bum cheeks they were, too, full yet firm from all that tennis and squash and horse-riding.

'Hmm?' She squirmed in enjoyment, letting all the sensations wash over her.

'Tell me what Maia did. In the kitchen.'

'I told you . . .'

'No, exactly. Tell me exactly what she did. I want to hear all about it.'

Melissa skewed her head round to give him a quizzical look.

'Why?'

'Can't you guess?' He chuckled. 'Because it turns me on, that's why. It's unbelievably sexy, thinking about you . . . you know, being with another woman.'

Melissa's face registered curiosity.

'It doesn't make you jealous?'

Slowly and luxuriously, Rhys slid one of the straps of Melissa's dress down over her shoulder.

'Not the *thought* of it, no. I'm not sure how I'd feel if I actually saw you fucking a woman, though.' He smiled, a wicked, sexy smile. 'I'd probably get amazingly horny and fuck both of you!'

The shoulder-strap now hung loosely from Melissa's upper arm, revealing the swell of her left breast but not the aureola or the big pink nipple that he so loved to suck and bite. He turned his attentions to the other strap.

'Go on, tell me. Tell me what you and Maia got up to in the kitchen.'

'She wanted us to have sex.'

Rhys could feel his cock swelling, uncoiling. It was one thing thinking about Melissa getting it on with another girl, but it was far, far sexier to hear it from her own lips.

'And did you?'

'No . . . yes . . . not exactly.'

He slid down the shoulder-strap and marvelled at the beauty of her breasts, the creamy-white hummocks of flesh, their nipples still hidden by the soft drape of the black fabric. Slowly, hungrily, yet wanting to make the moment last, he drew down the front of her dress. Her pink teats leapt out, eager and hard and oh-so-kissable. He stroked them gently with his fingertips, listening to the sound of her breathing, watching her eyes half-close as the pleasure began to overtake her.

'Tell me. Everything. I want it to be as if I'm there, watching you both.'

'I . . .' Melissa hesitated for a moment, uncertain. Would Rhys really be turned on by the idea of her and Maia together? Or would he sulk when he realised just how close she'd come to giving Maia exactly what she'd wanted?

Rhys bent to lick her nipples and she felt every ounce of her resistance ebbing away. What the hell, she thought. And the episode came flooding back, somehow sexier than before, denuded of guilt.

'She told me she knew what I needed – and that what I needed was her,' Melissa began, remembering how unexpectedly good it had felt to have Maia's fingers on her breasts.

'Did she touch you?' Rhys lapped like a kitten at her nipple, and she felt all her unsatisfied desire rekindling, desperate for release.

'Oh yes, Rhys. She touched me. She kissed me and I could feel her nipples pressing into me. They were so big and so hard. And then she pulled up my dress . . .'

'Go on.' Rhys pushed Melissa gently down onto the bed and let his hand fall onto her thigh, still licking at her nipple as he began sliding up her skirt.

'She pulled it up and started stroking my thigh. I wanted to tell her to stop but I couldn't. It felt . . .'

'How did it feel, Melissa? I want to know. Can't you see how you're turning me on? You're driving me crazy.' He took hold of her hand and placed it on his penis, now bone-hard and shiny with sex-juice.

'It felt good. It felt so, so good.'

'As good as this?' Rhys let his fingers walk teasingly up the inside of Melissa's thigh until they were resting on her pubis. Then, very slowly, he began to rub her through the damp red silk of her panties.

'Oh . . . oh, Rhys.' Melissa's breath escaped in a gasp

of unstoppable desire. Maia's fingers on her pussy had felt good, but this, this felt like heaven. 'Good! It feels . . . oh!'

'Don't stop.' Rhys moved his hips a little, sliding his cock in and out of Melissa's encircling fingers. That felt good too. But not as good as it felt to have his fingers between Melissa's thighs, slowly wanking her as he listened to her telling him all about Maia.

'I was so excited, my panties got all wet. And when she touched me they got wetter and wetter, I just couldn't control myself any longer. She seemed to know all the right places to touch me to drive me wild. She was stroking my clitoris through my panties . . .'

'And then?'

Melissa let go of Rhys's cock and kissed him, forcing her tongue into his mouth, tasting the tang of red wine.

'And then I pushed her away.'

'But why?'

'Because it's you I want, Rhys. I don't need anyone else to give me pleasure. Only you . . . your cock inside me . . . your tongue on my clit. I want you so much . . .'

Rhys rolled onto his back, pulling Melissa on top of him, making her take the initiative.

'If you want me,' he smiled, 'Come and take me.'

The thighs which straddled him felt as strong as steel and smooth as silk and he sank back onto the mattress in the perfect luxury of sensual self-indulgence. For an instant she held his cock-tip at the entrance to her sex, tormenting him with the wet heaven of her pleasure-palace.

'Please,' he groaned.

'Patience,' she said, smiling, and rubbed herself on his

glans, her wet furrow anointing him with a clear, sweet slick of love-juice. It was pure torture, feeling her inner labia teasing and tickling the head of his cock like a wicked tongue.

And then, at last, she gave a forward thrust of her hips, taking him so deep and so quickly inside her that he let out a cry of astonished pleasure.

Melissa was so right. What did they need other lovers for? With Melissa's beautiful pussy-lips kissing the shaft of his prick, he had all a man could ever want . . .

It was late the following morning when they came down to breakfast, pleasantly exhausted after a long night of passion.

Rhys picked up the morning papers from the mat and followed Melissa into the kitchen.

'Caffeine,' he yawned. '*Lots* of caffeine. That's what I need.'

Opening the cupboard he took out a jar of instant coffee and began to spoon it into a mug. 'OK for you?'

'Yes, coffee's fine.' Melissa took a brioche out of the breadbin and started slicing it up. 'You know, we've got to make a decision about what we're going to do . . . you know, about the money.'

'Well, it's your money really,' Rhys pointed out.

'*Our* money,' Melissa insisted. 'And it could be our passport to a new life. How long have we been in London? Five years now, and neither of us really likes it. We've always said one day we'd up sticks and go and live somewhere nice. Our own place in the country . . .'

'Ah, but there's your career. What about that Regional Sales Manager's job you've been drooling over for months?'

Melissa sat down at the table and spread a thick layer of butter on a slice of brioche.

'I've already told Peter Galliano I'm not interested. To be honest, I don't really want to work with the guy any more. I'd like a new challenge, somewhere different . . . And the North Yorkshire region needs a new Senior Rep. It would still be a challenge for me, opening up a new territory.'

'North Yorkshire.' Rhys scratched his head. 'Sounds tempting – all that open space and long winter nights in front of a log fire. But there aren't many jobs for a journo up there – unless you like writing about lost dogs and prize marrows.'

'You could go freelance again.' Melissa leafed through the morning paper. 'God, I hate Saturday papers. They're always full of adverts for garden sheds and toupees.'

'Freelance? I guess I could . . .'

'Well, we don't have to go anywhere if you don't want to. We'll maybe look for somewhere a bit bigger down here and I'll stick it out at Jupiter until something more interesting comes along.'

She flicked over the next page and was just about to fold the paper up and put it away when something caught her eye. It was a tiny photograph, postage-stamp sized, above a small ad on the property page, but something about it seemed to draw her like a magnet.

'Here you are, sweetheart, coffee triple strength – just how you like it.' Rhys placed a mug of black coffee on the table and sat down opposite Melissa.

'Hey, Rhys, look at this.' She pushed the paper across the table.

'What?'

'That advert. Look.'

Rhys read it. ' "Elizabethan manor house in need of total refurbishment. Extensive grounds, superb situation in North York Moors." Hmm, it looks pretty, but what a heap! You can hardly see the house for the overgrown gardens.' He looked up. Melissa's eyes were shining. Oh no, he knew that look. He knew it only too well.

'Melissa, you're joking! A place like that, it'd take every penny we've got and then some more.'

'But it's beautiful, Rhys. It's just what I've always wanted.'

'It's falling down, Melissa, and it's miles from anywhere. You can't be serious.'

But, in his heart of hearts, he rather hoped she was.

Chapter 3

Candice Soulbury watched her boss through the half-open door to his inner office.

Peter Galliano hadn't been the same these last few weeks. Hadn't been the same since the day when he'd summoned that Melissa Montagu to his office. An 'appraisal interview' he'd called it but Candice could think of other words to describe it.

She wasn't blind. As Galliano's PA, she was fully aware of his fondness for recreational sex. But this Montagu woman had really got to him, that was obvious. These last few days he'd flown off the handle at every small thing and when he wasn't shouting and throwing things he was mooning about in his office.

It wasn't right. And Candice Soulbury, for one, was overjoyed to hear that Melissa and her journalist husband were thinking of moving all the way up to North Yorkshire. The word was that they'd come into some money and had gone up north to look at some crumbling manor house. If they liked it, she was going to confirm her transfer to the north-eastern sales territory.

Good. If Melissa Montagu was working up there and trying to restore some ancient heap of a house, she wouldn't have time to go running after Peter Galliano, would she?

Which was just how Candice wanted it. Because for a long time now she'd known that sooner or later – though he might not realise it yet – Peter Galliano was going to be hers.

Melissa looked out at the scenery, flashing past the car window.

'Pinch me,' she sighed. 'I still can't believe I'm here.'

Obligingly, Rhys took his left hand off the steering wheel and gave Melissa's nipple a playful pinch.

'Ouch! Beast...' She limited her retaliation to a meaningful glare – she knew what Rhys's driving was like when he was distracted and she didn't want them to end up in a field.

It was just about as perfect a spring afternoon as you could get up on the North York moors; not warm, certainly, but flooded with a golden-yellow sunshine that seemed to pour down out of an eggshell-blue sky. They had enjoyed a pub lunch at the Mallyan Spout Hotel in Goathland and were now heading across country towards the village of Highmoor, several miles west of Whitby.

Village? To judge from the road map it wasn't much more than a hamlet: a pub, a telephone box, a tiny sub-post office and a scattering of houses, clustered together about a crossroads in the middle of wild and beautiful moorland. And as for Highmoor House, well, that was still more remote, situated at the end of an unmade road, a half-mile or so from the outskirts of the village.

Rhys glanced at his watch.

'It's almost half-past,' he commented. 'Best go straight to the house – the estate agent said he'd meet us there. If we're a bit early we can have a snoop round on our own.'

'Sounds good to me.'

'Oh, and the agent says he has some other properties to show us if we don't like Highmoor House.'

Melissa wondered how she could possibly *not* like Highmoor House. The countryside alone had won her over already. Rolling moorland extended as far as the eye could see, heather and bracken and gorse with here and there a patch of exposed rock, yellowed with lichen. Sheep were dotted over the landscape and seemed as much a part of the landscape as the isolated, whitewashed cottages Melissa could see in the distance.

'It's wonderful,' she decided, winding down the window and breathing in the sharp air. There was just a hint of salt in it, reminding her of the sea not so many miles away.

'Steady on,' urged Rhys. 'You haven't even seen the house yet. "In need of major refurbishment", that's what it said on the spec. And you know what *that* means. It probably hasn't even got a roof!'

'Yeah . . . maybe.' Melissa gazed dreamily out at the fluffy cotton-balls of cloud scudding overhead, across the pale blue sky. 'But I hardly care. It's wonderful just being out here, away from grimy London. A real escape.' She stroked the nape of her lover's neck. 'Rhys. Rhys, *darling* . . .'

Rhys let his hand slip onto Melissa's thigh and she gave a low growl of pleasure.

'What, sweetheart?'

'I feel sort of . . . horny.'

Rhys took hold of Melissa's hand and placed it in his lap.

'Me too. Can't you feel? I've been hard for you ever since we left home. Don't see what we can do about it here, though.'

Melissa smiled. 'You know what your trouble is, don't you, Rhys? You've got no imagination.'

'That's not what you said last night in bed...' Rhys chuckled as he let his fingers explore, the side-split in Melissa's skirt affording a welcome entrance to the silken charms of her thigh. 'Just you wait and see what games I think up later tonight.'

'We don't have to wait until later.' She squeezed the stiff stalk of his penis. 'You could have me right now.'

Rhys was looking straight ahead but in his mind's eye he was already undressing Melissa.

'Here?'

'Hereabouts.'

'We'd be late for the estate agent.'

'He'll wait. He wants to sell us a house, doesn't he?'

Rhys glanced in the rearview mirror, slowed the car down and brought it to a halt in the next passing-place. With the engine off, the silence and seclusion of this place really struck him for the first time. It was like being on some other world, some other planet where ordinary values had no meaning.

He released his seat belt and it slid back with a sharp click. Leaning across the front seat, he put his hand on Melissa's thigh and pulled her towards him, their lips meeting in a kiss of pure hunger.

Her scent intoxicated him. It was the scent of her sex, the special, intimate perfume she exuded whenever she was really hot for him and it always turned him on. Here, now, it was driving him half crazy.

Drawing away from Melissa's full, moist lips with the greatest reluctance, he slid his hand down over her shoulder and onto the full curve of her breast. Melissa had truly magnificent breasts, firm globes so large and heavy that two hands were inadequate to cup them. The ivory-white flesh spilled over his palms, the pink muzzles of her nipples nosing out between his fingers, succulent and unashamed.

Today she was wearing one of his favourite outfits: the black, side-split skirt with an écru skinny-rib sweater, modestly high in the neck but tight enough to hug every curve, betraying the hardness of her nipples. He tugged the sweater out of the waistband of her skirt and slid his hand underneath.

Her bra was a flimsy affair in stretchy cotton, so insubstantial that he wondered why she bothered to wear it. It wasn't as if she needed to wear a bra at all – despite their fullness, her breasts stood proud, their nipples upward-thrusting, as though demanding to be sucked.

Melissa gave a blissful sigh as Rhys's hand slipped under her sweater, moving determinedly upwards until it reached the generous overhang of her breasts. She arched her back slightly, expecting him to slip his hands round behind her and unhook her bra, but instead he let his impatience take over, seizing the bra and lifting it up over her breasts, so that the elasticated band lay across the tops of them, squashing and pushing them out.

His touch was a little rough but all the more exciting for that. She met his kiss with hunger, her lips moist, the muscular tip of her tongue eager to explore his mouth. As eager as his cock was to explore the hot, wet tunnel of her sex.

'Do you remember the first time?' whispered Rhys. 'The

very first time . . . in my old car?'

Melissa remembered. It had been their very first night out together. She didn't make a habit of going all the way on a first date but Rhys had been different somehow. She'd lusted after him all night at the club where she first noticed him, watching him dance with girl after girl; but she'd been with another guy and he'd hardly seemed to notice her. But on her way home she'd found a scrap of paper in her jacket pocket: 'Rhys Davies, 009-9043. Call me soon.'

She wasn't going to call him, she emphatically wasn't. But of course she did. And the following night she'd gone out with him for a meal. He'd offered to drive her home and, although nothing was said, they both knew what they wanted to happen next. The trouble was, Rhys shared a flat with another guy and Melissa had only just moved down to London and was sleeping on a friend's floor. There was no way she could ask him in for 'coffee'. No way at all. Only, she wanted him like crazy and it wasn't difficult to see that he wanted her too.

'I remember,' she replied with a smile.

'You seduced me,' said Rhys in mock disapproval. 'Right there, in the front seat of my old Escort, you put your hand on my cock.'

'And you put *your* hand up my skirt,' Melissa pointed out.

'Your panties were *so* wet,' reminisced Rhys. He was wet too, just at the memory of it. His cock was oozing thick sex-fluid all over the inside of his boxers.

'And then we got into the back seat and made love.' Melissa took Rhys's hand and placed it back on her thigh. 'You took my panties off, do you remember?'

PARADISE GARDEN

'How could I forget?'

'Why don't you take them off me now?'

Rhys slid Melissa's skirt right up to her backside and spent a few moments just drinking in the delights of those stocking-clad thighs. The most chaste pair of white cotton panties imaginable adorned her pubis, the cotton so thin – and so damp – that he could make out the little kiss-curls of corn-blonde, slightly gingery hair and the long, dark-pink crease between her pussy-lips.

Eagerly he hooked his thumbs under the sides of Melissa's panties and slid them down, releasing more of the delicious fragrance that made his cock throb with sympathetic lust.

She wriggled her bum and the panties slid easily down over her hips, her thighs, and into Rhys's covetous hands. It was strange how, even after three years of living together, just the scent of Melissa's soiled panties was damn near enough to make him ejaculate. Sometimes, when she was away on business trips, he even liked to wrap her panties around his cock and masturbate, surrounding himself with the feel and the scent of her, imagining that it was Melissa's hand on his cock, Melissa giving him pleasure.

He gave her a sidelong look.

'Ah, but now I've got them, what am I going to do with them?' He pressed them to his face and breathed in deeply. 'They're *very* wet – perhaps we should dry them off?'

Teasingly he held them out of the car window, watching the white cotton fabric flutter in the breeze. Then, with deliberate mischief, he let go of them and a strong gust took hold of them, sending them fluttering off across the road and into the gorse.

'Beast!' Melissa raised a fist as though to pummel him, but he caught and kissed it.

'I'm a beast if you want me to be,' he replied.

It was Melissa's turn to be playful.

'So you're the Beast of Highmoor?'

'If you like.' He growled menacingly.

Melissa licked her lips.

'Fancy a walk on the moor?

'What? I thought . . .'

'We've never done it in the great outdoors, have we? Never had sex in the open air. Wouldn't that be an adventure?'

Rhys gaped at Melissa.

'On the moors? Right now? But it's . . .'

'Cold? Broad daylight? We won't feel the cold, Rhys, believe me. And no-one will see us. It's obvious that hardly anyone ever comes this way, especially not this time of year.'

Without waiting for his response, she opened the car door and got out, the chilly air sending pleasurable shivers all over her body as it caressed her bare thighs and sex.

Climbing the bank, she stepped onto the open moor. Rhys joined her a second later, slipping his arm around her waist and nuzzling her neck.

'Know what you are? You're an exhibitionist, Melissa Montagu.'

'And . . . ?' Melissa's heart was thumping. She hadn't been this aroused in ages. Suddenly the one thing she wanted to do was to fuck, right in the middle of this beautiful, empty moorland.

'And I *love* it.' Rhys unzipped his flies. Melissa was right. He didn't feel the cold, not one bit. The furnace heat of his lust was enough to keep both of them as warm as toast. Fingers clumsy with desire, he pulled out his erect penis. 'Would you like to suck my cock, Melissa? I'd really love to spurt my come down your throat.'

Melissa's response was to kneel down on the heather in front of him, ignoring the discomfort of the scratchy twigs under her knees. She was suddenly so thirsty, her mouth and throat dusty-dry, and the only thing that could slake her thirst was the taste of Rhys's semen.

Before Rhys had time to think, she had taken the tip of his penis into her mouth, tightening the red 'O' of her lips about his shaft and then suddenly, gloriously, engulfing its entire length in her greedy throat.

Rhys let out a cry of startled pleasure, then instinctively began to thrust, answering Melissa's licking and sucking with slow, hard movements of his pelvis. He'd always liked having his penis sucked – what man didn't? – but Melissa had never been quite so eager to do it for him before. And this felt exquisite, like if he wanted it could go on for ever.

Melissa savoured the taste of Rhys's manhood on her tongue. The thick, slippery, salty fluid tasted so good that she probed with her tongue-tip, drinking down each new drop that oozed from the glans. Her fingers curled about the base of his penis, pressing on the root in the way that she knew gave him pleasure, brushing the hairy sac of his balls as they tensed and readied themselves for their explosive tribute.

She rubbed her thighs together, instinctively stimulating her own pleasure, the way she had done when she was a child. As her thighs clenched, her labia pressed together in an intimate kiss, and the pink, fleshy hood of her clitoris slipped back and forth, teasing and tormenting her towards a climax.

Rhys gripped Melissa's shoulders, watching his dick disappearing then emerging from between the tight sheath of her imprisoning lips. As he thrust into her with long, slow strokes, he noticed how her breasts jiggled and quivered inside her tight sweater; and he wished he had two dicks, one for her mouth and the other to thrust between those succulent, firm breasts.

Only a few moments more and he knew he would be at the very summit of his desire. He stroked Melissa's golden mane and her blue eyes told him how close she, too, was to pleasure. A few more strokes of his dick, a few more thrusts into that willing mouth . . .

A strong breeze blew across the moors, catching Melissa's golden hair and blowing it about her face like ripe corn, swirling in a summer wind. A cloud had drifted across the sun but neither of them noticed the raw, frosty chill in the air. Nor did they notice the designer jeep as it drove past, slowing down momentarily before accelerating off in the direction of Highmoor.

Christopher Maudsley was having an irritating day. As if dashing about like a blue-arsed fly between the Whitby and Pickering offices weren't bad enough, he had to be over at Highmoor by half-past three to show some young London couple over the big house.

Whilst he didn't share George Mainprize's superstitious dislike of Highmoor House, he didn't particularly enjoy going up there either, if only because he had little faith in anyone actually buying it and moving in. It had been five years now since the last couple took it over. They'd hardly lasted six months before they decided they'd made a mistake and sold out to some big leisure company who planned to develop the place as an upmarket country hotel. For some reason or other that had come to nothing and now the house was on the market again. It seemed a shame really. It was a nice house – or it would be, if it hadn't been left to fall to bits.

Genuine Elizabethan it was, too. There weren't many of those around this neck of the woods. You'd think people would be queueing up for a chance to live there. But, over the years, Highmoor House had had more owners than George Mainprize had had free pints of ale. Perhaps it was the old stories, the legends about mysterious disappearances, that put people off. All Christopher Maudsley knew was that he wished he could get this over with and go home. He was seeing that new barmaid from the Black Lion tonight. Janice, her name was – Jazz for short. *Very* nice legs.

The jeep took the hill, swerved round the corner and bounced onto the bumpy road between Goathland and Highmoor. Fingers drumming on the dashboard, Maudsley hummed along to the radio. It was pretty up here, maybe it wasn't such a bad day after all – sun on the heather, fresh air . . . hang on, what the bloody hell was that?

He slowed down to overtake a grey Audi parked by the side of the road and, as he looked left over the moor, he saw something. No, not something – someone. Two someones, in fact.

'Well, I'll be . . .' He whistled, half in disbelief, half in dumbstruck admiration.

A moment later he had driven past. He would rather have

liked to go back and take a second look but that would be kind of obvious. Still, it wasn't every day you saw a man and a woman having oral sex in the middle of the North York Moors . . .

'You didn't tell me this was going to be an assault course,' complained Melissa, wrestling with the wheel of the Audi as it bumped over the unmade track.

'You wanted to up sticks and live in the country,' retorted Rhys. 'The question is – can you take it?'

'Oh, I can take it,' replied Melissa. 'I'm just not sure the car can. If we do come and live here, we'll have to get a Land-Rover or something.'

Towards its end, the lane curved sharply right. Behind a stand of huge, gnarled trees appeared tall gateposts, half-hidden by vegetation. In the distance Melissa could make out the shape of Highmoor House, its barley-sugar twist chimneys poking up from behind the tangled tree tops, silhouetted against the pale sky.

It was not a particularly large house, but it was easy to see how magnificent it could be, given time and a great deal of hard work. Although overgrown with ivy, the stonework was more or less intact and the house seemed to exude a friendly, reassuring presence. But it was clear that nature had completely taken over the grounds. The garden walls had crumbled away to let in the creeping moorland vegetation, which now mingled with a riot of overgrown garden plants.

It was almost impossible to see where the gardens ended and the moors began. And with twelve acres of overgrown grounds to contend with, Rhys could see that Highmoor

PARADISE GARDEN

House would be a challenge even for the keenest amateur gardener – which he definitely wasn't.

A trendy Japanese jeep was parked beside the gate and, as they drove up, a man got out. He must have been in his late twenties or early thirties, thought Melissa, a little above average height, with broad shoulders and smooth brown hair combed back from his forehead. He wasn't exceptionally good-looking but had a rugged attractiveness which Melissa found rather appealing.

'That must be the estate agent,' commented Melissa, parking the Audi. 'What did you say his name was?'

'Maudsley. Christopher Maudsley, I think he said. He looks a bit ... well ... surprised, don't you think?'

Christopher Maudsley was surprised all right. Surprised that Rhys and Melissa had turned up at all (given that they were half an hour late) and more surprised still to recognise them as the couple he had seen on the moors, so deeply wrapped up in their own pleasure. Well, at least he now knew why they were so late.

He composed his face into an expression of professional friendliness and approached, hand outstretched.

'Christopher Maudsley, Rennitt and Creasey. And you must be ...' He consulted his Filofax, though he knew their names off by heart. He was slightly worried that if he looked them in the face he would burst out laughing. Or was it something else he was afraid of? Was he afraid of how profoundly sexy he found Melissa Montagu?

Rhys shook hands with Maudsley.

'Melissa and Rhys Montagu. Pleased to meet you.' Head on one side, he contemplated the distant house. 'Is it as bad as it looks from here?'

Maudsley laughed, a little nervously.

'Well . . . not all of it,' he said. 'The previous owners – a couple from South Wales – made a start on restoring the house. Some of the ground floor has been refurbished, together with one of the bedrooms. Oh, and the bathroom isn't *too* bad.'

'It's a lot of money you're asking,' said Melissa as they walked up the drive towards a side door. 'Leastways, it's a lot of money for a wreck.'

'Oh, it's hardly that,' Maudsley assured her, searching for the right key on his key-ring. 'Structurally speaking, it's basically sound and I think you'll agree that it's a very reasonable price when you've seen inside the house. And think of the investment potential. A genuine Elizabethan property . . .'

'A genuine Elizabethan building-site,' commented Rhys as the door opened and they went inside. The kitchen itself wasn't that bad but there was builders' equipment all over the place.

'The owners . . . er . . . made quite a sudden decision to sell up,' volunteered Maudsley. 'All of this would of course be cleared out before you move in. Now, why don't I show you the dining room?'

Until she stepped into the dining room, Melissa had been unsure about Highmoor House. It could have been any one of a dozen run-down old properties, begging for love and attention. But the dining room . . . now that was something special.

'As you can see, it has been fully refurbished in the style of the period.' Maudsley consulted the specification. 'Some of the rooms in the house have suffered from rather unsympathetic refurbishment over the years, but I think this room gives some idea of the house's original beauty.'

Melissa just stood and stared, her eyes travelling over the ornate oak-panelling lining the walls, the decorative plasterwork on the ceiling, the sculpted fire surround and the black oak chest, intricately carved, which served as a window seat. Tendrils of ivy wove a thick skein over the outside of the small-paned windows but golden afternoon light filtered into the room, making the woodwork gleam beneath its thick layer of dust. Even denuded of most of its furniture, the room exuded a stately yet romantic beauty which Melissa found irresistible.

'Who are they?' Rhys indicated two portraits, hanging on either side of the fireplace.

'Oh, that's Reuben Fairfax – he designed and built the house, back in the 1580s. And the woman is his mistress, Perdita. He built the house for her.' Maudsley winked. 'Nice and secluded, you see – a good long way from prying eyes.'

Melissa looked at the portraits more closely. Perdita smiled down at her from her dusty frame, more enigmatic than the Mona Lisa and a good deal prettier. Melissa turned to look at Reuben Fairfax, dark and bearded and indecently handsome in black velvet and a crisp white ruff. He seemed to be whispering to her from the canvas: 'Why hold back any longer, Melissa? Why delay when you know you've found what you've been looking for?'

Rhys blew the dust from an old framed engraving, a little tattered now but still hanging on the wall by the window. It showed a lush walled garden, where exotic fruits and flowers hung on every tree, and beneath the laden branches two lovers embraced, their naked limbs intertwined, their mouths joined in a passionate kiss.

'Paradise Garden,' Rhys made out with difficulty, turning back to look at Maudsley. 'What's that?'

Maudsley shrugged.

'There's supposed to be an ornamental garden in the grounds of the house somewhere, but it's so overgrown I'm not even sure where to look for it. Fairfax created it for Perdita – they used to go there when they wanted a little extra privacy, if you know what I mean. I think he called it the Paradise Garden.'

'It must have been beautiful,' said Melissa, looking at the engraving.

'I suppose it must.' Maudsley looked from Melissa to Rhys and back again. He smiled as he remembered what he had seen up on the moors. 'Well, they do say that Highmoor is a house for lovers.'

'I wish I could be sure.'

Melissa turned back from the window, gazing sightlessly into the darkness beyond the car park of the Black Lion Inn.

'I thought you were. You said you loved the house . . .'

'I know, Rhys, and I do. It's just . . . well, it would take every penny we have and how would we pay for all the restoration work?'

'We could do it ourselves.' Rhys could hardly believe he was saying this. He *hated* DIY – didn't he?

'Could we?'

'I don't see why not. It would take time but what the hell? We've got all the time in the world.' He sat up in bed, lifting up the covers on Melissa's side. 'Come to bed. We don't have to make a decision right away. And I've just thought of this wonderful way to take your mind off it . . .'

She sat down on the edge of the bed and he eased off her robe. It slid off with a soft whisper of pink satin and underneath she was naked, still moist and fragrant from her bath.

'Oh Melissa, every time I see you naked I realise I'd forgotten how beautiful you are.'

He made to pull her down onto the bed but she got to her feet and took a step further away.

'Is something the matter, Melissa?'

She shook her head, smiling. It was that same, mischievous smile she had given him that afternoon in the car.

'Do you remember what we did this afternoon, on the moor?'

'Melissa – I could hardly forget!'

'Did you enjoy having me suck your cock?'

He got up and embraced her, his stiffening cock pressing against the softness of her belly as he thought of just how good it had been.

'Darling,' he whispered, kissing her eyes, her throat, her breasts. 'Darling, it was amazing.'

'Would you do the same for me?' She took his hand and guided it down to the warm forest of her pubic curls, shuffling her feet a little way apart so that his fingers entered the moist haven between her thighs. 'Would you lick me out, Rhys?'

His reply was to slide to his knees before her, darting a trail of kisses from throat and breast to belly and thighs. Silently, excitedly, he explored her pubis with his tongue, winding the short, golden hairs about its tip, tugging at them gently so that the plump, sensitive flesh of her labia was stimulated.

She was breathing in short, thick gasps, her breasts rising and falling quickly, her thighs trembling and her fingers stroking his hair convulsively, as though they longed to be stroking her clitoris, seizing the pleasure which was now his and his alone to give. Slowly, painfully slowly, he let the tip of his tongue penetrate the deep crease between her outer labia, and was rewarded by a low moan of gratitude and a warm, sweet trickle of honeydew as the lips parted to admit him.

Melissa's sex tasted sweeter, juicier than the most exotic fruit. Her fragrance made his head spin with excitement, made him so aroused that he had to force himself not to throw her down on the bed and have her. And curiously, he knew that that was not what he really wanted anyway. What he wanted was this, this long, slow, luxurious sex-play which excited him just as much as it excited Melissa – perhaps even more.

As the tip of his tongue glanced over the head of her clitty, she began to move her hips, at first very slowly and then more quickly, until she was thrusting against him quite hard, clasping his face against the fragrant garden of her pubis as she took her pleasure.

He knew that she was coming, perhaps even before she knew it herself. He could feel the tension building up in her, the muscles of her thighs growing taut, trembling, her pussy lips gushing their honey-sweet juice onto his famished tongue.

And suddenly she opened herself to him, her sex gaping wide before clenching in the first of a series of powerful spasms.

'Oh darling, oh, Rhys, Rhys!'

No longer caring if she was overheard by any of the other residents of the Black Lion Inn, Melissa threw back her head and cried out the power of her ecstasy.

'Yes, yes, YES!'

She fell into his arms and they rolled onto the floor, over and over on the carpet, kissing and laughing. And then Rhys was astride her, his cock searching out the heart of her desire, entering her, thrusting, coupling, driving towards the ecstasy that only they could share.

It was just after two-thirty when Rhys awoke. He remembered that distinctly, because he glanced at the travelling clock on the old washstand.

At first he wasn't sure what had woken him up. Then he saw the gleam of light through the half-open curtains and heard it again, this time more distinctly.

'Oh. Ohhh . . .'

He slipped out of bed, trying not to wake Melissa, but as he lifted her arm from round his waist she murmured in protest and her eyes flickered open.

'Rhys . . .'

'It's all right, Melissa. I just heard something outside.'

He got to the window and drew the curtain aside. Outside, the garden of the Black Lion was flooded with the orange-yellow glow from a light in one of the downstairs rooms. But it wasn't the light that made Rhys blink and rub his eyes.

'Well, well, well!'

'Rhys?'

'Come and look at this.'

Melissa got out of bed and crossed to the window. There, outside on the grass, were two figures. Two naked figures: a woman with long red hair and a swarthy man, their bodies locked in a passionate embrace. As the man turned towards the window, Melissa saw that he had a long, white scar running down the side of his handsome face.

'Well!' Rhys scratched his head. 'I don't believe it. Getting it on out there stark naked – they must be freezing.'

'That doesn't seem to bother them,' remarked Melissa, remembering how easy it had been to ignore the cold up on the moors that afternoon – not to mention any fears of discovery.

The man and the girl seemed totally oblivious to everything around them. Their bodies coupled, they kissed as they fucked, their thighs intertwined and their skin soaked with sweat. Melissa had never seen either of them before, yet there was something curiously familiar about them. As she realised what it was, a frisson of *déjà vu* made her whole body tingle.

They looked exactly like the couple in the engraving they had seen at Highmoor House. The engraving of the Paradise Garden.

Chapter 4

Playful fingers of May sunlight crept through the curtains to caress the two sleeping lovers, casting ever-changing patterns on their bare flesh.

Melissa lay in the crook of Rhys's arm, her corn-blonde hair tousled and fluffy and her skin still a little moist from the sweat of their passion. It had been a long night, long and sensual; their bodies intertwining again and again in the darkness, feeding off each other's passionate hunger.

Neither of them had quite understood the unstoppable desire which had surged through them. Perhaps it had been anticipation of the new life which they were about to begin. The new life with its new challenges and freedoms, its uncertainties and excitements. In two days' time, they would be waking up in the master bedroom at Highmoor House. The thought made Melissa shiver deliciously and her hunger for Rhys seemed to burn even more fiercely within her. As they remade their life together, it was as though they were starting to see each other in a new light, too, falling in lust all over again . . .

As the warm sunshine flickered across her eyelids, Melissa stirred in her sleep, gave a little sigh and awoke, turning onto her side to kiss Rhys's bare chest. His skin was very smooth, very taut, with just a sprinkling of mid-brown hairs around and between his nipples. A little trail of hairs led down from his navel to the base of his belly, where the juicy fruits of his manhood awaited her touch to swell into ripeness.

She took his left nipple into her mouth. It was a tiny pink button, nothing like the great saucer-shaped, coral discs of her own nipples, that erected at the slightest touch into thick, rubbery crests almost an inch long. Nevertheless, Melissa knew how much Rhys loved having his nipples sucked and bitten, and wondered to herself if it felt the same way as it did for her, having lips and tongue and teeth playing around the sensitive flesh.

Did he feel the same electric tingling that she did, the same buzz that seemed to run from each nipple right down to the epicentre of need between her thighs? She tongued his nipple with infinite gentleness, as though it were very fragile and precious; and the warmth of need spread through her body as she felt the flesh grow, pucker, harden from a flat pink button into a hard pink pearl.

'Mmm. Oh Melissa . . . oh that feels good, you wicked girl.'

Rhys surfaced into wakefulness with the feeling that something very, very nice was happening to him.

Melissa smiled.

'I thought you'd never wake up.'

Then she went back to pleasuring him with her tongue, lapping at the salty sweat that had dried about his nipple.

Rhys stroked the hair back from her forehead and watched her lips part to reveal her darting tongue, its tip finding again and again the most sensitive, the most susceptible spot.

She paused for a moment and kissed his chest, his belly.

'Nice?'

'Feel how nice.' Rhys took hold of her hand and guided

it down over his belly until she felt the swollen stalk of his penis. He kissed her forehead. 'Not bad for an old guy of twenty-nine, huh? How many times was it last night . . . ?'

Melissa let her fingers curl about Rhys's cock. It felt right, somehow, to have his sex in her hand, to feel in its hardness the power of her own sexuality.

'Darling,' she whispered. 'Who's counting?'

To Rhy's disappointment, she stopped stroking his dick and rolled away.

'You've stopped!'

'Your turn,' she said. And she pushed the duvet off onto the floor, baring her slim thighs and the golden triangle of curls at the base of her belly. 'Your turn to pleasure me.'

'Oh it is, is it?' Rhys's heart was pounding. He ought to be exhausted after last night but he wasn't. He felt rejuvenated, ready to make love to her all day as well as all night. God, but he wanted her.

He let his fingers run, very slowly, right down the length of her body from shoulder to knee, savouring the silky-smoothness of her skin. He could feel Melissa trembling under his fingers, her whole body vibrating as though the energy within her was building up, demanding release.

Melissa watched him slide down to the foot of the bed, then felt a pleasurable tickle as he started kissing her feet. She giggled and wriggled.

'Rhys! Stop it – it tickles!' But she didn't really want him to stop. And the longer it went on, the more she felt the transformation from child's play to a far more sensual game.

Rhys took her big toe into his mouth and started playing with it, very gently at first. She felt the warm wetness of his mouth trickling over her skin and then he started licking and sucking. This wasn't something he had ever done before and quite honestly it had never occurred to Melissa that it might be so pleasurable. It had always seemed something of a joke.

But as Rhys licked and caressed her, taking each toe in turn into his mouth, she began to discover just how erotic it was to have his caresses on her skin there, and just how sensitive that skin was. A sensation a little like pins and needles ran over her as he nibbled at her littlest toe, sucking and biting at it simultaneously. When he took his mouth away, the cool morning air chilled the wetness on her skin and that, too, stimulated her excitement. She could feel her sex – already wet from the night's lovemaking – oozing a fragrant cocktail of semen and fresh sex-juice, as though it too longed to be the object of Rhys's intimate kisses.

At last he drew away, then began kissing the arch of her foot, her ankle, her calf and shin and knee. Each kiss lasted for several seconds, the wetness of his darting tongue lingering on the skin as though to show that his kisses could never be forgotten.

She knew what he was doing, knew where his kisses were leading. First one leg then the other: foot, ankle, calf, knee, thigh ... A few inches from the fold of her groin, where thigh met vulva, he paused, teasing, waiting.

'Oh, Rhys, please ...'

His tongue lapped slowly and tantalisingly at the inner surface of her thigh, tasting the essence of sex that had trickled down, drying on the skin.

'You want me to kiss you again?' he teased.

'Oh yes!'

'Where do you want me to kiss you?'

Melissa took hold of Rhys's hand and placed it on the mound of her pubis.

'I want you to kiss me there, Rhys.'

'On your pussy lips?'

'I want to feel your kisses on my pussy, Rhys. *In* my pussy, right inside.'

Rhys rubbed gently on Melissa's mound of Venus and she squirmed as the inexorable waves of pleasure washed over her, the slow trickle of clear sex-fluid becoming so abundant that it gushed out of her onto the sheet beneath her, staining the cotton a darker shade of blue.

Parting her thighs, he knelt between them and explored her sex. The whole of her pubis and outer labia was deeply forested with bright curls of wiry golden hair, but between lay the deep, dark crease which marked the entrance to her most intimate secrets. Rhys opened up her sex, very gently, prising it apart with his thumbs. Inside her flesh was coral-pink and as shiny as molten glass, glossy with her copious spendings.

He let his finger explore the delights of her inner labia, tracing the deep pink folds and frills, moving lightly over the delicate flesh so that his fingertip just brushed it.

It was enough to awaken desire but not nearly enough to satisfy it. Melissa gave a low, shuddering moan and drew her knees up further, exposing her sex to Rhys's greedy caresses and kisses.

He touched her, very lightly, on her clitoris. Instantly she let out a cry of distress and he drew back, faintly alarmed at the reaction he had provoked.

'So, so sensitive,' gasped Melissa. 'I can hardly bear it.'

Rhys moved his finger a fraction away and began circling

the engorged stalk of Melissa's clitty, so lightly and gently that he was scarcely touching the flesh. Yet Melissa moaned and clutched at the bed as pleasure overtook her and she felt herself dangerously, desperately, close to orgasm.

'Please, Rhys. Your tongue. I want to feel your kisses . . .'

Rhys needed no persuading. He had always loved the taste of Melissa's honeypot. And it increased his own pleasure many times over to feel and taste the excitement flooding out of her as he lapped up the sticky oozings of her climax.

He began by pushing just the very tip of his tongue into the well from which her desire was oozing and trickling. It was sweet yet spicy, its strong flavour a mingling of the pleasure they had shared all night long. He lapped it up, feeling the juices hardening his cock even as they melted on his tongue.

Just the tip. Just the very tip. Make it last. His tongue flicked and rolled just inside the entrance to her vagina and he felt the way her sex-muscles tensed, almost imperceptibly, as though trying to draw him deeper inside her.

It was not hot in the bedroom but sweat was trickling between Melissa's breasts. She was in heaven, her mind and body transported to a land where only pleasure mattered. Rhys's tongue-tip was stimulating the most sensitive part of her vagina – the very entrance, where even the slightest touch could make her writhe and moan with excitement. Her breasts quivered as she moved her hips, trying to force Rhys to release the tide of ecstasy inside her, but Rhys was biding his time, making her really ready for him.

His fingers slid over her inner thighs, brushing the

abundant yellow curls which fringed the secret jewel-box of her sex. He longed to throw himself on top of her, to pull apart her thighs and push into her in one long, smooth stroke, but Rhys knew that waiting, making it last, would bring greater pleasure for them both.

Slowly, he pushed his tongue a little deeper into Melissa's hot, wet haven.

'Oh. Oh, Rhys. Oh, do it to me . . .'

Just a fraction deeper, he told himself. Now stop. Twist and turn your tongue inside her, that's it. Feel how she's moving her hips, making you fuck her with your tongue. It feels good and, oh, the taste of her. So strong and sweet.

'Rhys, fuck me. Please fuck me, I'm aching for you.'

He pushed the rest of his tongue inside her, so deep that his face was pressed right against her vulva and he could hardly breathe for the warm wetness and the all-pervading scent of her. Not that he cared. All he cared about was the way she was making him feel, the way he was going to make her feel.

For a little while they lay like that, Melissa with her knees drawn up and Rhys between her legs, his tongue pushed into her up to the hilt and moving slowly in and out of her, like an eager penis.

Then he withdrew from her. The sudden, brutal loss made Melissa gasp and clutch at him, trying to draw him back into her.

He kissed her pubis, toying with her fragrant curls, winding them about his tongue-tip whilst the very tip of his finger played with the entrance to her sex.

'Do you want it, Melissa?'

'I want *you*.'

'Do you want me to fuck you with my fingers or with my tongue.'

'I want you to fuck me with both.'

Rhys gave a throaty chuckle.

'Greedy girl,' he murmured. 'I'm *so* glad you're a greedy girl, Melissa.'

His finger slipped into her like a hot knife into butter, in one swift movement which took him inside her right up to the knuckle. A second finger followed, then a third, and he spread them out inside her, stretching the elastic walls of her vagina.

'Feels good?' he enquired, twisting his wrist through ninety degrees so that Melissa could feel his fingers moving inside her.

'Feels like heaven,' sighed Melissa. 'But I want to taste you, Rhys. I want to give you pleasure too. Won't you let me take you into my mouth?'

Rhys's cock jerked at at the very thought of Melissa's warm and welcoming mouth closing about its tip. If she wanted to suck him off, he certainly wasn't going to pretend he didn't want her to.

'You want my dick in your mouth?'

'Oh *yes*.'

'You want it now?' He withdrew his fingers from her and knelt up so that she could see his cock, trace the upward-curving sabre of flesh as he cradled it in his hands and began stroking it.

Melissa stretched out her hands, beseeching.

'I want it now, put it inside me,' she begged.

Rhys kissed her, then turned round so that he was kneeling astride her, facing Melissa's feet. Slowly he lowered himself over her face so that his cock-tip was dangling just about her mouth. She put out her tongue and planted a kiss on the glans.

'There is nothing in the world so beautiful as your cock, Rhys.' It was true, too, thought Melissa. Rhys's might not be the biggest cock she had ever had inside her, not the thickest or the longest, but it was beautifully formed and iron-hard. It had the power to turn her on even when she thought she wasn't really interested in sex, and when she yearned for a night of passion, she knew that Rhys would never let her down.

Rhys lowered himself a few inches further and felt Melissa's wonderfully soft mouth engulf him. Instead of the cool air of the bedroom, he felt the hot, slick wetness of her tongue surrounding him, drowning him in a warm ocean of pleasure.

He parted Melissa's pussy-lips with his fingers and buried his face in the fragrant heaven of her sex. Slipping his index finger into her vagina, he began slowly finger-fucking her, whilst lightly kissing her inner pussy lips.

As Rhys bore down on her, Melissa took his cock deep, so very deep, into her mouth. So deep that its tip nudged hard against the back of her throat at every tilt of Rhys's pelvis, every thrust that took him just a little closer to orgasm. He tasted of purest sex, the strength of his taste surprising her as she sucked on him and savoured the memory of a long night's coupling. Both of them were in that taste, the unique taste and fragrance of their fucking.

It excited her to feel the lubricating fluid dripping from Rhys's glans and trickling down her throat. It was very smooth and slippery, a little salty, but she loved it, wanted more and more. But Rhys was very hard, steel hard, as he always became shortly before coming; and Melissa could feel her own climax approaching as his tongue wound its way ever closer to the pleasure-centre of her sex.

She felt Rhys's tongue making circular movements about her clitoris, never quite touching it but coming breathtakingly, unbearably close. How could she hold back when her lover was kissing and caressing the heart of her sex and each movement made the hood of her clitoris slide back and forth across the swollen nubbin of flesh?

Caressing Rhys's heavy seed-sacs, she sucked hard on his prick, feeling his smooth shaft become still harder in those few, breathless seconds between the realisation that there is no turning back, and the dazzling fulfilment of ecstasy.

Almost. So close. So close, feel the pleasure building up, the ache in the belly, the tingling, the expectation.

'Aah!' Melissa let out a sharp cry as at last Rhys's tongue-tip flicked over the head of her clitoris. She felt the electric thrill as her whole body tensed and then, suddenly, it was like stepping into bright light, falling and tumbling through ecstasy as her vagina tensed in the first of many delicious spasms.

Rhys felt her tighten about his finger and then her honeydew was inundating his fingers, filling his mouth, flowing so abundantly that he could scarcely lap it all up and swallow it down. Her lips too were tight, tight about his cock, sucking, licking, biting . . .

He was so delighted by the spectacle of Melissa's pleasure that the sudden rush of semen took him almost by surprise, shaking his whole body, making him feel as though his entire being were rushing out of him and into Melissa's willing mouth.

Afterwards they lay together for many minutes, each delighting in the other's taste and touch, each still warmed by the afterglow. Rhys drew Melissa towards him, kissing her, sharing with her the taste of her own desire.

'I've got an idea,' he said, lazily stroking her flank.

Melissa snuggled close, sleepy and warm, the morning sunshine peeping at her shamelessly from behind the half-drawn curtains.

'Mmm?'

'Do you remember the day we first moved in here?'

Melissa scanned the room, remembering their excitement on that day, almost three years ago. This was the first house they'd bought together, the first . . . and tomorrow they would be moving to Highmoor House. It was like a dream, an unbelievable dream come true.

'I remember.'

'And do you remember how we . . . celebrated our new home?'

Rhys ran his hand down Melissa's backside, appreciating the firm smoothness of her rounded buttocks.

Melissa thought for a moment, then chuckled.

'You mean . . . ?'

Rhys held her very close, the stiffening rod of his penis pushing impatiently into the base of her stomach.

'That's right, Melissa. We were so excited we just couldn't stop ourselves. At the top of the stairs – remember? – you took off your panties and hitched up your skirt . . .'

'. . . And you had me right up against the wall.' Her excitement rekindled by reminiscence, Melissa ground her belly against Rhys's swollen penis. 'So . . . ?'

'So shouldn't we say goodbye to the old house?' said Rhys slyly. 'Properly?'

'You know, I think we should,' said Melissa, smiling. And taking Rhys by the hand, she led him out onto the landing.

A day later, Rhys and Melissa found themselves unlocking the front door of Highmoor House.

It was a typical late spring day up on the moors – bright but a little chilly with a cutting breeze which rustled the heather and sent the sheep scuttling off into the cover of dry-stone walls and stunted trees.

But at Highmoor House, behind the sheltering walls and towering trees, only the sunshine seemed to matter. The air was still and sweet and fragrant with the scents of wet leaves and grass. Rhys and Melissa stood for a long time on the driveway, watching the removal van make its bumpy way back along the track to the main road.

'Looks like this is it,' said Rhys, drawing in a deep breath.

'Are we really here?' asked Melissa.

Rhys took a look around him. It really was like some fantastic dream.

'I think so,' he replied. 'It hasn't quite sunk in.'

'How do you feel, now we're here at last?'

'To be honest,' Rhys admitted, putting his arm round Melissa's shoulders, 'I'm shit scared. What if we've made the wrong decision? We've sunk everything we've got into this place.'

'It's a bit late to change our minds now,' retorted Melissa, planting a kiss on the end of his nose. 'And besides, we *have* made the right decision, I know we have. It's the chance of a lifetime.'

They strolled up the front driveway, hastily cleared by a local contractor so that there would be somewhere to park the car, and gazed around at the overgrown jumble which might once have been a rather nice front garden. As far as the eye could see, in every direction, stretched the verdant jumble that had once been flowerbeds and formal gardens and grassy walks between tree-lined avenues.

'Just look at it! It's completely out of control – looks like the Triffids have moved in. You can hardly see the house for overgrown bushes and trees. And you'd never think there was an ornamental walled garden somewhere in the middle of that wilderness.'

Melissa smiled and shook her head.

'We'll sort the grounds out. It'll take ages but we'll do it. It'll be fun.'

'It'll be fun watching you,' replied Rhys archly. 'You know how I hate gardening!'

Laughing like kids, they walked round to the back of the house and went in through the kitchen door. It was still a crazy jumble but at least they'd managed to turn on the water and the gas cooker seemed to be working, after a fashion. Better still, the leisure company's partial renovations had left them with a few luxuries – a rather splendid Edwardian-style bathroom, power points for Rhys's fax and computer, and a perfectly comfortable master bedroom, complete with a slightly rickety four-poster bed which – if you could believe Christopher Maudsley – was an Elizabethan original which had actually belonged to Reuben Fairfax and his mistress.

'I'm bushed,' Melissa announced, sinking onto one of

the kitchen chairs they had brought from the old house. It wasn't until they'd moved in that they realised how very inadequate and silly their ordinary, modern furniture was going to look in a place like this, alongside the few antique pieces which had been left behind by previous owners.

'Bed?' suggested Rhys hopefully.

Melissa laughed, taking the pony-tail ring from her hair and letting it fall free.

'Is that all you ever think of?'

'Mostly,' replied Rhys with disarming honesty.

Melissa ran her hand through her hair.

'Food would be nice,' she said. 'But I haven't got the energy to drive into Whitby. I guess we'll have to eat at the Black Lion.'

'Maudsley said he'd try and get us a loaf of bread and some milk,' Rhys pointed out, inspecting the bare kitchen table. 'I guess he forgot.'

'What do you expect? He's an estate agent, not a fairy godmother. But I'll try the pantry.' Melissa got up and walked across to the pantry door, opening it and taking a look inside.

It was an immense walk-in pantry, big enough for a room in itself. Slatted wooden shelves lined the walls, with marble slabs at waist-height to store perishable foods.

'Come and see this!' she exclaimed.

Rhys appeared at her shoulder.

'What?'

'This.' Melissa stood aside. 'It seems our Mr Maudsley's more generous than we gave him credit for.'

Rhys let out a low whistle. Ranged on one of the marble slabs were a huge slab of farmhouse Wensleydale cheese, a loaf of crusty bread, an uncut ham and a dusty bottle of wine. Next to this was a huge earthenware bowl filled to the brim with all sorts of fruit.

'That Maudsley must fancy you something rotten, that's all I can say,' observed Rhys. 'Not that I blame him,' he added, taking Melissa in his arms.

'Want to eat?' suggested Melissa.

'I'd rather fuck.'

'Sounds good to me . . . but how about a bath?' Melissa's blue eyes searched his face, full of merriment. 'It's a huge bath. You know, it just might be big enough for two.'

Melissa stretched out on her belly in the immense iron bath and relaxed as Rhys soaped her back.

'You have such a lovely back,' he told her, rubbing the cake of soap over her skin in smooth circles and watching the creamy bubbles of lather trickle down into the water, making opaque swirls about Melissa's naked body. 'And an even lovelier backside,' he added, pushing the cake of soap just a little further down this time, so that it slid edgeways into the deep crease between her bum cheeks.

Melissa was enjoying the sensual luxury of this first bath in their new house. Even if they had had to wait hours for the elderly boiler to heat up the water, it was well worth it.

The sensations produced by the bar of soap on her skin were quite novel. It was a creamy white soap, studded with granules of rough oatmeal, which stimulated the surface of the body like the tips of a lover's fingernails. As the soap-cake slid between the cheeks of her backside, she felt its roughness abrading the super-sensitive membranes of her arse, making its secret mouth alternately purse and dilate, like the mouth of some sea-creature.

He pushed the soap a little further down and now she could feel it at the entrance to her vagina, the soap stinging just a little and the rough grains of oatmeal tormenting her vulva with the most curious sensations.

'Rhys, please!' She wriggled so furiously that the softly splashing water turned into a turbulent ocean and began splashing over the sides.

Rhys held the soaked fabric of his shirt between finger and thumb, shaking his head with a mischievous smile.

'Look what you've done,' he declared. 'I'm soaking wet. I suppose I'll just have to get undressed now . . .'

He stripped off shirt and pants and Melissa watched him, licking her lips in anticipation as he peeled down his underpants, revealing the smooth, hard baton of his cock.

Melissa moved to roll onto her back but Rhys stopped her.

'No. Don't move. Stay where you are.'

He climbed into the bath, slopping yet more water onto the tiled floor – but at this precise moment neither he nor Melissa could have cared less about the state of the bathroom floor. Melissa felt her lover's weight on her, his thighs sliding astride her backside, squeezing her tightly in the narrow space of the bath.

His fingers fumbled, grown awkward and inept in the water, slick with creamy lather and scented bath-oil. Then he found the place and pulled her bum cheeks apart, feeling down, down, down until he found the irresistibly wet haven of her sex.

Melissa gasped and splashed, propping herself up on her elbows to stop the water getting into her eyes and nose. But she didn't want this to stop, oh no. She thrust out her backside to meet Rhys's exploring fingers, the nuzzling snout of his cock. And when he slid into her, she squealed her pleasure, no longer caring who heard them – and in any case, who could possibly overhear them in the middle of the wild North York Moors?

'Just think, Reuben Fairfax and his mistress might have made love in this room,' panted Rhys, scything in and out between Melissa's silken pussy-lips. 'Do you think he ever had her like this . . . ?'

Melissa did not reply. She was imagining the house as it must have been in late Elizabethan times when Reuben Fairfax had created it for his lover. She pictured Perdita, beautiful Perdita with the laughing eyes. Had Fairfax thrown her down on the floor of this room, lifted her skirts and taken her with rough hunger? Or had she straddled him with her creamy thighs as he lay on the ground, taking him up inside her and riding him until she drew the seed out of him, leaving him drained? Had she looked to him as her absolute master, or had Fairfax been Perdita's slave, a slave of the passions which had raged within him, insuppressible and unchecked?

There were so many questions, questions that there was no time to answer for Rhys was hard and strong inside her and the hot, white lava of his pleasure was bubbling and spurting out of him into her womanhood. And she was crying out, laughing and weeping for pleasure as her own body answered him, her climax taking her over, shaking her like a helpless rag doll.

Wonderful, wonderful, wonderful pleasure . . .

Rhys helped Melissa out of the bath and towelled her dry

with a rough tenderness which enchanted her. They embraced, and the towel fell to the floor in a damp heap of pink cotton. Rhys planted kisses on Melissa's breasts, her throat, her eyes, the nape of her neck, whispering as he kissed her:

'Are you still hungry?'

Melissa shook her head and smiled.

'Not for food.'

Rhys cupped her right breast in his hand and bit and sucked the nipple until it was a bright-pink cone of rubbery flesh.

'Then whatever shall we do to pass the time . . . ?'

'Let's go to bed.'

They walked out of the bathroom and down the long corridor which ran almost the entire length of the upper floor. At the far end was their bedroom. They hesitated outside the door. Melissa was about to open it, when Rhys took her hand gently away.

'Let's do this properly,' he said softly. And he gathered her up in his arms, lifting her off her feet. 'Now open the door.'

Melissa reached out to turn the handle and Rhys stepped inside, carrying her across the room to the old four-poster bed. Melissa had made it up with crisp cotton sheets and an antique velvet bedspread she had inherited from her grandmother. Wine-red and opulent, its jewel-bright embroidery caught the last rays of the sun, picking out patterns of flowers and fruits.

Rhys laid her down on the bed and as he lay down beside her, the bedspread rumpled, revealing a triangle of bedsheet underneath. He gasped.

'What is it?' enquired Melissa, drowsy and sensual from her bath.

Rhys pulled the bedcover a little further across and shook his head in astonishment.

'Well, I'll be...'

Melissa rolled onto her belly and blinked in disbelief. Instead of plain white sheets beneath the bedspread, she saw drifts and drifts of pink rose-petals, each one heavy with musky scent.

Incredible though it seemed, someone, somehow, had come into the house and filled their bed with rose petals.

Chapter 5

Candice Soulbury stood in front of the bathroom mirror, her hand shaking slightly as she put the finishing touches to her make-up.

She put the top back on the mascara, slid it into her bag and stepped back to gauge the effect. Her lips were glossy ox-bows, crimson and moist and juicy as wild berries. Her brown eyes, which she had always thought a little small, seemed wider tonight, the artfully applied mascara and kohl lending her an expression somewhere between sensual innocence and exotic mystery . . . which was exactly as she had planned it.

Her lips curved into a smile. They looked fuller with the glossy red lipstick, their outline drawn with a smudged pencil line, filled in with a soft lip-brush, just the way she had been taught by the beautician when she went for that very expensive make-over. Candice had been preparing for tonight for a very long time.

Picking up her comb, she teased a lock of hair back into place then set the elaborate style with a spritz of hairspray. She didn't normally wear her hair pinned up like this but, then, this *was* a special night. Her hair glistened, mirror-smooth, in the electric light, chestnut highlights burning like a slow flame in the heart of each perfect wave and curl.

Her eyes travelled downwards, to the choker she was wearing around her neck. It wasn't anything special – just a length of dark-blue velvet ribbon, but her grandmother's pearl and sapphire brooch, pinned in the centre, lent it a touch of class.

The dark, flashing blue of the sapphire perfectly complimented the midnight-blue of her dress. Candice had spent an age choosing it, visiting every designer shop in the West End until she'd found exactly the right style to compliment her elegant figure. It was a figure-hugging sheath in dark-blue watered silk, lightly boned in the low-cut bodice so that it made the most of her small but apple-firm breasts. The skirt was tight enough to make sitting down a real problem – if it weren't for the side-split which ran from knee to hip, exposing a long sweep of slim thigh.

Panties were also a problem, of course, in such a revealing dress. Which was why Candice wasn't wearing any. It would never do to spoil the line of the delicate watered silk with even the faintest suggestion of a panty-line. Apart from her stockings and suspenders, Candice Soulbury was perfectly naked underneath her dress.

She checked that the seams of her stockings were straight, and wriggled her toes into the navy-blue, high-heeled shoes. Not *too* high, though, she wouldn't want to be as tall as her escort. Tonight, she wanted to be both deeply sensual and infinitely vulnerable . . .

The sound of the doorbell made her heart pound. Swiftly she made a last check in the mirror: hair, dress, elbow-length white gloves . . . One final dab of perfume behind each ear and a little between her breasts as an afterthought, then she was picking up her evening bag and walking across her living room to the front door of her apartment.

She opened the door. Peter Galliano was standing outside

with a bottle of champagne, the keys to his Porsche jingling in his hand. She felt his eyes travelling all over her, devouring her, clearly astonished by the transformation from coolly elegant PA to sex siren.

'Good evening . . . Peter.' It was difficult not to keep on calling him 'Mr Galliano' – after all, she had been his PA for almost four years now and it was kind of hard to break the habit.

'Hello, Candice.' Galliano seemed ever so slightly stunned by this new, smoulderingly sexual, Candice Soulbury. 'Ready?'

Candice picked up her jacket from the hall table and slung it about her bare shoulders. This was her moment, her triumph, at last. That scheming bitch Melissa Montagu was well out of the way and now Peter Galliano was falling under her spell. At long, long last it was all beginning to happen, just as she had known it would one day.

'Oh yes, Peter,' she breathed. 'I'm *absolutely* ready.'

'Good day?'

Melissa opened the passenger door and Rhys kissed her then climbed into the car, dropping his portfolio and portable PC onto the back seat. He let out a long sigh of relief as the car moved away from the front of York railway station.

'I'm bushed! You know, we're going to have to get a second car if I have to keep travelling to meet clients.'

Melissa swung into the one-way system, windscreen wipers swishing back and forth in the torrential rain. It had been like this for a couple of days now. If it kept up much longer, Highmoor House would have not so much ornamental gardens as a fully-fledged jungle.

'How did *you* get on, though?'

Rhys smiled.

'I knocked 'em dead.'

Melissa gave him a sideways look.

'Really?'

'Really. It turns out that they're desperate for freelancers who can write on ecological subjects – their ecology correspondent's buggered off to join a commune in Mid-Wales and design windmills or something. There's as much work as I can handle, for the time being anyway.'

'You're brilliant!' As the car idled at traffic lights, Melissa leant over and gave his ear a playful nibble. 'Does that mean we can afford to get a contractor in to help clear the gardens?'

Rhys laughed.

'You and your gardens! Steady on Melissa, what about all those missing slates on the west wing? If we leave it much longer, we'll need a whole new roof.'

Melissa sighed.

'I guess.'

Rhys patted her hand.

'No sweat. All in good time. We'll get the gardens looking great, just you wait and see. But the first thing we need to do is stop the house falling down about our ears . . .'

The lights turned to green and Melissa turned left through the city walls and towards the town centre.

'Where are we off to? I thought we were going home.'

'I'm taking you out to celebrate. You've got some freelance work and, guess what, I got a definite maybe for an office refit in Kirbymoorside.'

'You did? Oh Melissa, well done, I knew you could do it!'

'Hang on, it's not in the bag yet,' smiled Melissa. 'But the client liked the product, and I think he liked me.' Melissa grinned broadly. 'I don't suppose it's very ethical, but I'm glad I wore this short skirt.'

'Told you,' said Rhys a little smugly. 'There's not a man alive who could resist those legs.'

They left the Audi in a car park by the river and walked towards the city centre, huddling together under Rhys's golfing umbrella as the rain pounded down around them.

'What do you fancy – Indian? Italian?'

Melissa considered for a moment.

'Italian. There's that place just off the Shambles – you know ... the one we went to when ...'

'Oh yes.' Rhys remembered it with a nostalgic pleasure which made his cock twitch with lust. 'It was when we came up to York on that dirty weekend – you were supposed to be developing business contacts and I was supposed to be researching a piece about the railway museum. Neither of us got much research done that weekend, as I recall.'

'Oh I don't know.' Melissa let the back of her hand brush surreptitiously over the front of Rhys's trousers. 'I learned a thing or two ...'

The Casa Romana was exactly the way they remembered it – a tiny shop-front, almost hidden in the gloom of an old snickelway, with only the sound of opera and the delicious scents of Italian cooking to indicate its existence.

Shaking out his umbrella, Rhys pushed open the door and ushered Melissa inside, into the steamy warmth.

'Ah, Signor, Signora!' The proprietor greeted them as though they were long-lost relatives and ushered them to a table by the fire. 'I take your coat, Signora, yes? And now I bring you a little wine . . .'

'Not for me, I'm driving,' protested Melissa.

'It's OK, you enjoy yourself,' said Rhys. 'I don't mind sticking to mineral water. Anyway, it's my turn.'

Melissa accepted the proferred chair and was about to sit down when something caught her eye.

'Look, Rhys – over there.'

'Where?'

'By the window – isn't that . . . ?'

'Chris Maudsley? Yes, you're right. Blimey, look at the girl he's with. Isn't that the barmaid from the Black Lion? I wouldn't have thought she was his type, would you?'

Melissa followed his gaze to the girl with the cropped black hair, dangly silver earrings and skin-tight leather pants. There was no mistaking Janice Summersdale – or Jazz, as she preferred to be called. She was the talk of Highmoor, with her biker-chic and the Honda Goldwing she roared around the moors on, even in the depths of winter. There wasn't an ounce of spare flesh on that wiry, athletic frame, and Melissa felt a twinge of envy as she was reminded just how good Jazz looked in those so-tight, so-macho biker leathers.

'Oh look, he's seen us.' Melissa smiled and waved, and – making a brief apology to his companion – Maudsley got up and came across.

'Melissa . . . Rhys . . . great to see you. What brings you to this neck of the woods?'

Maudsley nodded to each in turn, hands in pockets, shock of wavy, light-brown hair slipping over one eye. He really wasn't a bad-looking bloke, thought Melissa. Not really her type, mind you, a little too young and innocent-looking, but the sort of guy you wouldn't kick out of bed. She was willing to bet there was a nice body under that oversized tweed jacket and those baggy chinos.

'Oh, just a small celebration,' replied Rhys. 'Between us, we've just about earned enough to have the roof mended.'

Melissa laughed.

'And now we've come here to squander it all on high living.'

'Having your own celebration?' Rhys arched a quizzical eyebrow in the direction of Jazz Summersdale.

Maudsley nodded.

'Sort of. I've been working at the Malton office today, and Jazz has been sort of . . . you know, helping me out with some admin. I thought I'd bring her here tonight as a thank-you.'

I *bet* she's been helping out, thought Rhys, watching Jazz lift her wine glass to her lips. That T-shirt she was wearing was very, very tight and although Jazz wasn't what you might call hugely endowed, the pert little bee-stings of her breasts looked extraordinarily sexy, pushing against the tight white cotton.

As a rule, Rhys's tastes were directed towards more overtly feminine women, women like Melissa with pillow-soft breasts and shapely curves. But there was something about Jazz Summersdale that demanded attention. She was a disturbing combination of the boyish and the feminine and stirred up feelings in Rhys that he wasn't at all sure he wanted to acknowledge. Looking at her, lusting after her like this, was just a little like lusting after an adolescent boy, longing to explore the delights of his soft red lips, his lively cock, that tight little backside. And that was a side of his sexuality which Rhys Montagu hardly dared even contemplate.

'Oh, by the way, Chris, we meant to thank you,' said Melissa.

Maudsley looked puzzled.

'Thank me? What for?'

'For the food you got for us. You must let us know how much we owe you.'

Maudsley's brow cleared. 'Food? Oh, you mean the pint of milk and the sliced loaf? It wasn't much, I'm afraid . . .'

'No, not that,' cut in Rhys. 'All the other stuff – you know, in the pantry.'

'The ham and farmhouse cheese, and all that wonderful fruit, and the bottle of red wine . . .' Melissa giggled. 'And I bet it was you who put the rose petals in our bed too, wasn't it?'

Maudsley scratched his ear.

'I'm sorry, I'm not quite with you. Wine? Ham? I think there's been some mistake.

'Like I said, the only things I left for you were a pint of milk and a Mother's Pride. And *rose petals*?' He chuckled. 'I wish I'd thought of it, but I'm afraid I didn't. Believe me, Melissa, if anyone left rose petals in your bed, it certainly wasn't me.'

Peter Galliano slid his key into the lock and opened the front door of his apartment, reaching inside to turn on the light. He twisted the dimmer switch a little to the right – well, he didn't want it too bright, not for what he had in mind.

Candice had been a revelation to him tonight, he was willing to admit that to himself, if not to her. He'd never really noticed her before, just accepted her as part of the office furniture, something satisfyingly reliable and not unpleasant to look at. But over the last few weeks he'd been forced to notice Candice. What man wouldn't? She'd seemed to blossom before his eyes, changing the way she dressed, her make-up, the way she did her hair, even the colour of her hair. And it suited her, this new sexy image.

Now, Peter Galliano was only human. He'd always believed that any damn thing was fine as long as it was between consenting adults, and over this last week or so he'd got the distinct impression that Candice would consent to anything he cared to suggest. He couldn't quite understand why – Candice had always seemed the career type to him, not really interested in men. At one point he'd even wondered if she was a dyke and in a funny way that thought had rather turned him on.

Like most men he knew, Galliano occasionally liked to fantasise about watching two women getting it on together and then joining in at the climactic moment, putting his cock where a woman's tongue had been, bathing it in the juices of saliva and sex. Teach them what real pleasure was like. Yeah, that would be great. Even now, as he cast his mind back to that old, favourite fantasy, it made his manhood tingle with delectable anticipation.

But Candice Soulbury was no dyke, that fact had become increasingly obvious. As he stood back to let her walk into the hallway of his penthouse apartment, he watched her elegant backside swaying inside her tight blue dress. Watered silk it was, Italian probably, stylish definitely. But not as stylish as the body inside it. Look how the swirly patterns in the fabric caught the light, shimmering like a snake's skin, iridescent and sinuous. Listen to the way it rustled as her body moved, smoothly and oh-so-classily, inside the midnight-blue sheath.

He closed the door and took off his jacket, flinging it across the back of a chair. Then he eased off his tie and hung it over the outstretched leg of a thirties' statuette – one of those athletic-looking girls in tight shorts, balancing a beach-ball on her toe. That statuette had cost a bomb, but what did that matter? It was only money and, thanks to the family fortune, Galliano had a pretty inexhaustible supply of it. What's more, he was on the way up in Jupiter International and a loyal, obliging colleague like Candice Soulbury deserved the right to share in his good fortune.

Galliano flicked an unobtrusive switch and music came on, soft and slinky, music to get undressed to. He hoped Candice wouldn't be too slow in getting the message.

'Drink?'

Candice let her jacket slide from her shoulders and onto the arm of the sofa.

'What – *more* drink, Peter? Any more and I'm apt to forget myself and do something . . . silly.'

Which is exactly what we both want, thought Candice to herself. *Exactly* what we want.

'I'll have a brandy,' she said. 'A double.' And she walked slowly round the room as Galliano poured the drinks, casually examining all the glamorous paraphernalia of his daily life.

He had surprisingly good taste, all things considered. And his substantial private income gave Galliano free rein to indulge his every whim. That was a *real* Modigliani on the wall over the fireplace, Candice could tell just from the style of the brushwork. The Soulbury family too had once had money but that had all gone to pay her uncle Dominic's gambling debts. All that was left by way of an inheritance was good taste and that didn't pay the bills. Candice had long since learned that a woman had to make her own way in the world.

Not that seducing Peter Galliano had anything to do with money – well, not much anyway. She wanted him because of the passion that had been burning within her ever since she had first started work in his private office. She wanted him because just listening to him made her wet between her thighs, because every night she dreamed that he was in her bed and because of the deliriously sexual exhilaration it would give her to have power over such a powerful man.

Candice accepted the generous measure of brandy but did not sit down. Instead, she stepped a little closer to Galliano and raised her glass, looking straight into his eyes as she clinked it against his.

'Cheers,' she smiled, and swirled the brandy around her glass a few times before draining it at a single draught.

Her lips were wet with brandy and she licked the drops away, slowly and lasciviously.

It was driving Galliano mad, she could see that, and it was not just the brandy which warmed her belly, burning a trail of fire down into the secret pleasure-palace between her thighs.

She placed the empty glass on a side table.

'Let's dance,' she suggested and she began to move slowly in time to the music. As she danced in the rose-pink light from the table lamp, Galliano marvelled again at her transformation, at this creature made from pure sex, maddening him with her body. She pouted resentfully. 'Don't make me dance on my own.'

Galliano kissed her, his hands roaming over her backside whilst his lips explored her breasts, her throat, her large and sensual mouth. Candice shivered at his touch, the fulfilment of all her dreams. As he pulled her tightly against him, she could feel the hardness of his cock, a slanting pole of flesh that began at his groin and lay flat on his belly, its tip almost reaching the waistband of his trousers.

Galliano desired her. That thought alone was enough to make Candice quiver with pleasure, at last she was living all the fantasies she had rehearsed over and over again throughout the years she had been working for him.

'You look wonderful,' Galliano whispered, his teeth teasing her earlobe, twisting and turning her earring in the soft flesh, sending little electric shocks of excitement to breasts and belly and eager womanhood.

Candice's reply was to press her belly against his, her pelvis tilting and grinding as they moved together, swaying and turning to the music though all that truly mattered now was the silent music of their own sexual hunger.

She put her hands behind Galliano's head and pulled him towards her, devouring him with her kisses, making love to him with lips and tongue, nipping his lower lip between her teeth, possessing him.

'I want you,' she murmured. 'Do you know how long I've wanted you?'

'You have wonderful tits.' Galliano stroked his hand lightly over the bare, rose-white swell of her breasts. 'I'd love to see them. I'd love to suck them.'

He reached behind her and groped for the tag of the zipper. It yielded easily and the dress opened with a soft swish as he pulled it down, baring her back down as far as the deep crease at the base of her spine.

No longer held against her body by the zipper, the bodice of the tight silken sheath peeled away and fell down, held up at the waist only by the tight fabric still clinging about her hips. Beneath, her breasts were bare, the nipples long and insolently hard, inviting kisses.

Galliano gave a low moan of hunger as his greedy hands explored the small, firm domes of flesh, sometimes letting the nipples protrude between his fingers, sometimes teasing them by brushing his open palms very lightly over their sensitive tips.

'Do you know what I'd like to do to you, Candice?'

Heart thumping, her sex oozing juice, she smiled at him, shameless, provocative.

'Tell me.'

'I'd like to shoot my spunk all over your tits, that's what.' He swallowed, his mouth suddenly filled with saliva. 'And then I'd make you suck me hard again, so I could pull off your panties and slide right up inside your beautiful pussy. And I'm so sure it *is* beautiful, Candice . . .'

Still smiling, Candice took hold of the blue silk sheath which covered her from the waist down and wriggled it over her hips, like a snake shedding its skin. Galliano watched, entranced, as millimetre by millimetre, she exposed herself to him.

Underneath the sheath dress she was wearing a scarlet suspender belt, its satin and lace deliciously tarty after the sleek sophistication of her dress. She was wearing dark-blue seamed stockings and high-heeled shoes, but her thighs and pubis were quite naked, her maidenhair a dark and tempting triangle on her mound of Venus.

She stepped out of the dress and kicked it away.

'You see, there's no need to pull my panties off, darling,' she observed coquettishly.

Galliano seized her round the waist and she allowed him to lower her onto an exquisite Chinese rug in front of the fire. Why fight it? Let him think he had power over her, let him believe that he was the one who was initiating this, when in truth she was the powerful one, the complete mistress of his sexuality.

She watched with impatient hunger as Galliano knelt over her, so greedy for her that he did not even take the time to undress. He fumbled with his trouser belt, unbuckling and unzipping, reaching inside his pants and pulling out a long, beautiful, purple-tipped cock which Candice yearned to suck.

She could hear his breathing, shallow and rapid, felt the powerful pulse in his thigh as he straddled her, squeezing her breasts very tightly about the long, stiff shaft of his penis. It excited her beyond belief to have him astride her, his large, smooth shaft sliding between her breasts, leaving a clear slick of wetness on her bare skin.

'I'm going to fuck you,' Galliano whispered, repeating the words over and over again, in time with the rhythm of each thrust, almost as though the words were some sort of mantra. 'Fuck you, Candice, I'm going to fuck you . . .'

Candice put out her tongue and licked the tip of Galliano's cock as it emerged from the deep valley of her breasts. He shuddered, brought to the very brink of orgasm by her shameless audacity.

'Come all over me,' she whispered, squeezing her breasts a little harder about his cock. 'Come all over me, darling. I want you to spurt all over my breasts and my throat and my face ...'

Galliano withdrew his cock and masturbated, those last few, delicious strokes. With a gasp of sudden pleasure he tensed, his eyes closing for a split second then opening very wide, as his cock jerked once, twice. Pearly-white seed spurted out, covering Candice's breasts, her throat, her parted lips, with a sheen of opalescent droplets.

Candice lapped Galliano's seed from her lips with greedy enjoyment, her hips bucking and writhing as her clitoris pulsed with frustrated hunger.

'Now, my darling,' she breathed. Her heart pounded with the ecstasy of triumph. 'Now, you may fuck me.'

Galliano slid his still-hard cock between Candice's thighs, more than happy to answer her sensual need. But what Candice did not realise was that, even as he was fucking her, even as his fingers were rubbing her swollen clitoris, he was thinking about Melissa Montagu.

I want you, Melissa, he told himself as he slid in and out of Candice's hungry pussy. *I want you and I have to have you.*

And if it takes a little persuasion, well, so be it. I'll find a way to persuade you, Melissa. I'll find a way of showing you that I'm the only man you'll ever need.

Melissa put down the duster and the jar of beeswax polish and stretched her aching back. She glanced around the dining hall, her pride and joy, admiring the ornate plasterwork of the ceiling, the dark, lustrous sheen of the polished oak panelling. The rest of the house might be in a state of neglect, but this room alone showed how magnificent Highmoor House was going to look when it was restored to its former glory. Though how long that would take, was anybody's guess . . .

Something drew her eyes towards the open window, to that curious shadow on the wainscoting which you only really noticed when the sun caught it at a certain angle. It was an instantly recognizable shape – the shape of a large, heavy, old-fashioned key, and there was even a rusty hook set into the wooden panelling, showing where it had once hung. Melissa wondered to herself what that key had once opened and where it was now.

'What's this then – have you come out on strike?' Rhys breezed into the room in a pair of torn white overalls, spattered here and there with multicoloured splashes of paint. 'When's lunch?'

Melissa responded by sitting down on the old oak chest which formed a seat underneath the window and folding her arms defiantly.

'Cheek! I've been cleaning this place ever since breakfast. What makes you so sure it's *my* turn to make lunch?'

'It'll be fried-egg sandwiches again then,' warned Rhys. 'You know it's the only thing I can cook. Anyhow – ' He flicked the hair back from Melissa's face and bent to kiss her. 'I'm not that hungry. I'd rather go to bed, wouldn't you?'

'Honestly,' laughed Melissa. 'Anything to get out of cooking. If it was up to you, we'd never get out of bed.'

Rhys nuzzled her neck and stroked her breasts with painty fingers.

'Mmm. Sounds OK to me.'

Melissa felt her nipples swelling at his touch. It was no good pretending she wasn't aroused by him. Ever since they'd left London and come up here to live, their desire for each other had taken on a whole new lease of life. Freed from some of the constraints of a nine-to-five existence, they had taken to satisfying their desires in all sorts of places, at all hours of the day.

But this time – well, this time, she really shouldn't give in.

'There are so many things I need to do,' she protested, getting to her feet and pushing Rhys half-heartedly away. 'You said you'd move this chest so I could clean behind it.'

'The romance of it,' sighed Rhys, surveying the chest. It looked heavy – bloody heavy. Solid oak with brass bindings, and enormous with it. 'If it's full of books or something, I'll never shift it,' he protested.

'I'm sure it's empty – but take a look inside. It's about time we found out what we've inherited along with the house.'

'It's probably locked.'

'Well, you won't know unless you try.'

Strange how neither of them had wanted to open the chest. It was as though they had both sensed something about it, something mysterious, something just a tiny bit worrying.

Rhys hesitated.

'What if there's a dead body in it – you know, one of those people who's supposed to have disappeared from here?'

'Don't talk rubbish! Here, *I'll* open it.'

Melissa knelt beside the chest and lifted the lid. It was very, very heavy, but not locked, and as she pulled with all her strength she felt it give, opening with a creak of rusty hinges.

The smell which wafted out was curiously sweet, curiously exciting.

The first thing which met Melissa's eyes was a drift of scarlet satin, a little crumpled but still in perfect condition. She took hold of it and lifted it out of the chest.

'It's a sort of . . . petticoat thing,' commented Rhys. The garment was tight at the waist, with a wide skirt trimmed with black lace. He took hold of it and pressed it to his face, breathing in the scent. A woman's scent . . .

'Look, Rhys – look at all these . . . what are they?'

Melissa threw back the lid of the chest and the light from the window above flooded in, illuminating a strange collection of objects. Ivory, silver, jade, ebony, rose-quartz, obsidian, haematite, leather and iron: a vast array of colours and textures met Melissa's curious gaze.

She picked out a curious confection of polished brass and leather.

'What . . . ?'

Rhys took a look at it.

'It's like a horse's halter,' he said, 'But I've never seen one quite like that before, it's the wrong shape. It's almost as if . . .'

'As if what?'

'I don't think it was made for a horse to wear, Melissa. I think it was made for a person.'

Melissa rummaged through the artefacts in the chest.

There were smooth ivory balls, the size of billiard balls but linked by a leather thong. As she held them in her hand, the warmth of her skin awoke their scent, the scent of sex, and Melissa realised what they must be.

'These must be love-eggs!' she exclaimed. 'I've seen pictures. You know, they're for putting inside . . .'

Rhys reached in and took out a beautiful dildo, fashioned from polished rose-quartz. Swirling patterns seemed to inhabit the heart of the stone, pink and white, ever-changing as he turned the beautiful object over in his hand and the light shone into it, making patterns in its clouded depths.

He touched his cheek with it, ran it over his skin, felt its coolness, smelt its residual fragrance. Who had used this exquisite love-toy? Whose body had welcomed it as the instrument of its pleasure? How many lovers had used it to coax or bully or caress ecstasy from each other's bodies? Even the thought made him feel excited, as though in touching the dildo he had plugged in to the erotic memories locked within it.

'Look,' whispered Melissa. 'A little harness to put round a man's dick. The leather's so very old . . . And here's a riding-crop with a solid silver handle. And little golden clips with such sharp teeth. I can't begin to imagine what you'd use those for . . .'

'You know what this is, don't you?' said Rhys quietly.

'What?'

'It's a toy box. A grown-ups' toy box. I don't know . . . maybe even the box of toys which belonged to Reuben Fairfax and Perdita. Can you imagine that?'

Melissa picked up the leather harness, turning it over and over in her hand, wonderingly. She had heard of such toys, of course she had, had even seen pictures of them, but she had never really thought of experimenting with them. She wondered . . .

'Let's go to bed,' she said.

'I thought you'd never ask.' Rhys got to his feet, still holding the pink quartz dildo. It felt warm in his hand now, warm and full of an irrepressible energy, as though it, too, was hungry to fuck.

Together they left the dining hall and the morning sunlight filtered in through the open window, casting dancing patterns on the walls and floor as the overgrown trees outside waved their branches in the breeze.

And as the curtain blew inward, exposing one section of panelled wall, even the casual observer could not have failed to notice something rather curious.

A huge, ornate iron key, hanging on a hook by the window.

Chapter 6

Rhys had never wanted Melissa more than he wanted her right now. It didn't matter that she was dressed in old jeans and one of his cast-off shirts; if anything, the scruffy old casual clothes enhanced her beauty. She looked utterly natural, utterly vulnerable, even a touch childlike and he desired her so powerfully that his balls ached with longing for her.

The bedroom had never seemed further away, more impossibly out of reach. Melissa felt her clitoris throb more urgently with each step as her outer labia rubbed together, exciting her desire. She was still holding the little cock-harness, its leather smooth and supple between her fingers despite its great age, and the old scent of sex and leather a new and exciting aphrodisiac.

Pushing open the bedroom door, Rhys led her inside. The windows were ajar and the morning rain had spattered onto the window sill, covering it with large wet droplets which glittered diamond-bright in the noonday sunlight. Sunlight fell, too, on the red velvet draped over the four-poster bed, creating a great pool of warmth into which two eager lovers might sink and drown and never again emerge.

Without a word they undressed, fingers fumbling automatically with buttons and zips that were infuriatingly slow to yield. Melissa undid two buttons of her shirt, then pulled it off over her head, throwing it in an untidy heap on the ground. Her ripped jeans followed, Rhys watching mesmerised as she wrenched them over her shapely hips and slid them down to her ankles.

White cotton panties and a plain white bra were all that veiled her from him now. As she reached behind her to unhook the clasp of her bra, Rhys watched in agonised excitement. It seemed so slow, so painfully slow, like a film being played out frame by frame.

At last he saw the white elastic side-straps spring forward and the cups grow loose about her breasts. She leant forward just a little way and let the straps slide down her arms until, at last, the bra cups fell away, leaving her heavy breasts unfettered.

Her panties were little more than a triangle of white cotton, so thin that it was plain to see where the damp ooze of her desire had soaked into the fabric, making it semi-transparent. Curls of corn-blonde hair had escaped from the gusset of her panties, curls which Rhys longed to kiss and press his face against, breathing in their very special, erotic perfume.

In a few moments, Rhys had thrown off his paint-spattered overalls and was down to his T-shirt and shorts. Melissa watched with growing excitement as he peeled off the T-shirt, pulling it off over his head. After a long morning's hard work, there was a light seasoning of sweat all over his body and Melissa thirsted for its taste on her tongue, yearned to lick him all over until he begged for her mercy.

He unzipped his jeans and slipped them off. Underneath, he was wearing a pair of plain red cotton briefs, tight enough to leave nothing to the imagination. There was something very, very erotic about looking at her lover's manhood, stiff and erect, yet imprisoned by its tight covering of red cotton. She could quite clearly make out the line of his foreskin, and the patch of dampness on his pants where his glans had leaked wet, sticky droplets of lubricating fluid.

Rhys's balls seemed very heavy, very juicy. Melissa glanced down at the leather harness in her hands. It too was an instrument of imprisonment, a toy of sensual bondage, and she longed to see the leather straps pulled and buckled tight around her lover's penis and testicles.

But before that could happen, Rhys had other games to play. He had brought something else from the carved oak chest: a set of thick, supple leather thongs.

'Do you want me, Melissa?'

'Oh yes.'

'But do you trust me?'

'Of course.'

'*Completely* trust me?'

'You know I do.'

'Then do everything I ask. It's only to give you pleasure, Melissa, I swear it.'

Melissa looked at him quizzically, head tilted, mind racing.

'Whatever have you got in mind?'

'If you lie down on the bed I'll show you.'

She pouted playful defiance, her full breasts thrust out, her nipples turned to pert pink stalks.

'And what if I don't?'

Rhys took her in his arms and hooked his thumbs under the elastic sides of her panties. They slid down easily, almost gratefully, over the firm half-moons of her arse cheeks and he slipped the very tip of his finger into the secret valley between. She wriggled but he kissed her resistance away.

'Then I shall have to make you, shan't I?'

There was no menace in his words, only a playful warmth, but his embrace was strong and the power of Melissa's own lust stronger still. They had never played a game like this before. Perhaps they should have done. Perhaps if they had experimented with the full gamut of their desires, she would never have been tempted that foolish, fateful day in Peter Galliano's office.

Putting up just a token show of resistance, a sexy little wriggle here and there, Melissa allowed herself to be laid down on the four-poster bed. Sprawled across the bedspread, she found herself staring up at the canopy overhead. She'd seen it dozens of times before, of course, but this was the first time she'd really paid it much attention.

Like the rest of the carved oak bed, the canopy was old, very old – perhaps Elizabethan or even earlier. Rhys knew a little about antiques and he had been stunned to find it in the house. He could see it would be worth serious money to the right buyer – maybe enough to pay for a goodly portion of the repairs that needed doing on Highmoor House. But Melissa had been adamant – she wouldn't part with the bed for anything. She'd fallen in love with it the first time she saw it, had felt something warm and strong and welcoming about it.

Now, as she looked up at the canopy, she saw the designs on its underside in detail for the first time. The sun's angle threw the carved figures into relief – the huntsmen and the stag, and the beautiful naked woman kneeling in supplication at her captor's feet, her hands bound behind her back, helpless and vulnerable. Only now did Melissa notice the man's hugely erect phallus disappearing into the woman's mouth . . .

Rhys touched her, fleetingly, between her thighs and Melissa moaned with pleasure. For once in her life, she wanted to be naked and vulnerable like the woman in the old carving, her whole body open to the vagaries of her lover's masterful desires. She wanted to abandon herself utterly to her own pleasure, abdicating all responsibilities, all duties, finding freedom in total submission.

Rhys knelt over her, running his hands over her body, enjoying her through touch and scent. Then he took hold of her wrists, pinning her to the bed.

'What do you want from me, Melissa?'

'I want you to *take* me.'

'What if I tied you up? You'd be completely helpless . . .'

Melissa looked straight into his eyes.

'That's exactly what I want.' She paused, smiling up at him, enjoying the game. '*Master*.'

Although he had never had much experience of sexual power-games, Rhys found himself profoundly excited by Melissa's pretended submission. Excited, yes, and perhaps a little scared too. She lay before him like a blank canvas, her body his to do with as he chose. Her pleasure was in his hands now, his tongue, his dick – limited only by the boundaries of his own imagination.

Carefully he wound the leather thongs about her wrists, attaching them quite loosely to the posts at the head of the bed.

'Tighter, Rhys,' begged Melissa, excited beyond imagining by the feeling of her own helplessness.

Rhys bent to kiss her as he pulled on the leather straps.

'Tighter, *Master*,' he reminded her. 'If you're insolent I may have to punish you.'

He looked down at the remaining strips of leather in his hand. About eighteen inches long, they were supple and very, very soft: soft enough to soothe and caress, but thin and flexible enough to bite like a whip. He lifted his hand, trailing the ends of the leather strips across Melissa's face, and she caught one between her lips, wetting it with her saliva before letting it go.

'Punish me,' she breathed. 'Please punish me, Master. You know how much I deserve it.'

Rhys could smell her excitement. It was more than just the ordinary wetness of her pussy lips. This was something muskier, more compellingly sensual, as though he had unwittingly tapped in to some deeper level of her sexual need.

Drawing back, he raised his arm above his head. Melissa's creamy-white nakedness lay there before him, her wrists tied tightly to the bedposts and her legs, although left free, spread wide as though pleading with him not to spare the soft and fragrant heart of her womanhood.

Punish me. Melissa's words rang in his head, sending ripples of guilty excitement through his body. Ought he to be feeling like this? Should it really turn him on quite so much to have his lover completely at his mercy? Shouldn't they be equals in this game of love and lust?

And then, as he drew back his arm and brought the leather thongs swishing down through the air, Rhys realised that they *were* equals. It was as much Melissa who was controlling the game as he. It was she who was driving him crazy, making him as much a captive of his own lust as she was of the leather bands about her wrists.

Swish. Slap!

The bunch of soft leather thongs struck Melissa's belly and she arched her back, letting out a shuddering gasp.

'More. More, Master, please . . .'

He struck her again, watching her skin redden a little where the stinging tips of the leather thongs had hit home. His heart was pounding, his dick hardening to stone at the sight of his lover writhing and moaning beneath him, begging him to do it again, again, again.

The leather kissed Melissa's breasts and she gave a sharp cry.

'Yes! Oh Master, yes, yes!'

Melissa's thighs were spread very wide, her back arched a fraction off the bed as her whole body tensed in pleasure. He could see her shuddering, quivering, like a steel wire stretched too taut and about to break. She was so, so very close to orgasm.

Her eyes reproached him as he laid down the leather thongs.

'Why? Please don't stop.'

He kissed her and she pushed her tongue hard into his mouth.

'Patience.'

The dildo of rose-pink quartz was lying on the bedside table. Melissa's eyes had travelled to it even before his fingers stretched out and picked it up. Odd how it still felt warm to the touch, though he had placed it there many minutes ago. It had none of the coldness he had expected and even its smooth surface felt more like the smoothness of living flesh than ancient stone.

As he picked it up the sunlight caught it, striking flashes of pinkish-white light from its heart. In the cloudy-pink, swirling depths of the stone phallus, Rhys thought he could make out the faint reflections of naked, writhing bodies but, like cheap holograms, they disappeared as he tilted the dildo a fraction of an inch. When he moved it back, he could no longer see them.

He ran his fingers along the smooth, hard shaft.

'Is this what you want, Melissa? Do you want this inside you?'

Melissa did not reply straight away but there was no mistaking the light in her eyes. Her lips parted, just a little way, and her tongue flicked over her parched lips.

She was staring at the pink stone dildo, coveting its pleasure-power, these ten smooth inches of rose-quartz, fashioned into this most exquisite surrogate penis. So thick was it that even a man's hand might have difficulty in spanning its girth. It curved like a sabre, taut and tense as straining flesh, with a bulbous glans divided by a deep fissure which you could almost imagine oozing juice. Melissa longed to taste and stroke and lick and fuck that beautiful stone prick . . .

A faint, warm odour of sex rose from the rose-quartz penis as Rhys began rubbing it over Melissa's body. In places her skin had reddened where the leather thongs had struck it, and, as sunlight blazed through the quartz, it cast a blush of rosy pink on her creamy breasts and thighs.

'Look what I'm doing to you, Melissa,' breathed Rhys, so unbearably excited that he knew he must soon taste sexual release or die of frustration. 'Feel what I'm doing to you. This is my dick rubbing over your skin, your Master's dick.

And it can do anything it likes to you, *anything*, do you understand?'

'Oh yes, Master, I understand.'

Rhys ran the tip of the dildo over Melissa's nipples. Already erect, they lengthened and hardened at the kiss of the smooth stone. Round and round he moved it, with a circular motion, then down over her belly.

Slowly and luxuriously he moved it over the taut flesh, from the base of her breasts to her navel; pushing the tip of the dildo into the little dark well, causing her such curious sensations that it felt as though an electric current was tingling and buzzing through her body from belly to thigh. She drew her thighs together as he caressed her lower belly, trying to stimulate her poor, neglected rosebud by rubbing her labia together. But Rhys gently prised her legs apart.

'Bad girl,' he chided her. 'Your pleasure is mine, remember, Melissa. I will decide when you are to have an orgasm . . . that is, *if* I decide . . .'

Rhys reached out and opened the drawer of the bedside cabinet. This was where Melissa kept her favourite silk scarves and gloves. Selecting a patterned black scarf, Rhys folded it into a thick band.

'Raise your head,' he said.

'But . . . ?'

'Don't be afraid. You're not afraid of me, are you?'

'No, of course not, only . . .'

With no further protests, Melissa lifted her head, allowing Rhys to bind the silk scarf over her eyes. At first she thought he was only going to tie it loosely, that she would be able to peep underneath like she had done when she was a child, playing Blind Man's Bluff. But Rhys bound it tightly – not uncomfortably but very securely, shutting out all light. Now she had entered a mysterious, dark world where anything might be possible.

Despite her apprehension, it was her sexual desire which most terrified Melissa. She had realised by now that she could no longer control it, that only Rhys could give her the release she craved. She was almost weeping with frustration, her body writhing and jerking on the bed as Rhys pushed the dildo down to the margin of her pubic curls, and then began rubbing it, quite hard, across the dome of her pubic bone.

There was skill in that caress. Although he drove her to distraction, augmenting her sexual desire until her sex wept tears of yearning and her puckered arsehole opened and closed in a kiss of welcome, he never brought the tip of the dildo quite near enough to stimulate Melissa's clitoris.

Being in such a state of arousal was almost painful in its intensity. Melissa wondered if she could ever bear to feel even the slightest, lightest touch on her hugely swollen clitoris. It seemed to pulsate with an insistent hunger that burned with a slow, yet red-hot flame. Even the faintest breath, the touch of a single hair on that distended flesh would send her into the most delicious spasms of orgasm. Surely anything more than that would turn her pleasure into torment . . .

Suddenly, she felt something hard force itself between her thighs. Something smooth and thick, with a domed head that seemed much too large to push its way into the heart of her sex.

'Rhys, I . . . !'

Rhys's fingers smoothed and soothed the sensitive flesh

of her inner thigh but his voice was darkly sensual.

'I'm your Master, Melissa. Everything is for your pleasure, but you must do as I say. You must let me do anything I want to do to you.'

The rose-quartz dildo pushed between Melissa's outer sex-lips and into the entrance to her vagina. Here, in the most sensitive part of her sex, it lingered for a long, long time, twisting and turning in the hot wet slick of love-juice which oozed from the well-spring of her desire. Her clitoris ached and burned, but Rhys made no attempt to touch or caress it, preferring to torment her with the dildo, almost but never quite thrusting into her, awakening layer upon layer of sensation that she had never even dreamed existed.

When, at last, he pushed the dildo into the depths of her haven, Melissa screamed aloud – with release, with anguish, with unbearable pleasure. It felt so good to have the dildo inside her and yet it felt so huge, so very long and thick, distending her sex lips, stretching the elastic walls of her vagina to the point where she wondered if it would tear her apart.

And yet she offered herself to it utterly, rejoicing in the excitement as it slid further and further into her, so far and so deep that she was sure she could take no more. She could feel its domed head pushing against her cervix, at first lightly then harder, harder, harder, filling her up, stretching her, possessing her.

'No, no, I can't!' she gasped as Rhys pushed the dildo even further inside her.

'You can, Melissa. Trust me, you can. Just relax and feel the pleasure building up inside you.'

It was true. For all her terror at the size of the dildo inside her, for all the discomfort of being stretched so tight, the overwhelming sensation which Melissa felt pouring into her was that of pleasure. Pleasure that would be so much greater, if only her cruel Master would touch the throbbing head of her swollen clitoris.

'Please touch me, Master,' she sobbed.

'Touch you?' For the sake of the game, Rhys feigned incomprehension. He was enjoying it every bit as much as Melissa was. 'Touch you where, Melissa?'

'Touch me,' she repeated. 'Please touch me.'

'Where? Tell me where.'

'On my clitoris. I want you to touch my clitoris. You know I can't come if you won't touch my clitoris.'

'Ah.' Rhys pushed the dildo a little further and watched Melissa's sex-muscles swallow it up, drawing it right inside her until only the very end of it remained visible between her thighs. 'You see, Melissa, I knew you could do it. I knew you could take it all inside you.'

'Please,' begged Melissa.

Rhys slid off the bed and picked up the leather thongs from the floor where they had fallen. They were a little damp with sweat, and the moisture had released from them an ancient perfume of sex. What games had they seen? What pleasures had they been witness to?

'Spread your legs, darling,' he whispered. 'I'm going to make you come.'

Melissa drew her thighs further apart and raised her knees. She looked so very beautiful like that, thought Rhys: helplessly vulnerable, and yet so powerful in her beauty. Her sex was a work of art, a treasure-casket fringed with corn-gold hair, in the heart of which glistened the perfect, rose-pink pearl of her desire.

He drew back his arm, aroused yet curiously nervous. It wasn't like him to be so adventurous, so ... dominant. Oh, he liked to call the shots sometimes, sure he did – what guy didn't? – but he could also recall plenty of times when all he'd longed for was for Melissa to be on top, absolving him of all responsibility for his own pleasure, riding him hard, her large, soft breasts hanging like ripe fruit over his greedy mouth.

Swish.

The leather thongs sliced down with sudden precision, to plant their first burning kiss between Melissa's thighs.

'Aah!' Melissa's voice was a shrill scream of ecstasy as the first, brutal pain turned to astonished delight. 'Oh yes, yes, YES!'

Rhys watched with covetous hunger as her sex opened wide like a blossoming flower, contracted and then opened again, pouring forth a great tide of the sweet honeydew he loved to lap from her coral-pink lips.

Hurriedly, with clumsy, fumbling fingers he unfastened first the silk scarf then the leather thongs which bound Melissa's wrists. Throwing himself on top of her he kissed her passionately, holding her to him, searching with the tip of his cock for the slippery-wet haven between her thighs.

But there was a new light in Melissa's eyes – playful, mischievous, just a little wicked. Rolling sideways, she wriggled from his grasp.

'Melissa!' protested Rhys, his cock throbbing with the need to fuck, his whole body aching with release.

Melissa reached down onto the floor and picked up the leather cock-harness she had taken from the oak chest.

'Put it on,' she whispered, planting a trail of kisses leading from Rhys's lips, down his chest and belly to the mid-brown tangle of his pubic curls. 'Put it on for me. Make it really tight.'

He took it from her, a little hesitant.

'You really want me to . . . ?'

'Please put it on, darling,' repeated Melissa, a little more firmly this time. 'Do it for me. For your Mistress.'

Rhys saw the bunch of soft leather thongs in her right hand and understood what was in her mind. They were going to play that wonderful game all over again – only this time, Melissa was taking charge.

It was mid-afternoon by the time they came down from the bedroom, bathed and dressed but still scented with the faint perfume of their coupling. The passion they had shared had been a surprise to them both. Maybe Maudsley was right. Maybe Highmoor House really was a place for lovers.

'I'll put these away, shall I?' Melissa indicated the dildo, harness and leather thongs which she had brought downstairs.

Rhys returned her smile a little wistfully. That had been fun, *boy* that had been fun.

'OK,' he said. 'But I want you to promise me we'll do it all again soon.'

Melissa lifted the lid of the chest and replaced the sex-toys with all the others. The chest was a real treasure-trove – there would undoubtedly be plenty more sensual adventures to be found inside it.

'Very soon,' she promised. '*Master*.'

Just as she was replacing the lid of the chest, Melissa noticed a curious thing. As she brushed against the curtain, pushing it back, she saw that beneath the wall-hook there was no longer a shadow on the wooden panelling. Or if there was, she could not make it out, for in its place hung a key.

'Look, Rhys – how on earth did this get here?' Melissa held the curtain back and Rhys stepped forward to have a look.

'The same way the rose petals got into our bed?' Rhys crouched down and took the key off the hook. It was huge: a real old-fashioned thing of wrought iron, impossibly heavy but with not a trace of rust. 'I think someone around here's playing games with us, Melissa.'

But Melissa wasn't listening. She had taken the key from Rhys's hands and was reading the label over and over to herself. There were only three words written on the tattered label, in a spidery brown hand –

THE PARADISE GARDEN

Chapter 7

Maia Kerrigan liked champagne. She liked it better still when it was Krug and when Jim was licking it out of her navel.

She had grown to like her job in computers too – it gave her a sense of power she found intensely sexual – but everything could become tedious if you had too much of it. Even Jim.

The problem with sexual freedom, she had discovered, was that pretty soon you found you'd tried just about everything and there were no more adventures to be had, or at least no surprises.

Or were there? She thought with a smile of Melissa and that night in the kitchen at Rhys and Melissa's house. Melissa had certainly been a revelation that night, far more sexual and receptive than Maia had anticipated. If she had played it a little more slowly, seduced Melissa rather than trying to rape her; if Melissa didn't have quite so many stupid, childish hang-ups . . .

If, if, if. What good was if? Maia believed in making things happen. If you wanted something, you had to go right out there and grab it before someone else stole it right from under your nose. She spread her legs wide so that Jim could lick her pussy. He so loved to lick whipped cream from between her labia and she had to admit that it always felt pretty good, having his tongue flick back and forth over the head of her clitoris.

Melissa. Mmm, yes, pretty Melissa with the big, big breasts and that soft, yielding pussy which dissolved into guilty wetness at the merest touch. Maia felt a pang of regret. She felt cheated by Melissa's silly, repressive guilt. It could have been fun.

She thought of the letter on the hall table. 'No hard feelings,' Melissa had said. 'We were both a little drunk. Let's forget all about it. Why don't you both come up and see us sometime, when you're up north? Rhys is having terrible trouble with his new computer – he's always saying he could do with your expertise.'

My expertise, thought Maia with a secret smile. And what about you, Melissa Montagu? Couldn't you use a little of my expertise, too?

Jim had brought her very close to climaxing and she lay back to enjoy it. Suddenly she was feeling really good again. Maybe afterwards, if he gave her multiple orgasms, she'd suck Jim off and then let him watch her getting it on with the Swedish au pair.

And maybe she'd take Melissa up on that offer to visit Highmoor House. If Melissa wouldn't succumb to her seductive skills, perhaps Rhys would offer the sexual challenge she'd been looking for . . .

'You're right,' said Rhys, contemplating the gardens of Highmoor House. 'We're going to need one hell of a lot of help to clear this lot – you need a machete to hack your way through it.'

'Ah, well, I'm always right,' replied Melissa with unbearable smugness.

'What – even about that "really nice" Indian restaurant

by the British Museum? The one with the cockroaches?'

'OK, nearly always right,' retorted Melissa. 'I mean, I was right about Highmoor House, wasn't I? It's perfect – and now, at long last, we're actually going to take a look at this so-called Paradise Garden.'

'If we can find it. Pity no-one thought to mark it on the map we got with the deeds. And it's no use asking anyone in the village – the minute you mention it, they all clam up.'

'I bet I know where it is. Or at least, where it used to be.'

Rhys stopped in mid-stride.

'Where?'

'There's an old red-brick wall right by the southern edge of the grounds, you know, where the moorland's almost taken over. It's just a bit further on from that stone gazebo thing. I noticed it when I was trying to follow one of the old paths. It's really overgrown, though, like everything else round here.'

'It's worth a look anyway,' conceded Rhys. He winked. 'And I quite fancy getting lost in the undergrowth with you on a sunny afternoon.'

'Ah, but will I be safe with you?' demanded Melissa.

'Definitely not. I'm the Beast of Highmoor, remember?'

'Oh good.'

They walked on, along half-forgotten paths so overgrown that they were barely detectable among the tangle of riotous vegetation.

'Does anything strike you as odd about this place?' asked Rhys.

'You mean apart from rose petals in the bed and reappearing keys? No, not really. Why?'

'It's amazingly overgrown.'

Melissa shrugged.

'It would be. No-one's bothered with it for yonks and there's acres and acres of it.'

'Yes, but this is up on the North York Moors! You don't get many tropical rainforests in North Yorkshire.'

Melissa giggled.

'Don't exaggerate.'

'Yes, all right, but just look at it – talk about green fingers. The land round here's supposed to be so poor and scrubby even the sheep don't like it, yet Highmoor House is practically swamped by trees and bushes and God-knows-what. Don't you find that a bit . . . peculiar?'

'Perhaps it's just in a sheltered spot.'

'Perhaps,' said Rhys doubtfully, thinking of the bare-limbed, stunted trees he had noticed all the way from Whitby – poor, twisted things, all bent permanently sideways by the prevailing wind. 'But somehow I doubt it.'

'All right clever clogs, what's *your* explanation?' demanded Melissa, rounding on him, hands on hips, glossy lips pouting a challenge. 'You're supposed to be the ecology specialist.'

Rhys took a look round him, at the thick trunks of the trees, their branches so interwoven overhead that he could scarcely make out the latticework of lapis-lazuli sky.

'Search me. Maybe it's magic.'

'And maybe I'm Marilyn Monroe,' retorted Melissa drily.

'No, no, definitely not Marilyn Monroe.' Rhys drew her to him and stroked her flank from breast to thigh. 'You're a thousand times sexier than her.'

Laughing, they made their way through what had once

been landscaped lawns, now turned over to dog-rose and thistle, towards the southernmost edge of the grounds. They had been so preoccupied with the house since their arrival that they had scarcely given much thought to the sprawling acres of land which went with it. Other than having the front driveway cleared, they hadn't bothered much with the grounds, though they had wondered from time to time about the legendary Paradise Garden.

Making their way along a narrow path which branched left to a crumbling section of dry-stone wall, they came upon the old stone summerhouse. It was an odd structure of indeterminate age, decorated with ornate carvings of nymphs and satyrs – the sort of pretty but pointless folly some mad nobleman might have had built just for the hell of it. It was completely enclosed, except for one side, which stood open where there had once, perhaps, been a wooden door.

Melissa poked her head inside. A stone bench ran the length of the interior, bare but durable. Over the centuries it seemed to have suffered remarkably little from the depradations of time and neglect. Even the outside of the summerhouse was remarkably free of mossy cushions or the greyish-orange scales of age-old lichen. Tangles of ivy and wild rose caressed the stonework, pink and yellow and white flowers forming a rustic arch over the doorway.

Seeing something glitter, Melissa bent down and picked it up, carrying it outside to look at it properly in the daylight.

'It's an earring.' She turned it over in her palm.

'Old?' enquired Rhys.

'You're kidding. Woolworth's finest, circa last week.' The clip-on earring really was very tacky – a sort of flat, square disc with blue enamel stripes, from which hung an enamelled oval hoop.

'So somebody's been in our summerhouse then . . ,' Melissa kissed him.

'You sound like Daddy Bear. I guess they have. And you can imagine why – it's a wonderful place for a discreet bit of hanky-panky.'

'Maybe they were the ones who put the roses in our bed.'

'I guess. In this place, anything's possible.'

Melissa pocketed the earring and they walked on a little further, through an increasingly dark tangle of ivy and ground elder.

'There! I told you,' announced Melissa triumphantly. 'This must be it.'

Almost obscured by dripping skeins of ivy stood a wall, a little over six feet high, its reddish bricks crumbly and in places cracked by age and frost, but still intact. Rhys weighed it up with a practised eye.

'I could climb over that.'

'No, don't, let's look for the gate.'

'If it's still there.'

'It will be,' Melissa assured him. 'I can just *feel* it.'

They followed the line of the wall through tangled greenery until they reached a corner and it turned off suddenly left. As Rhys and Melissa turned the corner Rhys stumbled and fell against the wall. Reaching out to break his fall, his hand met first a cushion of leaves, then something hard underneath: something that wasn't brick.

'Here, Melissa. Look.' Rhys tore away the ivy and there, underneath, was a door.

Rhys felt somehow disappointed to have found it so easily.

He'd almost hoped that the Paradise Garden might remain a mystery, a seductive legend never to be sullied or spoiled by the harsh light of reality. He ran his fingers over the surface of the door.

'This must have been replaced at some time. It can't be Elizabethan, it's in such good condition. Look, the iron banding's not even slightly rusty and the wood looks good as new.'

'It *is* old though,' said Melissa. 'I can tell. Look – the ironwork matches the pattern of the key perfectly.' She fumbled the key into the lock, its huge heaviness making it difficult to handle.

At last it slid in, slotting home with a satisfying clunk. It took the strength of two hands to turn the key in the lock but at last it yielded, the levers clicking round in the ancient tumblers.

Rhys pushed the door. It gave a creak of protest but did not budge. Melissa pushed a little harder and this time it moved inward, but only a foot or so before it was impeded by a thick tangle of leaves and branches. It took the two of them, pushing together, to force the door inward on its protesting hinges.

'So this is it? The Paradise Garden?'

Melissa stepped into the verdant jumble of overgrown bushes. It was a mess, there was no other word for it. Where there had once been tidy arrangements of herbs and trees and shrubs, there were now great swathes of ground elder, ivy and couch grass, winding and tangling about the overgrown flowerbeds, choking and almost completely obscuring the plants underneath.

In the centre, barely discernable beneath a thick layer of

slime and dead leaves, lay an ornamental pond, filled to the brim with stagnant water and debris. And the climbing plants that had once decorated the high, encircling wall with a delicate tracery of flowers now all but obliterated it.

Rhys gave a low whistle.

'Now this is going to take some clearing up.'

Funnily enough, it wasn't the neglect that Melissa noticed, it was the beauty. The beauty that had burst through the chaos of greenery. There were flowers everywhere – pink and white and yellow and every shade imaginable, mirroring the whole spectrum of the rainbow. Defiant splashes of colour everywhere relieved the uniform green of weeds and unpruned bushes. And their scents surrounded her, making her dizzy – the heaviness of a musky rose, the lightness of lavender, the sharpness of lemon verbena, the honeyed fragrance of creamy-yellow broom, biscuity and sweet.

She brushed against a branch and it quivered, raining down a shower of palest pink petals which settled on her face, her hair, her clothes.

'Can you feel it?' she asked Rhys.

'You mean . . . you mean the warmth?'

Melissa nodded. It had been the first thing she noticed when she stepped into the garden – how amazingly warm it was in here, even for early June. Out on the moors, a cold wind snapped at the heels of the unwary traveller, even on summer days, but here in the cocooning shelter of the Paradise Garden, it was eternal, tranquil summer . . . or that was how it seemed to her fertile imagination.

'It's beautiful here,' she sighed. Or at least, it must have been once and it could be again. If only we could make it as wonderful as it used to be . . .'

She pulled Rhys to her and they embraced under a confetti-shower of fragrant, pinkish-white blossoms. The sun seemed to laugh overhead in the burnished blue sky and suddenly Melissa felt filled with the most immense sense of well-being.

Rhys surprised himself by replying with more enthusiasm than he could have imagined. After all, he hated gardening ... didn't he?

'We'll do something with it,' he promised. 'Together. We'll make it even more magnificent than it was before, just you wait and see.' And a flood of warm desire seemed to wash over him as he held her in the warm embrace of the Paradise Garden.

Rhys opened the door to the old library and blinked in the dusty atmosphere.

'If anything's been written about the garden, it ought to be in here.' He sneezed as he picked up a book from the floor and blew the dust off it. 'Jed down at the Black Lion says he's sure somebody once wrote a book about the house. Maybe there'll be something in it about the gardens.'

Melissa followed him in. The library was one of the rooms she'd been avoiding since they moved to Highmoor House. Quite frankly it was in a horrible state of disrepair.

There were several small holes in the ceiling, where pigeons roosted, and lumps of once-fine plasterwork lay littered about the floor. In places damp had made the old wooden panelling part company from the wall, revealing sections of wattle from the original timber framework of the building. Indeed, this was said to be one of the very oldest rooms in the house, one of the first to be created in the 1580s when Reuben Fairfax began the Paradise Garden.

'Is it safe?' enquired Melissa, treading gingerly on floorboards which sagged and creaked alarmingly as she stepped on them.

'It had better be!' replied Rhys. 'The cellars are right under here, remember.'

Previous owners of the house had clearly set little store by Highmoor House's extensive library, leaving it to moulder in the damp. Books with mildewed covers and curling pages filled one entire wall, with others scattered around on the floor or piled up on the library table which stood towards one side of what must once have been an impressive room.

Rhys balanced precariously on a pair of library steps which had seen better days.

'Most of this stuff looks like nineteenth-century sermons,' he remarked, scanning the spines, many spotted with greenish mould. He took one out and examined the decaying leather binding. 'Even so, they don't deserve to rot. It's a crying shame.'

He replaced the book and scanned along the shelf, then stepped up a rung to take a look at the topmost row of books.

'Mind you don't fall,' Melissa called.

He grinned down at her.

'Want to swap places?'

'No fear. Just don't fall off, OK? The nearest casualty department's about forty miles away!'

'Ah – here's something.' Very gingerly, Rhys slid out a chunky volume bound in tan-coloured leather. Wobbly letters, embossed in gold-leaf on the spine, read: 'THE HOUSE AT HIGHMOORE'.

PARADISE GARDEN

He handed it down to Melissa then climbed down the steps, jumping the last two.

'Any good?'

Melissa made a space on the library table and set it down. The flyleaf read: 'BEING A HISTORY OF THE HOUSE AT HIGHMOORE, ITS ARCHITECTURAL MERITS AND MEANS OF CONSTRUCTION. LONDON, 1806'.

'Damn.' She flicked through the book. It was full of engineering drawings and tiny print. 'It's purely about the way the house was built. It doesn't even mention the gardens.'

'Never mind, we'll keep it out. It might be interesting.'

Melissa made a face.

'I doubt it.'

She was just taking the remaining books off the library table when one caught her eye. A little smaller than the rest, it sat inconspicuously under a pile of nineteenth-century encyclopedias. She smoothed the dust off its cover and saw that it was very old: not a printed book at all, but a bound set of manuscipt pages. She lifted open the heavy cover.

'What's that?' enquired Rhys.

'Search me, it's all in Latin, and the writing's all spidery and old-fashioned. I can't read a word of it.'

'Ah. Look – it's about the house, it has to be. See? That's a sketch of the approach to the house, the way it must have been ... and that there, that's the stable block, do you recognise it?'

'But what does it *say*?'

'Haven't a clue. I failed Latin, remember. Maybe it doesn't matter.' Rhys could feel excitement building up in him as he turned page after page. 'But at a guess I'd say it's some sort of detailed description of the house in the very early days.' He flicked back to the front of the book, carefully prising apart two of the thick sheets of rag-paper, stuck together by damp.

'That's Reuben Fairfax!' Melissa stared at the faces which gazed back serenely at her from the page. They were unmistakable. 'Fairfax and Perdita!' Underneath was a little writing, larger and clearer than the rest: 'R FAIRFAX FECIT'.

But Rhys was already leafing through the book, more slowly and carefully this time, studying each page for any clues, wondering how long it had been since anyone looked between these ancient covers.

'The garden! Isn't that . . .' Rhys jabbed his finger at the open page.

'A picture of the Paradise Garden, yes, it must be. Look at it, it's amazing – knot gardens and a little maze and there's the ornamental pond we found. A sundial and lawns and trees and an orchard . . .'

Melissa snatched up the book to take a closer look at it and, as she did so, something fluttered out. Something once-red, now faded to a dusky pinky-brown. Something still fragrant with a potent sensuality.

Melissa picked up the pressed flower and held it to her face, breathing in its scent. It was musky, sweet, lingering like incense, creating strange moods, strange feelings . . .

'A rose,' she exclaimed excitedly. 'A rose from the Paradise Garden.' She stroked her fingers over the dried petals, filling her lungs with its perfume. 'Perhaps Perdita put it there . . .'

'We don't know that.'

'But it's something special, can't you feel it?'

'It's just a rose, it doesn't mean anything. Just a flower...'

But Rhys found his hand was shaking as he took it from her and the scent wafted into his nostrils. What the hell was happening to him – to them both? How could a single pressed flower make him feel the way he was feeling right now? His cock was stirring in his pants, uncoiling like a snake awakening from a deep sleep, refreshed, hungry, ready to spit its venom...

The scent was all-pervading, incredible for something as small and utterly insignificant as a dried flower, a rose crushed between the pages of an old book. It surrounded them like an erotic incense, no longer the scent of a rose but the perfume of purest, most intense sex, seductive and irresistible.

Melissa's hand smoothed over the front of his trousers, her fingers butterfly-light over the burgeoning swell of his prick. She did not speak but he could hear her breathing, the fluttering sigh of her desire as the dizzying scent filled her whole being, reducing her every thought, feeling, desire to a single need.

The need to fuck.

Slowly, tantalisingly, she drew down his zipper. He was beautifully hard for her, the tip of his prick already dampening the front of his silk boxers, the fabric semi-transparent so that the smooth flesh of his cock showed a deep and luscious pink through the wet silk.

He let her caress him for a few moments, just standing there, rejoicing in the feeling of flesh on silk and silk on flesh. His cock reared at her touch, nudging its way through the front vent of his pants and into her hand, dripping its slippery lubricant all over Melissa's fingers.

She used it to wank him, spreading the slick wetness over the head of his prick, then down the length of his shaft, smoothing it up and down with light, slow movements. She felt like she was in paradise . . .

Seizing her hand, he drew it to his lips, licking the essence of his own sex from her fingers, winding his tongue about each one individually, making her quiver with pleasure.

'Rhys. Oh Rhys . . .'

His tongue-tip traced a fine line from the tip of her index finger down to the middle of her palm and he pressed her hand to his mouth, kissing and gently biting the flesh.

'I want you, Melissa. I want you now.'

He stood behind her and cupped her breasts through her T-shirt. He loved it when she went bra-less, letting her large breasts move with a natural fluidity beneath the thin white fabric. Her nipples were as hard and as long as sweet almonds, and he toyed with them, rolling and pinching them between finger and thumb.

Melissa felt a tingling, burning, surging heat in her belly, as though there were electric wires leading from her nipples down to her navel and from there to the white-hot heart of her sex. Taking hold of the library table in front of her, she found herself leaning forward, so that the full weight of her breasts was in Rhys's hands and her backside was thrust shamelessly towards him, grinding against the bare stiffness of his erect prick.

'My darling hussy,' he murmured, letting go of her left breast and easing up the hem of her skirt. Underneath, she had on only the briefest pair of panties, a flirty, scanty pair he had bought her for her last birthday, all lace and ribbons and hardly any substance. They were held together at the sides with strings which tied into bows and he unfastened them swiftly, tugging so that the bows untied and the triangle of frilly lace fell away, revealing the glorious twin globes of her rump.

Melissa felt his hands move to her bum cheeks and a delirium of pleasure overtook her. Before her eyes danced Reuben Fairfax's picture of the Paradise Garden, its flowers and fruit, its verdant branches and soft grass forming the perfect setting for the lovers who embraced in the shade of an apple tree.

Rhys knew what he wanted – and what Melissa wanted too. It was all instinct now, with no need for words. Her buttocks were firm and juicy in his hands and he could not resist seizing them, squeezing them, pulling them wide apart to reveal the deep furrow between; and in its very heart, the secret amber rose...

His cock-tip was so wet that it slipped easily between Melissa's bum cheeks, nuzzling and nudging its way a little further down until at last it was pressing lightly against the entrance to Melissa's own secret garden.

'No, no, no,' whispered Melissa, but her words were barely audible, and in her head she was screaming *yes, yes, yes, do it to me, put your cock into me, do what you have never done to me before. What no man has ever done to me*...

Rhys could feel the blood pumping and thudding through his veins, swelling his cock almost to bursting point, until all he could think about was this wonderful, intriguing, forbidden pleasure he had never tasted before.

With a sudden, scything thrust he penetrated the tight sphincter of her anus, his penis sliding about halfway into her. Melissa cried out, but it was a cry of astonished excitement, not a cry of discomfort; and as his full length entered her with the second thrust, Rhys felt her begin to push out her backside, answering his thrusts with her own. He knew that she was signalling to him that she too shared this exotic, forbidden pleasure.

He slid his hand round in front of her and felt for the entrance to her vulva, parting her outer sex-lips with his fingers and letting his finger slide over her dripping-wet inner folds until he found the hard, slippery pearl of her clitoris.

Together they fucked, in perfect rhythm, lost in a world of sublime pleasure. And as they moved towards orgasm, they fucked harder, faster, aware now only of two realities: the pleasure bubbling and surging within them and the sweet, secret scent of an ancient rose.

Chapter 8

Melissa stretched out on her belly on the soft green grass, her silken skin sun-dappled with light and shade. Her blouse was unbuttoned and her knickers lay moist and crumpled on the ground. Her skirt was up round her waist, revealing the smooth white domes of her buttocks and the opalescent wetness trickling down her inner thighs.

Rhys lay beside her, his jeans still unzipped and pulled down onto his hips, the fat pink snake of his dick lying lazily across his thigh. Even though its pleasure was all spent, his hand stroked it almost instinctively, savouring the delicious glow of satisfaction as his other hand traced the curve of Melissa's backside. It seemed to Rhys that he was seeing her naked for the first time.

'It's so beautiful here,' whispered Melissa as he bent to kiss the nape of her neck. 'Just like paradise.'

Overhead in the tangled canopy of branches, a small russet-coloured bird was singing, its song as liquid and as melodious as the bubbling spring which they had uncovered by the southernmost margin of the wall, its crystal-clear waters feeding the lush vegetation they saw all around them.

'We really ought to go back to the house,' ventured Rhys, pressing his body up against Melissa's bare flank and rejoicing in the pulsating heat from her body. 'It must be well after twelve and I *have* to get some work done today. And, don't forget, Maia and Jim are coming this evening.'

'Mmm . . . I don't care, they can wait. It can *all* wait.' Melissa grabbed hold of Rhys and, rolling onto her back, pulled him on top of her. She loved to feel his weight bearing down upon her, loved to feel safe and secure within the protecting cage of his strong arms. 'It's Sunday, Rhys. Nobody works on a Sunday.'

Rhys bent to kiss her neck.

'Freelance journos do,' he told her. 'Or their editors kick their poor, underpaid arses into the middle of next week.'

'Couldn't we stay just five minutes more?' pleaded Melissa. It had been such a wonderful morning, here in the Paradise Garden. OK, so they'd come here meaning to weed and dig like crazy and ended up making love on the grass, but what did that matter?

'Five minutes.' Rhys kissed Melissa's throat, then slid down to kiss between her full breasts, bare and inviting beneath her open shirt. 'Now what could we do in five minutes . . . ?'

Melissa shivered as he slid down her body until his face was level with the base of her belly.

'Such a wonderful perfume,' he told her, breathing in deeply. 'Have you any idea what it does to me? You make me hard as iron for you, Melissa.'

A light breeze wafted through the tree tops, gently shaking the branches and making the leaves rustle. Sunlight filtered through them, making kaleidoscopic patterns on Melissa's flesh as Rhys bent to kiss his lover's plump and succulent labia.

The garden was a revelation on a day like this, when a full yellow sun beamed down out of a cloudless blue sky. Out on the moors, a strong breeze gusted over the open heath, but here within the cocooning walls of the Paradise Garden all was tranquillity, fertile and sensual excess.

Old English roses bloomed in profusion, clambering over the russet brickwork of the Elizabethan wall and half-obliterating it with pink and white flowers. Around the spot where the freshwater spring emerged from the ground, many-coloured marsh-plants flourished. Their curious flowers and brilliant-green stems formed a vivid contrast to the muted greys and greens of the sweet herbs which, when restored to their former glory, would once again trace out the intricate patterns of knot-gardens.

Woody thyme and lemon-scented verbena struggled to peep through the tangled drifts of couch grass and briar, ivy and columbine. Much, much more remained to be discovered beneath the enshrouding weeds and overgrown shrubs, but already the Paradise Garden was beginning to reveal some of its former beauty.

Against the southern wall a peach espalier stretched out its branches, already laden with small yet juicy fruits. And lying on the soft grass, Melissa felt as though she too were a part of joyful, burgeoning nature, welcomed and embraced and aroused by the abundant life around her.

Drawing up her knees, she spread her legs to accept the gift of Rhys's tongue, its tip daintily exploring the moist pink frills of her inner labia before darting to the very heart of her desire, the fleshy stalk of her clitoris.

His thumbs slid inside her vagina, pulling and stretching the elastic walls, teasing the ring of nerve-endings just inside the entrance. She was tight and yet yielding, her sex-muscles at first clenching tight about him then relaxing, inviting him to probe more deeply.

Rhys's tongue flicked over and over the head of Melissa's clitoris, very, very lightly and yet with such accuracy that Melissa wondered if she could bear it. The touch was so brutally pleasurable, such wonderful agony, that she twisted and turned, almost pushing Rhys away yet at the same time pleading with him to do it again, harder, harder, faster.

'Aah!' She let out a yelp of pain as Rhys's tongue-tip jabbed with a sudden, malicious delight at the very epicentre of her throbbing desire. 'Aah, oh no, no, no . . .'

Her voice rose to a crescendo that was almost a scream of terror, and then suddenly everything was sunlight and ecstasy, and the all-pervading scents of chamomile and lemon verbena, and sweet, sweet sex.

Arriving back at the house, Rhys and Melissa went straight upstairs to get washed and dressed.

'Three o'clock!' Melissa glanced at the old long-case clock on the stairs. 'It's later than I thought . . . Maia and Jim said they'd be here by six and I haven't even faxed those sales figures that I promised I'd send on Friday.'

They went into the office together. A long white ribbon of paper was dangling from the back of the fax machine. Melissa tore it off and scanned it.

'It's for you,' she said. 'From *Ecology Now*! They say, can you rejig it so it's only fifteen hundred words. Oh, and can you do it by tomorrow evening, as one of their regulars has let them down?'

'Blast!' Rhys took the fax and plonked himself down at his desk, in front of his computer. 'At this rate I'll be working all night . . . hang on, what's this?'

Melissa finished loading her sales figures into the fax

machine and leaned over his shoulder.

'What's what?'

'There's a message in E-mail ... good God!'

Melissa and Rhys stared at the screen as the message flashed up. No sender's name, no sender's code, it seemed as though it had been deliberately wiped clean of all identifying marks.

The message consisted not of words, but of an animated sequence of pictures. In the middle of the screen, a woman with corn-yellow hair lay on a black settee, her thighs and pubis bare. A man was lying between her legs, pushing, pushing, pushing into her, his long dick possessing her, making her writhe and moan.

Melissa could feel the blood rushing to her face. Surely Rhys could not fail to recognise the woman in the picture ... and if he realised who the man was, there was no telling how he might react.

'Bloody hell,' said Rhys softly, replaying the message again and again, watching the two figures fucking as though he were transfixed by the scene. Melissa could see his cock swelling under his dusty jeans. 'This is pretty horny stuff ... but why on earth would anyone want to send me computer porn?'

'I ... I've no idea,' replied Melissa, turning away and hoping Rhys hadn't noticed the confusion and guilt on her face.

Because she knew darned well that no-one had sent it to Rhys at all, they'd intended it for her. And only one man would stoop that low in the quest to satisfy his lust.

That man was Peter Galliano.

* * *

Maia Kerrigan watched Highmoor House loom up before her as the car turned onto the unmade track which led to the house. It was Maia's company car but Jim was driving. He enjoyed driving and, besides, Maia was saving her energies for tonight.

'Good of you to offer to help Rhys with his computer,' observed Jim ironically as they bumped up the track.

Maia smiled.

'What are friends for, if not to help you out in a crisis?'

'To screw?'

'Mmm, yes, now you mention it, I *would* rather like to get to know Rhys a little better.'

She stretched out her long, model-girl thighs, wriggling her pert backside on the leather seat as she thought about Rhys and the games she intended to play tonight. She still felt a small pang of regret when she thought of Melissa and the fun they could have had together. Such an aptitude the girl had, too. Such a well-developed sensuality. But Melissa Montagu was a silly young woman who let her inhibitions rule her life. Rhys might be equally inhibited, of course, but Maia was confident of her ability to charm him into submission, particularly as she and Jim had been invited to stay the night at Highmoor House.

'Looking forward to this?' enquired Jim.

He felt a faint stirring between his thighs as he thought of Melissa and Rhys . . . particularly Melissa. God, but he'd had a letch for her for years now, ever since Rhys had introduced her to him as his new girlfriend – it must have been, oh, four or five years ago. Like Maia, Jim couldn't understand why people were so reticent about having fun with their bodies. There was nothing he liked better than to watch Maia screwing some other bloke or getting licked out by some slim-hipped girl. Nothing turned him on more than seeing another man's semen trickling out from between his wife's pussy lips. Nothing except, perhaps, the thought of taking Melissa Montagu to bed.

'I intend to enjoy myself,' purred Maia. 'I've decided I'm going to have Rhys tonight. There's something about him . . . an innocence . . .'

'And if you can't have Melissa, you'll take Rhys as a consolation prize . . . ?'

'Quite.' Momentarily annoyed to be reminded of her failure, Maia glanced out of the window. How Rhys and Melissa could bear living up here, she couldn't begin to imagine, even if it was a rather fine Elizabethan house.

'Why don't you tell me what you want to do to him?' suggested Jim.

'I want to suck his cock. But I won't let him come, I'll just tease him for a long, long time until he begs me for mercy.'

'Rhys is one lucky guy,' murmured Jim, rubbing the front of his pants.

'And then, when he can't take any more, I'll make him fuck me in the arse. That'll *really* blow his mind, the poor darling. I don't suppose Melissa's ever let him touch her there, let alone bugger her. The poor girl doesn't know what she's missing.' She ran her fingers up Jim's thigh and the electricity of intimacy crackled between them. Through the games they played with other people's partners, they kept the sexual chemistry of their own partnership as fresh and as potent as it had been the first time they met. Her eyes met Jim's for a brief moment. 'So why don't you show her?'

Jim's lips curved into a half-smile.

'Me?' he replied in mock-surprise. 'Now what could I possibly teach Melissa Montagu?'

'You could teach her how to take ten inches of beautiful hard cock into that tight little backside of hers. And you're obviously more to her taste than I am...'

'Hmm, perhaps I *could* show her a thing or two...'

'Go on,' whispered Maia, deftly manipulating Jim's penis until it was just short of the blissful release of orgasm. 'Go on, do it. Drive her wild, make her beg you to put it up her arse. I want to see your spunk dribbling down her thighs. And when you've done, I want to lick your beautiful cock clean.'

The car turned into the driveway, past two gate posts topped with lopsided stone lions. Jim looked with interest at the Suzuki jeep parked outside the front of the house.

'Look – the others have already arrived. Who did Melissa say she was inviting? Some estate agent, wasn't it?'

Maia pulled a face.

'Something like that. He's bound to be boring as hell, especially if he's one of the local yokels.'

Parking the car, Jim switched off the ignition and got out. Maia followed a couple of seconds later, stretching her long, slender limbs as she stepped down onto the gravel path. She was one of those rare women who know and love their bodies, who are perfectly in harmony with every curve, every sensation, every graceful and sensuous movement.

Together they walked up to the front door, which opened just as they arrived.

'Melissa, *darling*.' Maia pecked three kisses onto Melissa's slightly reticent cheek and handed over a bottle of very good Australian Chardonnay. 'You're looking stunning.' Her hand just brushed the tip of Melissa's nipple, lingering a little too long to be a mere accident, and Maia suppressed a chuckle of amusement as she saw how Melissa shrank from the touch, terrified that she would once again enjoy it too much and find herself responding.

'Good to see you both again.'

'And you. This is quite some house you've got here,' observed Maia.

Rhys laughed.

'It will be one day, when we get round to finishing it.'

Rhys took Maia's coat and for a long moment Maia embraced him, her lips skating from his cheek to his lips. She could feel him responding, his body vibrating to the frequency of her tyrannical desire, and she felt almost disappointed. Perhaps Rhys wasn't going to be quite such a difficult conquest after all. She enjoyed a challenge.

'It was difficult getting through York,' remarked Jim, following Melissa down the corridor to the front sitting room. He watched the way her smooth, rounded bum-cheeks fought against the imprisoning fabric of her tight black dress, and his cock reared in his pants, refusing to be discreet. 'There's a race meeting on – Maia was convinced we were going to be late.'

'Not with Jim at the wheel,' replied Maia archly, directing her words at Rhys, refusing to let him break eye-contact. 'Jim doesn't believe in speed limits, do you darling? But then that's just like Jim. He goes at *everything* hell-for-leather.'

Melissa pushed open the door of the sitting-room and turned back to look at Maia and Jim.

'The others are in here. I'll just introduce you, and then I must go and finish the dinner.'

'Want a hand, darling?' enquired Maia with a wicked smile.

'No need for that,' replied Melissa hastily. 'Rhys will help me, won't you, Rhys?'

'What . . . ? Oh, yes, yes, of course I will.' He managed to snap away from Maia's hypnotic gaze and followed Melissa into the sitting-room. Maia glared after him but he did not turn back.

Christopher Maudsley got to his feet as they went in. Maia looked him up and down. Not bad-looking, a little ordinary for her tastes, but not so ordinary that she'd say no should the opportunity present itself. Quite tall, with wavy brown hair, and broad-shouldered under that tweedy jacket. No, not bad at all . . .

But it wasn't Maudsley who attracted Maia's attention. It was Maudsley's companion. Jazz Summersdale was so distinctive that she quite made Maia forget her determination to pursue Rhys. Yes, this girl was far, far more interesting than Melissa and Rhys put together.

The only concession Jazz had made to Melissa's dinner party was to change out of her biking leathers and into the shortest leather micro-skirt Maia had ever seen. It hugged her hips like a second skin, the hem so high that it barely covered her panties . . . assuming she was wearing any, and you couldn't make any assumptions about Jazz Summersdale. A chunky metal belt hung loosely around her waist and she was wearing a red crop-top in skintight Lycra underneath a black leather blouson jacket. Her jewellery was not so much attractive as aggressive and a small red garnet glittered in her pierced nose.

Introductions were made, but Jazz remained resolutely settled in her chair, offering only a brief nod of response. Maia lusted after her instantly. It was obvious that Jazz was a complete slut – and a slut who knew her own mind. For once, Maia felt as though she were the victim, the one waiting to be seduced, whilst Jazz had the upper hand, coolly aloof, utterly in control of the sensual powers which waited to burst out of her like molten lava.

Maia looked from Maudsley to Jazz and back again. How come a man so ordinary could get such an extraordinary woman to share his bed? The conundrum intrigued her.

'You're an estate agent, Chris?'

Maudsley made a face as he took a sip of his beer.

''Fraid so. But it pays the rent. How about you?'

'I'm a systems analyst.'

'You enjoy your work?'

Maia gave a husky laugh, filled with meaningful overtones.

'It's not so bad. I get to tell people what they want and give it to them.' She slipped off her glittery evening jacket, revealing bare shoulders and a neckline which dipped in an alarmingly deep V, almost to the waist. 'Before that, I used to be a catwalk model.'

'Really?' Jazz leaned forward, suddenly showing an interest. Or maybe it was Maia's unveiled body that she was showing an interest in. At least, that was what Maia hoped.

'Uh-huh.' Maia tucked an imaginary wisp of hair behind her ear. 'Actually, Jim used to model too, to make a bit of extra money when he was an engineering student. Soft-porn pics mostly. He's still got a nice body, don't you think so, Chris?'

Maudsley's eyebrows rose slightly at the question.

'I . . . er . . . yeah, I reckon so. Keep yourself fit do you, Jim?'

Jim smiled. It never ceased to amaze and amuse him, the way men refused to acknowledge that they found other men even remotely attractive as though admitting that you fancied a little same-sex recreation would make you any less of a man.

'Oh, I get *plenty* of exercise, Chris. We both do.' He winked at Maia. 'Isn't that so, darling?'

As if unsettled by Jim's words, Maudsley reached out and placed his hand on Jazz's thigh. What a tart you are, thought Maia, looking at the girl with her cropped hair and her bra-less tits. What a completely delicious, utterly shameless tart. Forget Rhys. Forget Melissa. It's *you* I'm going to have tonight, Janice Summersdale.

All through dinner, Melissa watched Maia. Even though she had rejected her friend's sexual advances, back at the house in London, secretly she still realised that there was something compelling about the woman, something that drew men – and other women – towards her like moths to a flame. And there was enough sexual power within Maia Kerrigan's perfectly proportioned frame to burn right through your soul.

Curiously enough, Melissa felt odd twinges of jealousy as she saw the way Maia looked at Jazz. And it wasn't just a one-way thing. It was perfectly obvious to anyone with half an eye that Jazz lusted after Maia too. Well, who'd have thought it? And whatever did Christopher Maudsley think about his girlfriend making eyes at Maia Kerrigan?

But Maudsley seemed not to have noticed, chatting with Rhys about the price of property, and a moment later Melissa's attentions were distracted by the touch of something soft, stroking its way over her ankle and calf.

She looked across the table and saw Jim smiling at her. Not so much a smile as a smirk, an invitation, a dare...

'Great dinner party, Melissa.' He raised his wine glass in a toast and when he put down the glass she couldn't help noticing how red and moist his lips were from the rich, ruby liquid. How succulently kissable too...

'Thank you,' she replied, trying to keep her cool. But Jim's stockinged foot was still stroking her ankle, creeping a little higher up her leg, and she hoped that Rhys would not detect the slight tremble in her voice. She tried moving her leg but Jim just kept on stroking her with his toes.

'You know, Melissa,' said Jim quietly. 'I've always believed that some things are . . . inevitable. You know, meant to be. Don't you think that's true?'

'Really? I don't know.'

'Really.' Jim picked up his chicken leg and wrenched off a great chunk of the flesh with his teeth, chewing and then wiping the grease from his lips with the back of his hand. There was something profoundly erotic in the act, something both obscene and compelling. 'Surely you believe that, Melissa . . . in lust at first sight?'

Melissa felt his toes sliding up her calf to her knee. She tried to move her knees together, to stop him, but her body refused to obey her and his caress was very insistent, very persuasive. Slowly his foot slid between her knees, between her thighs, his toes creeping up towards the heart of her pleasure.

'I'm not sure what you mean,' she lied, trying hard not to show the tumult of emotions within her.

'I mean ... that some things, some *people* ...' Jim smiled. 'People like you and me, Melissa. It was meant to happen and we shouldn't fight it.' He lowered his voice. 'Don't fight it, Melissa. You know you want it just as much as I do.'

'Jim! Please!' Melissa dared not raise her voice above a hoarse whisper, though Rhys seemed absorbed in his tedious conversation with Christopher Maudsley and Jazz was too busy flirting with Maia to be bothered eavesdropping on Melissa. 'Don't!'

'You don't mean that,' smiled Jim. And he was right. Melissa's hungry sex-lips were opening and closing in a kiss of welcome, the gusset of her panties moist with juice.

His foot wriggled into the tight space between her half-closed thighs and now his toes were a fraction of an inch from her pussy lips, from the wisps of corn-gold hair which had escaped from her panties and curled, dew-spangled and exciting, at the very tops of her thighs.

Oh yes, she wanted it. She wanted it like crazy. And it would be so simple just to ease herself forward the merest fraction on her chair, so that the apex of her pubis was pressing against his toes. So simple just to rotate her hips gently. No-one would guess. No-one would know but she and Jim when at last she brought herself to orgasm ...

'Melissa?'

Rhys's voice broke the spell and Melissa swung round. 'Oh! Oh, Rhys ... yes?'

PARADISE GARDEN

'Are you all right?'

'Yes, fine . . . any special reason?'

'Only you looked a bit . . . I don't know . . . out of it.'

Melissa eased herself, gently but firmly, away from Jim's foot. Out of the corner of her eye she could see the disappointment on his face but she knew, now that the charm was broken, that she couldn't go through with it. How she could possibly have thought she wanted him in that way she just couldn't imagine.

'I'll get dessert,' she announced and started clearing the plates away.

At the end of dinner, they chatted around the table for a while, drinking port and brandy.

'So – what about the grand tour you've been promising us, eh, Rhys?' demanded Jim. 'I thought you were going to show us this amazing garden of yours.'

Rhys shook his head apologetically.

'Sorry, folks, I know this is a terrible thing for a host to do, but could you spare me for a little while? I just have to print out an article and fax it off to the editor.'

'Tell you what, Melissa,' Maudsley cut in. 'Why don't you and Jazz and I take Maia and Jim to see the Paradise Garden? I know my way there, now you've shown me round.'

'Brilliant idea.' Melissa searched around for an excuse not to go. She didn't particularly want to be caught in the Paradise Garden with Jim Kerrigan when the sun went down . . . 'Only there's one or two things I need to sort out . . .'

'Later,' urged Jim. 'Come with us.'

'No, I really must,' she replied with unexpected resolution. 'I'll see you all later, when you come back to the house.'

*   *   *

In the warmth of a summer's evening, the Paradise Garden was suffused with a pale, rose-gold light.

Maudsley, Jazz, Jim and Maia stood in the middle of what had once been a lush chamomile lawn and surveyed the garden.

'It's beautiful but it's a mess,' Maudsley observed. 'It'll take a lot of work to get it back to the way it once was. The knot-gardens will probably need replanting and everything's so overgrown.'

Maia strolled along a moss-covered brick pathway, breathing in the scents of summer flowers and herbs and the spiciness of warm peaches and nectarines and damsons, ripening on heavy boughs.

'I like it,' she announced. 'It's a romantic place, surprisingly sensual...'

Jazz Summersdale threw back her head and laughed, her long silver earrings jangling and clinking.

'Romantic!' There was a sneer in her voice. 'What you mean is, you'd like to screw someone in here, am I right?'

Maudsley stared at her in stunned silence. It had been Jazz's unconventionality, her daring sexuality, which had drawn him to her in the first place and having sampled her skills in bed, he counted himself a lucky bastard; but sometimes, she went a bit too far...

'Jazz...' he began.

To his surprise she turned on him.

'Oh, for fuck's sake, Chris,' she spat, 'It's all manners with you, isn't it? All politeness and never saying what you really mean. And half the time you don't notice what's right in front of your nose!'

'Meaning?'

'Meaning Maia and I have been touching each other up all evening and you never even noticed. Do you know how that feels? Do you? You don't give a damn about me, do you, Chris? I'm just a sexy bitch you can show off to your friends . . .'

'That's not true!' protested Maudsley. To tell the truth, he was besotted with Jazz. The thought of someone else – especially a woman – laying hands on her body made him mad as hell. 'You're my girl, nobody else's. I mean, look here . . . !'

'No, Chris, you look here.' Jazz looked so, so amazingly sexy when she stood like that, hands on hips, breasts thrust out, lips pouting and scarlet and her black hair glossy in the evening sunlight. As he watched, she peeled off her leather jacket and threw it on the ground. The tattoo of a scorpion on her right shoulder was bright yellow and red against her winter-paled skin. 'This is my body, mine to use as I want. I don't belong to you or to anyone else – understand? And what I want to do right now is have a really good fuck.'

'You want to do *what*?'

'You heard.'

'Don't be stupid, Jazz. You're embarrassing Jim and Maia.'

Jazz laughed humourlessly.

'Not them, Chris. I'm embarrassing *you*.'

'Are you drunk?'

'Not yet. I don't need to be drunk to fuck. And I'm going to fuck, right? Here and now. I'm going to fuck with Maia and you can watch if you want. Isn't that right, Maia?'

To Maudsley's horror, Maia smiled and nodded. She was

already sliding down the side-zip of her dress.

'That's right, Chris. Don't be shy. It's all perfectly natural. Afterwards you can have me, if you like.'

Maudsley's head was spinning. Watch! Watch his own girlfriend screwing some other woman while he and Jim looked on? He couldn't, he just couldn't. The very thought made him feel angry, sick, betrayed.

And excited.

'You do what you want, Janice.' He only ever called her by her full name when he was angry with her. 'You do what you damn well want, but I'm not sticking around to watch, do you hear?'

He turned to go back to the house. If he had hoped Jazz would tag along after him, he was very much disappointed. She stood staring defiantly after him as he opened the gate, her nipples pressing hard with excitement against the fabric of her tight crop-top.

'Are you coming, Jazz?' There was a note of desperation in his voice.

'No.'

'Then don't bother coming back at all.'

The wooden gate slammed behind him and Maia listened to his footsteps retreating along the pathway which meandered through the grounds towards the house. There was a warm glow in her belly and her heart was thumping like a steam-hammer. This girl, this crop-haired leather-slut from the middle of nowhere, was more exciting by far than she had dreamed – though Maia was an excellent judge of character and she had sensed the sensuality within Jazz the first time she had set eyes on her.

But this little scene . . . this little drama in the middle of

Rhys and Melissa's garden – well! She certainly hadn't anticipated that things would move so quickly. Maybe it was something about this place, something in the warm, clean, sweet-scented air that caressed your body and filled your lungs like an expensive perfume; or the light, soft breeze that rustled the branches of the trees, and whispered wicked thoughts into your ears. It was a pity about Maudsley but then she hadn't really fancied him that much anyway. It was Jazz she wanted, Jazz's fingers and tongue . . .

It was Jim who spoke first.

'Did you mean that, Jazz? What you said?'

Jazz pursed her crimson-painted lips.

'I don't say things I don't mean.'

'And what would you say if I told you I'd like to fuck you, too?'

Jazz looked him up and down with a crazy half-smile.

'I'd say I'd never met a man who didn't want to fuck me. But then again, I've never met a man I didn't want to fuck.'

Maia's voice was barely louder than a whisper, but it seemed to echo around the walled garden, cutting through the balmy stillness of the evening.

'Darling Jazz. Sweet, darling Jazz. I can't begin to tell you how much I want you.'

Maia slid her dress down over her hips, giving them a little wriggle to free the tight crepe and then letting it go, so that it fell in a burgundy-coloured swathe about her feet. She stepped away from it, her legs impossibly long and smooth in their black stockings and high heels.

Jazz's eyes were full of hunger as she watched Maia pulling down her panties, sliding them right down over the swell of hips and thighs and then stepping out of them.

Underneath she was freshly shaven, the bare flesh of her sex clearly displaying the deep pink of her inner labia, protruding from between her outer labia like an insolent tongue.

Not to be outdone, Jazz pulled her crop-top off over her head. Her bee-sting breasts were almost childlike in their firmness, tiny, pert hillocks crested with puckered brown nipples that were hard as hazelnuts. She took off her belt and then unzipped her leather mini-skirt. Underneath she was wearing nothing but the tiniest of G-strings and a pair of spike-heeled black ankle boots which laced up the front.

She took a step forward, and very, very slowly took off her G-string. Maia's eyes feasted on the bounty within and she saw Jim's tongue flick greedily over his parched lips. Jazz too was shaven, and through her outer labia passed a heavy gold ring which distended the flesh and glittered as it caught the sunlight.

'Jazz,' began Maia. 'Why don't you . . .?'

But it was Jazz who was taking the initiative now.

'If you want me to fuck you, you'll do as I say, Maia. Kneel on the grass, that's it, just like the red-hot bitch you are. Hands and knees, bum thrust out. *Yes*, good girl.'

Jazz knelt on the ground behind her and pulled apart Maia's bum cheeks, quite roughly.

'Well!' she exclaimed. 'You *are* a hot little slut, aren't you?' She ran a long-nailed finger the length of Maia's intimate crease, from pubis to arse. It came away glistening with wetness and Jazz licked it off. 'Mmm, delicious. Such sweet cunt-juice you have, did you know that? It's almost like . . . like melted syrup.'

She placed a finger inside Maia's vagina. Behind them,

Jim was undressing, taking out his cock, smoothing and caressing it, stroking and playing with it as though it were a favourite mistress.

'Have you ever had a woman's fingers inside you, Maia?'

'I . . . yes,' gasped Maia, sliding back so that Jazz's finger was inside her up to the knuckle.

'Ah, but have you ever had a woman's *fist* inside you?'

Without waiting for Maia's reply, Jazz curled up her hand into a fist and plunged it deep into Maia's dripping-wet sex. She was tight, very tight, and only the extreme quantities of her own lubricating fluid prevented pleasurable discomfort from turning into pain. Maia cried out as Jazz's chunky silver rings twisted and turned inside her, pressing hard against the stretchy walls of her vagina. And then the ringed fingers opened out like the petals of an exotic flower, stretching the flesh still further, making Maia feel that she must surely be torn in two.

Jim could resist it no longer. Jazz's perfect backside was bobbing up and down in front of him as she fist-fucked Maia, her arse cheeks opening and closing to offer tantalising glimpses of the puckered brown rose of her arsehole.

He knelt behind her, kissing and biting her rump, loving the little white bite-marks that turned so quickly to the full and vibrant colour of a damask rose. He could hear Jazz's voice beneath Maia's, her gasps and moans lower-pitched than Maia's shrill cries of impending pleasure. She made no attempt to fight him as he pulled her bum cheeks further apart and started poking his tongue into the matchless areola. It was the most beautiful arse he had ever seen, the tightest, the most pleasingly formed, the most welcoming. Even Maia's tight and greedy arse had never delighted him as much as this one did.

At last, when his saliva was trickling from her anus right down to the well of her sex, he withdrew from her, gasping, and knelt up so that the very tip of his cock was pressing against the entrance to her secret gateway.

'Oh! Oh yes!' he heard Maia cry, and he felt Jazz's body tense as she began fisting her lover faster, faster, harder.

With one powerful thrust he buried himself in Jazz's receptive flesh, the long, smooth shaft of his cock disappearing up to its hilt and his balls jiggling excitingly close to the rounded swell of her backside.

It could not last long, not even here in this perfect, sunlit garden where everything seemed made for sexual delight. The pleasure was a little too intense, the need too urgent. He lost track of time. Perhaps it was minutes, hours, or only seconds; but too, too soon, Jim felt the familiar delicious ache at the base of his cock as jet upon jet of semen came powering out of him into Jazz's thrusting backside.

Maia sank to the ground, her own juices spilling from her in fragrant abundance onto the grass beneath her. Jim fell to his knees, panting, head swimming, cock still hard and throbbing. Jazz simply withdrew her fist from Maia's pussy and gave her fingers to Maia to lick. She lapped off the clear juice as though it were the finest, the sweetest honey.

'Good girl,' said Jazz with perfect composure. Getting to her feet, she stooped and picked up Maia's evening dress. It would do. Reaching between her legs, she wiped the ooze of sperm from her thighs and buttocks, then dropped the soiled dress on the ground in a crumpled heap.

Jim watched in stunned silence as Jazz got dressed with an almost military efficiency.

'Where are you going?'

'Back to the house.'

'But why? Why don't you stay here with us?' pleaded Maia, feeling cheated. There were so many things she still wanted to do with Jazz and to her ...

'I have to see Chris.' Jazz buckled on her belt and slung her jacket over her shoulder. 'Explain a few ground rules to him. But thanks anyway. You weren't bad.'

And with a smile that was as brief and as brilliant as summer lightning, she was gone.

Maia sat with her knees gathered up to her chin, gazing at the closed gate.

'I wanted to lick her out,' she pouted. 'I wanted to lick your semen out of her pussy.'

'I know you did, darling.' Jim got down on the ground beside her and started kissing her face, her neck, her breasts. 'And now I want you to suck my cock.'

'Shouldn't we go back to the house? I'm supposed to be helping Rhys with that stupid computer of his.'

'Sod Rhys and his bloody computer.' Jim pushed Maia gently backwards and she sank onto the soft grass. Kneeling over her, he pushed his cock-tip against her lips and she took it eagerly into her mouth. 'You know, I really like this place. I could stay here for ever just fucking you, my darling, darling slut.'

As Maia sucked at Jim's cock, the sun sank a little lower in the sky, turning the clouds to orange and magenta and softest peach. The breeze was stilled in the trees and a lone nightingale began to sing somewhere in the branches above them. A song for lovers.

And very soon it had grown too dark to see that on the

grass, where Maia's sex-juice had formed a moist and fragrant pool, a scattering of pearl-white flowers had sprung up.

As if by magic.

Chapter 9

Curiously, there was no sign of either Maia or Jim at the breakfast table the following morning. More to the point, there was no sign of them in their room either. Their bed clearly hadn't been slept in, there were no clothes in the wardrobe and their car had gone from the driveway.

Quite simply, they had disappeared.

'What on earth possessed them to go off like that? They might at least have said goodbye,' commented Melissa, secretly a little relieved to see the back of Jim and Maia. 'Maia didn't even stick around long enough to help you with your PC.'

Rhys gave a shrug of his broad shoulders.

'Maudsley said he had a bit of a bust-up with Jim – he wouldn't say what it was about.'

'Knowing Jim, it *had* to be something to do with sex. And did you see how lovey-dovey Chris was with Jazz when she came back from the Paradise Garden?'

Rhys did. He also recalled the sexy smell that had surrounded Jazz like the waft of an expensive French perfume. Only this wasn't out of a bottle – this was the scent of sex.

'Never mind,' said Rhys, dropping two slices of bread into the toaster. 'I expect Maia will spill the beans, all in good time. You know what she's like. You don't hear a word from her for months, then she's on your doorstep telling you you're "simply wonderful, dahling".'

At that moment there was a loud knocking on the kitchen door and Melissa went to open it.

'Hello?'

The young man standing on the back steps was casually dressed in check shirt and jeans, his shirt sleeves rolled up to the elbow, revealing forearms which were tanned and muscular. His hair was very dark and naturally curly, giving him a slight look of the gypsy. Pale grey eyes twinkled in a high-cheekboned face tanned to a deep gold by the moorland winds.

'Morning. Mrs Montagu, is it?'

'That's right.' Melissa's tongue-tip slid over the swell of her lips in an involuntary reflex. Mmm, but he was tasty, this young man with the impetuous grey eyes and the tanned, work-hardened body. Deliciously tasty. 'And you are . . . ?'

'Simon. Simon Allbright.' He spoke in a deep, sonorous baritone, accented with the local burr. 'Mr Maudsley rang me up the other day, see. Said you had a garden needed clearing?'

The young man's hand grasped hers in a vice-like grip as they shook hands. There's such strength in those calloused fingers, thought Melissa to herself. And the thought of his strength, of his strong arms crushing her to him, forcing pleasure from her body, made her head reel with sudden, guilty imaginings.

She tore herself away from the fantasy.

'Yes. Yes, we have. Do come in.'

'I won't, if you don't mind. It's the muddy boots, see – they'll trail muck all over your nice clean floor.'

Melissa turned back to Rhys, unconcernedly drinking

tea, his feet up on the kitchen table.

'It's the gardener,' she announced.

'Oh good!' Rhys swung his feet onto the floor and got up, brushing toast crumbs off his trousers. He walked across to the door and peered quizzically at the newcomer. 'Not too expensive, are you? Only we're a bit skint right now.'

Simon's face crumpled into a smile and he tapped the side of his nose knowingly.

'I'm sure we can come to some arrangement, Mr Montagu,' he said. 'Cash in hand suit you, would it? A couple of notes in my back pocket and nobody's any the wiser. OK by you?'

Rhys shook Simon's hand.

'Sounds fine. Do you want to make a start today? Only Melissa and I have to go out on business.'

'That doesn't make much difference to me,' shrugged Simon. 'I've got all my tools with me, so I'm ready to go. Just show me where you want me to work and I'll get cracking.'

The trio walked across the grounds together towards the old summerhouse and the walled garden beyond. Getting that woodland management contractor in from Leeds had been expensive but the difference was quite impressive. Now you could actually see the walls of the Paradise Garden almost from the house. Most of the old pathways had been roughly cleared and the patterns of the old formal gardens were beginning to reappear like artefacts in an archaeological dig.

The Paradise Garden, though, they had decided to work on themselves, with the aid of just one gardener. There was something special about it, something intimate that they didn't want to share with the world in general. And when it was at last restored to its former magnificence, they sensed that it would be as special to them as it had been to Reuben Fairfax and his mistress. It would be their place of escape, a secret world of purest sensual pleasure.

'This is it.' Rhys unlocked the gate and went in, Simon Allbright following and Melissa bringing up the rear. 'It must have been amazing back in the sixteenth century but, as you can see, it's been allowed to run riot these last few years.'

Simon scratched his head and surveyed the garden. It had been cleared in patches, but large areas still remained under bramble and weeds, the original plants either barely managing to survive or taking over huge areas of the garden.

'There's a lot of work here,' he commented. 'More than I thought.'

'We'll help,' Melissa assured him. 'And all we want are the weeds clearing away, we'd like to keep as many of the old plants as possible.'

'OK. I can do that. It'll take a while, of course, but no problem. I might as well make a start today, while this good weather holds.' He unbuttoned his shirt and peeled it off. Melissa's eyes never left him for a second, devouring the magnificence of his bare, tanned torso, the way his perfectly toned muscles rippled underneath his golden skin – and that flat belly which led so invitingly down beneath the tight-belted waist of his jeans.

He scratched the ground with the toe of his boot, bent down and scooped up a handful of earth, smelling it and rubbing it between his fingers.

'Funny that.'

PARADISE GARDEN

'What is?'

'This soil. It's really good stuff, soft and loamy and quite rich. Nothing like the usual soil around here. Whoever designed the garden must have had it brought in from somewhere else.'

He strolled around, examining plants, wading through knee-deep weeds, picking the odd sprig of thyme or basil and crushing it between his fingers to release the scent. Melissa watched him, suddenly hungrier than she would ever dare admit. What was it about this young man that made her whole body cry out for him? She wanted him, oh how she wanted him.

Melissa's excitement had not escaped Rhys. He could see how she lusted after the young gardener and, to his surprise, he found that he felt not jealous or resentful, but powerfully excited. Aroused beyond endurance by the mental image of his lover having sex with another man, here in this most sexual of places . . .

'It's important that we get the garden looking just like it did in Elizabethan times,' said Rhys. 'We've got illustrations to work from, so it shouldn't be *that* difficult.'

Simon looked up.

'Oh yes?'

Melissa nodded.

'It's a very special garden – I don't know if you've heard about it. It used to be known as the Paradise Garden.'

Rhys thought he saw Simon stiffen almost imperceptibly but perhaps he had imagined it.

'The Paradise Garden? There's one or two stories about it round here, yeah.'

'Stories?' Melissa's ears pricked up. 'What sort of

stories?' She laid her hand on Simon's arm and the hardness of the muscle beneath the smooth skin was shockingly erotic. 'Won't you tell us?'

'Oh, you know,' said Simon dismissively, almost as if he wished he hadn't said anything. 'About the guy who built this place for his mistress. They're supposed to have disappeared.'

'Yes, we know that.' The disappointment in Melissa's voice was obvious. 'But . . . aren't there any other stories?'

'Well . . . one or two.' Simon bent to pull up a hank of couch grass. 'There were those two teachers from the Academy. Last year it was. The last person who saw them said they were climbing over the south wall into your garden. They never did turn up again.' He stood up, stretching his back, and Melissa couldn't help noticing how beautifully pert and firm his nipples were. Firm enough to kiss, firm enough to bite. 'But I reckon they just ran off somewhere together – both married they were, see, but not to each other!'

Rhys glanced at his watch. He didn't want to leave the garden, he really didn't. For some reason, his bones ached with the need to stay here all day long, basking in the warmth from the big yellow sun that was rising over the tops of the apple trees and turning the old brick wall to a rich, fiery red. But he and Melissa both had work to do, money to earn, and, besides, he was afraid of what might happen if they stayed here. Afraid of the way he felt whenever he thought about Melissa and this firm-bodied, strong-limbed gardener.

Just look at the way his cock swelled inside his jeans. It wasn't even erect. Rhys found himself imagining Simon unbuttoning his pants, cradling a huge and swelling pink serpent in his hands, offering it to Melissa to suck . . .

He forced himself out of this disturbing reverie.

'I'd better go now. The libraries will be open soon and I've got a stack of research to do.' He shook Simon's hand. 'See you later, OK?'

'Sure. You just leave it all to me. 'Spect I'll be gone when you get back – I like to knock off around four.'

Melissa gazed longingly at the dark-haired hunk. What on earth was wrong with her these days? Galliano had been an aberration but ever since she'd come to Highmoor House she couldn't get enough sex – of any and every kind. Just how close had she come to letting Jim Kerrigan do anything he damn well liked to her? How close had she come to accepting his invitation to 'show him round the garden'? And the funny thing was that, until last night, she had never even realised that she found Jim attractive.

And now here she was in the Paradise Garden with Rhys and Simon and her body was going crazy, unable even to decide which of the two it wanted more. Perhaps it wanted both . . .

'I have to go too,' she said hastily, catching Rhys's eye and looking away, sure that he must have seen the lustful glances she was giving Simon. 'Or I'll be late for the sales conference in York.'

'Right you are, Mrs M. I'll see you both later.' Simon stooped to clear a patch of cow parsley and paused, hesitating for a moment before picking something up.

He held it out.

'Don't suppose this would be yours, would it?'

Melissa took it from him. At first glance it seemed just an old rag, a tangle of dew-sodden, burgundy-coloured fabric scrunched up into a ball and left lying on the ground for goodness knows how long. But, as she held it up, it released a hint of Givenchy perfume, mingled with other, far more intimate scents.

Burgundy-coloured *crêpe-de-Chine*. That oh-so-familiar Givenchy perfume. Melissa stared at the fabric and listened to the pounding of her own heart. Suddenly she knew what it was.

It was Maia Kerrigan's evening dress. The one she had been wearing the previous evening when she and Jim visited the Paradise Garden.

Rhys had spent a profitable morning in Whitby library. It wasn't much of a library in absolute terms but when it came to local studies it had just about everything a freelance journalist could wish for.

The editor of *Ecology Now!* had commissioned him to write a series of articles on local green issues and he had spent several hours poring over papers relating to the decommissioning of the Fylingdales nuclear early-warning station.

He had all he wanted now, absolutely everything he needed for the first two articles. By rights he should pack up and go and find himself some lunch. There were at least a dozen of the finest fish-and-chip shops in the entire universe around Whitby harbour. It would probably take him an hour to make up his mind which one to eat in today.

But just as Rhys was packing away his portable PC, a thought popped into his head. If the local archives were so good on green issues, maybe they would have something on Highmoor House?

He strolled over to the information desk. A coolly attractive redhead of perhaps thirty-five peered at him over the top of a rather sexy pair of tortoiseshell-framed reading glasses.

'Thanks for the files.' He handed them over.

'Any use?'

'Yes, thanks. I got everything I needed. But I was just wondering . . .'

'I'm afraid that's all we have on Fylingdales,' cut in the redhead.

'No, not Fylingdales. It just occurred to me – do you have anything on Highmoor House? You know, the old Elizabethan manor-house up on the moors.'

'I know it.' Rhys thought her voice sounded just a hint frostier, more distant. 'But I'm afraid we don't have very much. Most of our records on the house were destroyed in a fire in 1942.' She sounded almost relieved.

'So there's nothing then? Nothing at all?' Rhys's journalistic nose told him she was holding something back.

'Well . . .' The redhead got up from her seat, took off her glasses and slipped them into a neat little Laura Ashley case. She looked disappointingly less sexy without them, Rhys noticed, as though half of her appeal evaporated when the sense of mystery was taken away. 'I think we may have a small cuttings file somewhere.' She unlocked the top drawer of a filing cabinet and started flicking through the files. 'But nothing very much, you understand.'

'What about the local history society?' suggested Rhys. 'Would they have anything?'

The librarian shook her head.

'I'm afraid there's no great interest in Highmoor House

around here,' she told him, almost as though she were making an effort to convince herself.

'But . . . it's Elizabethan, it's got so much history . . .'

'Like I said, no-one around here is very interested in the house.' She flicked a glance at Rhys. 'Quite honestly, we were all rather surprised when it found a buyer recently.' She extracted a slim cardboard folder and handed it to Rhys. 'There you are, sir. And what, if you don't mind my asking, is your interest in the house?'

Rhys met her quizzical gaze.

'I bought it.'

Leaving the librarian staring at him like a startled goldfish, Rhys took the folder and sat down at one of the study tables. He wondered why everyone around here was so cagey about Highmoor House. OK, so Reuben Fairfax and Perdita were supposed to have disappeared and *perhaps* those two teachers had been on their way into the gardens – or then again, maybe they'd just run off together. Either way, it hardly constituted a great mystery, did it? People could be so superstitious and gullible. What did they expect – ghosts?

He opened the file and saw that it contained a handful of cuttings from local newspapers. The earliest, yellowing scrap dated from 1942: 'Local landowner's son and village girl feared abducted,' the headline proclaimed. Rhys read on but the details were sparse. The son of the owner of Highmoor House had, it seemed, defied his father's wishes and eloped with a village girl but their deserted car had been found on the moors. The age-old story. Rhys flicked through the others – every single one of them related to Highmoor House and every one relating a tale of mysterious disappearance. The very last one related to the two teachers who had apparently been seen entering the grounds of the house, one winter's afternoon, and hadn't been seen since.

He closed the file. As usual, the local rags had resorted to the very worst kind of tabloid journalism just to sell papers. If you read between the lines, every single one of those stories could be given a rational explanation.

He was sure they could . . .

Melissa's morning had started badly. Arriving at the Royal Hotel with only minutes before the sales conference started, she had discovered a ladder in her Christian Dior tights and had had to sit through the morning session hoping no-one would notice.

Luckily she was sitting next to Dan Greenway, her former colleague from the London office, and as they listened with half an ear to the speakers he filled her in on the latest gossip.

'Tony's shacked up with Steve now,' he whispered.

'No!' exclaimed Melissa, clapping her hand over her mouth to stifle a giggle. 'I thought Tony and Graham were madly in love and buying a house together.'

'Oh, they were. Until Graham came home and found Tony giving Steve the blow job of his life.'

'So how's *your* sex-life, Dan? Still trying to sweet-talk Vanessa into bed?'

Dan's face assumed a delighted smirk.

'I thought you'd never ask. Actually she moved in with me last month . . . er, we're expecting twins in January.'

'You sly dog! And after you swore blind you were going to give up trying to seduce her, too.'

'It was well worth it in the end, Melissa, believe me. Talking of triers, did you hear about Candice?'

'What – Candice Soulbury?' Melissa felt a vague twinge of unease. Talking about Candice made her think about Candice's boss – Peter Galliano. And thinking about Galliano brought a whole host of uncomfortable, guilty sensations bubbling to the surface. Not to mention the memory of that obscene E-mail message he'd left on Rhys's computer.

'The very same. She's finally managed to lure Galliano into her bed. Really blatant she is about it, too – keeps telling everyone she's going to marry him. I can't see Galliano going along with that, though, he's too much your international playboy type.' Dan lowered his voice to a conspiratorial hiss. 'You know, at one point I did wonder if you and he . . . you know, if you and he had a thing going.'

To her chagrin, Melissa felt herself colouring.

'Don't talk bollocks, Dan!' she hissed. 'As if I'd have anything to do with that slimeball . . . !'

'Methinks the lady doth protest too much,' replied Dan smugly.

'Oh shut up!'

'Didn't you even fancy him a teensy-weensy bit, then?'

'Well . . .' replied Melissa dubiously.

'Of course you did. Every woman at Jupiter Products fancies Peter Galliano. And some of the men. Graham's crazy about him, but of course he'll never get anywhere. Galliano's strictly a ladies' man.'

'Strictly a letch, you mean,' bitched Melissa and she started taking a sudden interest in the lecture on 'Modular Office Design: The Way Forward'.

At lunchtime, while the other delegates were hoovering up the free buffet in the hotel dining room, Melissa made her way across the road to a quiet café. She always did that at conferences or, at least, whenever she could. She hated all that shop-talk, all that back-biting, all that frenzied networking and neurotic empire-building. She'd had it with all that. From now on, she was doing her job strictly to help pay for a better life with Rhys.

As she sat sipping her cappuccino and reading through the conference agenda, the door of the café opened and she heard a familiar voice above the jangling of the shop bell and the fussing of the frilly-aproned waitresses.

'Table for one, sir?'

'No, no, don't worry about that. I've just spotted a friend over there. I'll sit with her.'

It wasn't until he was level with her table that she looked up.

'You don't mind if I share, do you, Melissa?'

Galliano! Before Melissa had had time to think of some excuse to get up and leave, he had pulled out a chair and was sitting opposite her, looking more coolly irresistible than ever with his glossy, blue-black hair and his sardonic smile.

'I . . .' she stammered. Galliano patted her hand. She wanted to shrink away from the touch but her body was whispering to her: hey, why not? You know you like it . . .

'All alone, Melissa? That's a damn shame. A good-looking woman like you should never be alone.' He picked up the menu and scanned it. 'Still, you're not alone now, are you? You have me.'

'Mr Galliano.' Melissa made an effort to steady her voice, to keep control, to sound cool and calm and collected. 'Fancy meeting you here.'

Galliano snapped his fingers and the waitress approached, simpering and flirtatious, her varnished nails fiddling nervously with her lacy cap. It was obvious the girl was completely besotted with this sophisticated man who commanded every room he entered, who could have any woman he wanted in his bed. Any woman except you, Melissa, she told herself firmly. You can get those thoughts out of your head right now, young lady!

'A pot of lapsang for me and I'll have the lobster salad.'

'Yes, sir. Right away, sir.'

She disappeared into the kitchen and Galliano amused himself by watching her retreating backside quiver and wobble inside her slightly too-tight black skirt.

'Peasant,' he said with affectionate contempt. 'Still, she has a certain rustic charm.' His eyes met Melissa's, refusing to let her look away. 'A little like the local men around Highmoor, perhaps?'

'And what exactly is that supposed to mean?'

Galliano's fingertips stroked her cheek.

'Come, come, Melissa. You don't expect me to believe you've been faithful to that dreary man of yours up there in the sticks? You must have taken yourself a lover or two.'

'No, of course not. I . . .' She knew Galliano must be able to see the confusion flicker momentarily across her face as she thought back to that morning, when she and Rhys had been in the Paradise Garden with Simon Allbright. Would she have taken off her white cotton panties for Simon if he'd asked her to? Would she have unbuttoned his 501s and engulfed his prick in her mouth . . . ?

'Not even one?' Galliano's smile was at once menacing and attractive. 'Not even one empty-headed himbo with the body of a Greek god? You disappoint me, Melissa.'

'I'm sure I do,' replied Melissa with as much coolness as she could manage. She took a sip of her coffee. 'But then again, I'm not a hard-faced bitch like Candice Soulbury, am I?'

Galliano chuckled.

'What's this, Melissa – do I detect a hint of the green-eyed monster?'

'Don't flatter yourself.' She smiled. 'Sir.'

'I don't need flattery, Melissa. I know I'm the best. Candice knows it too, that's why she's with me.'

'Good for Candice. I just hope she knows what she's letting herself in for.'

Galliano paused to acknowledge the arrival of his lunch, then continued talking.

'The trouble with Candice, Melissa, is that the stimulation she gives me is purely physical. Oh, she thinks she's clever – she thinks she was the one who seduced me – but really she's just a child when it comes to intrigue. Whereas you, Melissa . . .' He stroked her cheek and ran his fingertips over her glossy lips. 'You have the makings of a truly great courtesan.'

'I don't have to sit here and take this from you,' said Melissa.

'No, but you want to, don't you? You want to but you're afraid to. Why did you run away from me, Melissa?'

'Why did you send obscene pictures of you and me to Rhys's computer terminal?'

Galliano laughed, so suddenly that several of the other diners craned their heads to look at him.

'Did I? Well, perhaps I did. And perhaps I did it because

I wanted to remind you that I am the only man you truly desire. It's true, Melissa, isn't it? Tell me you don't want me to fuck you again, like I did that day in my office.'

'I don't want you,' replied Melissa weakly. 'I told you before, I don't.'

'But the wetness in your pussy tells me you do, Melissa.'

This time Melissa coloured to the roots of her hair. How could he know? How could he possibly have guessed that her sex was oozing juice, that her clitoris was agonisingly swollen and that with each slight movement of her buttocks on the seat of her chair, it rubbed deliciously against the inner surface of her pussy lips?

'I want you too, Melissa. I don't mind admitting it, so why should you? If you were to put your hand on my dick right now – and I sincerely wish you would – you would discover that it is perfectly hard for you. I could unzip my cock for you, Melissa. You could sit on my lap in some secluded corner, just slide aside your panties and I would slip right up inside you. Or would you prefer me to bugger you? That's what you really want, isn't it, Melissa? That's what you want – my dick in your arse, filling you up with my spunk . . .'

'Stop this!'

'Why should I? We both know it's what you want. Come back to London or, better still, I'll set you up in the country somewhere, somewhere discreet. I'll make sure you get a job too, a nice one – lots of money and not too much work . . .'

Melissa got to her feet, a little unsteadily, signalling to a waitress as she went past.

'The bill, please.'

'Just one moment, madam. If you could just wait...'

'Now!' She thrust a ten-pound note into the woman's hand. 'Look, keep the change, it doesn't matter.'

And it didn't. All that mattered was getting out of here right now, getting away from this man who made her sex burn with guilty, frustrated hunger, who called up deep, dark longings which she was far too proud and far too terrified to acknowledge.

'Goodbye, Mr Galliano,' she said.

'You're making a big mistake, Melissa.'

'Perhaps. But you're making a bigger one if you think you can buy me.'

And with that, Melissa turned and stalked out of the café, slamming the door so hard that it rattled in its frame.

When Melissa arrived home it was after six and Rhys was in the kitchen, drinking coffee and scribbling notes for his next article on the back of an old A4 envelope. He always worked best when inspiration struck him – and it tended to strike in the oddest places, at the most inconvenient moments.

As Melissa kissed him he sensed the hunger inside her, felt it in the vibrations from her body.

'Mmm, *darling*.' He pushed her lightly against the old oak table and bent her back over it, easing up her skirt so that he could press himself between her thighs as they embraced.

'I've missed you,' whispered Melissa.

'I *want* you.'

She tilted her pelvis, grinding her pubic bone with mischievous skill against the swollen stalk of Rhys's penis.

'Let's fuck,' she breathed.

Rhys started unbuttoning her blouse, fondling her breasts, but on an impulse she pulled away.

'No, not here. Let's fuck in the Paradise Garden.'

'What about Simon? He might still be working there.'

'No, no, he said he'd be gone by four, I remember him saying so.' Melissa rubbed the long, hard baton of flesh pushing against the inside of Rhys's pants and felt herself falling for him all over again, that crazy teenage excitement making her feel like a kid, hungry for sexual adventures.

'I'm not sure I can wait,' groaned Rhys. 'I want you now.'

But Melissa got up and took him by the hand, leading him out of the back door and along the path which led to the Paradise Garden.

Simon Allbright had not intended to work late but there was something about the old walled garden which had got him well and truly hooked, something wild and sensual in the tangle of leaves and flowers that seemed to wrap themselves around him as he worked.

It was a hot afternoon and sweat was pouring down his bare back and chest, tendrils of his dark curly hair plastered to his moist, tanned forehead.

There was no-one to see him here, so he had soon stripped off his jeans and was working in his boxer shorts, the white cotton fabric wet and clingy against his golden flesh.

Reaching the gate first, Melissa opened it and led Rhys through. The garden had undergone quite a transformation since that morning. Where there had been nothing but tangles of brambles and weeds, the outlines of formal beds could now be made out.

PARADISE GARDEN

The box hedge that had once formed the outer edge of a knot-garden had reappeared, shaggy and overgrown but clearly retaining the lines and swirls of the original design. The air was filled with the mingled scents of herbs and flowers and sap-filled leaves, so dazzlingly bright in the afternoon sunshine that they seemed like a million emeralds, translucent against the bright-blue sky. Rock-samphire and velvet rose blossomed and budded among gillyflower, cuckoo bud, lavender and quince.

Standing at one side of the garden, tending an ancient apple tree, stood Simon Allbright. At first he did not notice them, lost in his work, and Melissa spent a long, delicious moment rejoicing in the beauty of his young body.

He was quite naked except for his white cotton boxer shorts and the fabric was so soaked with sweat that it clung to his body and had become semi-diaphanous. It was all too easy for Melissa to make out the clean, smooth lines of his rounded buttocks with the deep crease between and the pink snake of his cock, lying along his belly, semi-erect as though he too were aroused by the sensual beauty of the garden.

'Simon . . .' began Melissa.

He turned and their eyes met. In that second she knew he felt it too and Rhys felt a burning excitement in his belly at the looks of pure lust exchanged between Simon and Melissa.

'I'm sorry,' he stammered. 'I thought I'd be gone by the time you got back . . .'

'It's all right, don't worry.' Melissa found herself walking towards him, as though drawn by some magnetic force which had passed between their eyes, locking their gaze together. 'You mustn't worry, Simon, everything's going to be just fine.'

Simon could feel his head reeling with a delicious dizziness. It was a little like being drunk, only much, much nicer. He was no blushing virgin, with a body like his he'd never had any trouble finding girls willing to share his bed, but all of a sudden he felt like a kid again. It was like the day he'd lost his virginity, at fourteen, to Jazz Summersdale. Even then, she'd had more sexual experiences than most girls ten years older than her. He'd felt kind of nervous, scared even, but so excited that he'd have done anything just to pull down those little panties and slide his dick into her welcoming haven.

That was how he felt right now, exactly how he felt. God, what would Rhys think if he could see inside his head, and realise just what he yearned to do to his wife? And yet Rhys seemed just as excited as he did, his cock straining fit to burst the zipper on his jeans. Look, he was rubbing himself through the denim, grinding the metal zipper against the sex-hardened flesh.

The next thing he knew, Melissa was kissing him, and he was undressing her with clumsy fingers as she slid his pants down, baring the unbearable hardness of his erection.

'What a lovely dick you've got,' she whispered in his ear. And he knew she wasn't lying, because it *was* a beautiful dick, eight and a half inches long and so thick that it would stretch a tight hole almost to tearing point. Her fingers started masturbating him and he began playing with her, fiddling with her bra-catch and seizing her big, soft breasts as they tumbled out

For a few, agonising moments, Rhys watched, caught between fear and excitement. What on earth was happening? Melissa was seducing a complete stranger, and he was masturbating as he watched Simon undressing her, watched Melissa fingering another man's cock. Yet Rhys was just an ordinary bloke, they were all just ordinary people. How could this be happening?

His own excitement seemed almost alien to him, a great force overwhelming him, urging him on, *making* him obey the instincts of his arousal. Seconds later he was beside them, his hands roaming over Melissa's body, taking his penknife from his jeans' pocket and cutting away her panties because to take them off any other way would be too slow, too agonisingly frustrating.

Then he undressed, very quickly and clumsily, throwing his clothes onto the half-cleared ground. It would have felt wrong to be clothed in the Paradise Garden now, when the sun caressed warm flesh with subtle fingers and the gently waving branches of the trees cast a potent scent around them like a protecting veil.

No-one spoke. There was no need for words, not any more. Everything seemed to be happening as though they were actors in someone else's dream, or in a slow, dreamy, erotic movie. Kissing and caressing each other's naked bodies, they slid gently down onto the ground, their hunger bruising the soft stalks of chamomile and savory, making them release their sweet, dizzying scent.

Melissa rolled onto her side and Rhys lay facing her, his kisses rough and urgent on her lips and his cock pressing with equal urgency against the base of her belly, demanding entrance. She lifted her right thigh and wrapped it about his hip and, with a sigh of pure pleasure, he slid inside her.

She felt Simon's calloused hands stroking her back, playfully toying with the firm roundness of her bum cheeks.

His cock felt very big, very hard in the small of her back, its wet tip skating over her smooth flesh, leaving a trail of sex-fluid which cooled in the light breeze, making her shiver deliciously.

Then she felt a finger slide down the broad crease between her arse cheeks, a finger with a roughened tip that felt harsh and sandpapery against the sensitive membrane of her arse. She wriggled, impaled upon the spike of Rhys's penis, and in doing so pushed herself onto Simon's fingertip, swallowing it to the knuckle in her most secret intimacy.

He thrust in and out of her in long, delicious strokes, and Melissa could feel his finger through the wall of her sex, Rhys in her vagina and Simon in her arse. Then Simon slid out his finger and started scooping up the trickle of sex-juice escaping from her vagina, using it to lubricate the puckered rose of her anus.

She knew what would happen next and welcomed it, oozing honeydew from her sex as she gently fucked Rhys and waited for Simon's smooth cock to slide its way deep into her secret haven. She closed her eyes and thought how beautiful Simon's cock was, with its fat domed head, the deep and glistening purple of a ripe plum pushing through the foreskin, and the thick, pulsating veins which ran along its underside, begging for a lewd tongue to tease them.

He pushed into her very slowly, very tantalisingly, making her moan and shake with excitement, his hands holding her buttocks apart, his shaft disappearing into her backside with agonising slowness.

And then two cocks possessed her, two men between whose bodies she was the willing captive, the slave of their lust and her own. Smoothly and slowly they moved together, luxuriating in the warm, sensual ecstasy of their coupling.

And the branches overhead swayed in the breeze, their rustling leaves whispering of pleasures still to come.

Chapter 10

As the gentle warmth of early summer melted into the scorching heat of July, Rhys and Melissa worked on the Paradise Garden at every possible opportunity. Somehow, imperceptibly, a new urgency had lent itself to their work. It had become almost an obsession, a desperate need to restore the garden they had seen so beautifully depicted in Reuben Fairfax's day-book.

There was something irresistible about the garden, too. Something that drew them back there again and again, day after day, night after night... It was as though the garden itself held some sensual, almost magical power to enchant and seduce the senses. How good it felt to make love on the soft grass, or among the heavy scents of herbs and flowers that wafted like incense along the many paths and shady nooks of the Paradise Garden.

One hot Saturday afternoon in late July, they pushed open the gate of the garden and stepped inside, pushing it shut behind them. This was their secret world now. They hadn't bothered much with socialising since the garden had begun to take shape, and when they hadn't heard from Maia and Jim it hadn't really bothered them at all. The garden filled their minds and their senses now.

'It's really coming along, isn't it?' commented Rhys, stroking along the soft blade of a perfect green leaf. 'I know there's a long way to go and these things take time, but ...'

'But it's beautiful already,' said Melissa softly, sinking down onto the fragrant softness of the chamomile seat. The seat was fashioned not from wood but from a skilfully shaped bank of earth, thickly planted with the sweet herb so that whenever anyone sat down on it, its bruised leaves would release their drowsy, heavy scent.

She scanned the garden. Now that it had been cleared of its entangling, intertwining weeds, it appeared much larger than it had done that first day, when she and Rhys had discovered it, neglected and untamed. It was in the shape of a long rectangle, surrounded by the high wall of russet bricks, over which ran spidery fingers of creeper and climbing rose, fruit espaliers and an old, knotty vine. In the centre was the sunken pool, its waters now clear and crystal-bright, fed from the freshwater spring. Waterlilies sailed gracefully upon the surface of the water, veiling the small silvery fishes who darted below their spreading circles of shade.

The garden was a mixture of lawns, formal flowerbeds, and grassy, tree-lined alleyways with statues and secret nooks. At each corner were intricate knot-gardens, now cleared and replanted according to the illustrations in Fairfax's book. It would take time and tending to make them as magnificent as they had been in the 1580s, but neither Rhys nor Melissa resented the work they had put into the garden.

Little pathways of sunken bricks wound between flowerbeds lush with a profusion of roses, hollyhocks, every type of herb and flower. Gnarled apple and walnut trees shaded leafy nooks where lovers might embrace in perfect secrecy. Peaches and apples, nectarines and quince bore fruit on twisted and ancient limbs, as yet untamed and unpruned.

And a cracked and weathered statue of Aphrodite smiled down on it all, beside the little path which meandered past the grassy maze to a second gate in the wall and led by a shady path to the old summerhouse.

Melissa lay on her belly on the chamomile seat, basking in the warmth which soaked into her not only from the white-gold disc above her, but from the sun-warmed leaves below. Their scent was as sweet and musky as incense; as heady too, for it made her mind swim and meander like the fishes in the cool, clear waters of the sunken pond.

Rhys lazed beside her, stroking the long, corn-gold waves of her hair, which fell in a bright sweep across her face and shoulders.

'We should really do some work on the garden,' he whispered as he pushed back her hair and began teasing the tiny, flaxen hairs at the nape of her neck. 'Really we should . . .'

'Mmm,' murmured Melissa, her body rippling like a snake's on the soft chamomile bed, first her shoulders arching, then the small of her back and the smooth, firm swell of her buttocks, tightly encased in the white cotton drill of her shorts. 'I suppose . . .'

'But I can think of things I'd rather do,' Rhys whispered, bending over his lover and running his tongue over the back of Melissa's neck. It tasted slightly salty, seasoned with droplets of warm sweat that evaporated almost the second that the sun kissed her flesh. 'Can't you?'

Melissa rolled over, her body relaxed and floppy like a sleeper's, her eyes half-closed, her breathing a shallow purr which turned to a low growl of pleasure as Rhys began to fondle her breasts.

'Wicked boy,' she sighed luxuriously, the rose-pink buttons of her nipples swelling and toughening at his touch.

Rhys gazed in wonderment at Melissa's breasts. Even veiled by the tight, stretchy material of the body she was wearing, their full, firm shape was clearly visible, her nipples showing a deeper pink where their hardness had stretched the white cotton jersey more thinly. He opened out his hands and ran the palms lightly over the very tips of the hard pink crests, and Melissa began to moan, twisting and turning under the torment of his caresses.

Some madness seized him and he grabbed hold of great handfuls of her breast flesh, kneading and squeezing it as though it were warm bread-dough, every bit as soft and firm and yeasty beneath the sweat-moistened fabric. There was something fantasmagorical about these huge, firm, juicy breasts, as though they had a life of their own, and were trying to force their way from beneath the fabric and into his hands, their sexuality aggressive and almost menacing, yet seductive and soft too.

As he took her right breast between both hands, squeezing it at the very base, he saw how it bulged out into an almost perfect sphere, as though it were separate from Melissa's body. Yet Melissa was writhing and weeping with excitement, her knees drawn up, arms thrown back, nipples distended and hard as bullets under the white T-shirt. Beneath her, the soft grey-green leaves of chamomile released their seductive perfume, surrounding them both with a sweet mist of fragrance which was both langorous and urgent.

Rhys felt increasingly excited. Lowering his face, he opened his mouth and took Melissa's nipple between his lips. He began licking it, the enshrouding material rough against his tongue but he didn't care, all he wanted was to taste her, to have her. Overcome by his hunger, he bit into her flesh through the white cotton, and she let out a long, high wail that was both pain and pleasure. Letting go of her nipple, he took the fabric between his teeth and began biting and tearing at it, trying to rip it away from Melissa's delicious flesh, but it would not yield.

His heart was pounding, his cock ramrod-stiff and wet-tipped in his pants. All thoughts of gardening now forgotten, he scrabbled at the stubborn covering which veiled Melissa's breasts from his greedy caresses.

'Please, please,' he murmured. 'You have to let me, Melissa . . . now, please . . .'

She smiled at him and to Rhys she seemed suddenly beatific, gracious, angel-soft yet as wickedly sensual as Lucretia Borgia.

'If you want me, you'll have to undress me,' she whispered.

Rhys needed no further encouragement. Already his fingers were unfastening the top button of her shorts and sliding down the zipper. Underneath, he could quite clearly make out the corn-gold triangle of curly pubic hair, pressed hard against the taut crotch of the body. And her scent . . . oh how it tormented him, filling his lungs, making his head swim, torturing him with mental images of what they might do together. No. What they *must* do together, for his own desire was reaching bursting-point and he knew Melissa felt the same way. He could smell the desire in the oozings of her sex, taste it in the sweat that seasoned her sun-gold skin.

Melissa raised her backside a fraction of an inch and he slid her shorts down over her buttocks and hips, marvelling at the taut firmness, at the swell of well-honed muscle beneath the smooth, golden skin.

He slipped off her shorts and dropped them on the ground. She slid her arms around his neck and pulled his face down to hers, kissing him, possessing him with her lips, drawing his tongue into her mouth and sucking it hard, as though it were a tiny, questing dick.

His hands smoothed down her belly and into the deep valley between her thighs, feeling for the three poppers which he knew held the body taut across her pubis. Finding them, he seized them between finger and thumb and gave a shiver of delight as, one by one, they yielded to his urgent hunger.

'I'm wet for you, my darling,' murmured Melissa. 'So wet. Can't you feel?'

She took hold of Rhys's hand and guided it between her legs. His fingers met the cold dewdrops spangling her maidenhair, and the warm slick of juice oozing out of her onto his exploring hand. He could have spent forever just toying with her, running his fingertip lightly along the deep-pink inner lips of her sex, teasing them, making her clitoris swell and strain and pulse with growing excitement. But he wanted more. He wanted so much more.

'Sit up,' he urged her and he took her hands, pulling her up until she was sitting on the edge of the chamomile seat. One foot was on the ground and the other still resting on the seat, her knee flexed so that her sex lips pouted shamelessly at him, daring him not to kiss the secret treasure within.

He pushed up the white cotton body, pushed it up over her belly, her waist and then over the beautiful firm swell of her breathtaking breasts, the stretchy cotton imprisoning them for just one more, unending moment, before releasing them so that they sprang free, their pink tips eager for his kisses.

Melissa pulled the body off over her head and then, very softly and very gently, began to caress her lover, stroking his hair, his face, kissing his closed eyelids and his throat. Slowly she pulled his face towards her, burying it in the deep valley between her breasts, squeezing them hard about his face so that he was her captive, her willing pleasure-slave, his tongue lapping greedily at the little trickle of sweat that ran from throat to navel.

For many long minutes they remained like this, Rhys with his face buried between Melissa's firm, white globes, she with her hands on her own breasts, caressing and kneading them, teasing the nipples into ever-greater hardness. Above them, the branches of the old, gnarled apple trees swayed in the gentlest, the most imperceptible of breezes, their leaves shimmering in the heat haze, their boughs dipping down with heavy, swelling fruit.

At last Rhys drew away, Melissa clinging to him, silently beseeching him not to let her go; for her desire was reaching fever pitch, her womanhood aflame with the need for his sweet kisses.

Glancing to his right, Rhys saw tendrils of ivy wrapped loosely around the statue of Aphrodite and in a flash he knew what he most wanted to do. Instinctively he knew how much it would excite Melissa, too.

He tore at the ivy and it came away in long, flexible stems which were perfect for his purpose.

'My darling,' he murmured. 'My darling Melissa. You have the most beautiful breasts I have ever seen. Won't you let me make them even more beautiful?'

He knotted the ivy stems into one long, slender rope – whiplash thin, yet strong and pliant. This he threaded under Melissa's arms and wound around her torso several times, beneath the firm overhang of her breasts. Then he began winding the ivy-rope between her breasts and round her back, forming a figure-of-eight pattern so tight that her breasts began to swell and distend, standing out on her chest, pushing forward into white, veiny globes with reddish-pink, engorged nipples.

'Oh! Oh Rhys, oh do it to me harder, oh yes!' gasped Melissa, shuffling her bare backside on the chamomile seat, relishing the feeling of the scratchy stems entering the sensitive valley between her legs. Rhys had never suggested playing this game before, and Melissa had never even dreamed of having her breasts bound but this was a pleasure she would not have missed for all the world. 'Harder now, much, much harder! You mustn't stop.'

Rhys bound the ivy-stems as tightly as he could, then knotted them behind Melissa's back so that they would not slip. He moved back a little, admiring the breathtaking results of his handiwork. Melissa's breasts seemed huge, covered in a tracery of bluish veins like fine marble, the nipples enormous and blushing red yet utterly shameless in their sexuality, as though she had painted them with a dusky red lipstick.

'I'm going to masturbate over your breasts,' Rhys told her as he kissed them, at first lightly and then more fervently, nipping the flesh with eager teeth then soothing it with a light film of saliva. 'Is that what you want, Melissa? Is that what turns you on? Do you want to feel my hot spunk dripping down your tits?'

Melissa smiled at him. They both knew how much it was turning her on, both understood that this new game was their most exciting yet. How could they ever have imagined, in those days back in London, that their sex-life could become so much more exciting, experimental, dangerous even? Coming to Highmoor House was the best thing they had ever done. And restoring the Paradise Garden seemed, by some unknown alchemy, to have put them in touch with that same source of erotic inspiration which Reuben Fairfax had shared with his mistress, Perdita. Even their sexual encounter with Simon Allbright had seemed not shocking, but simply natural.

'Whatever we do will turn me on,' she promised. And she began to undress him, kissing each new inch of bare flesh as she exposed it. First the shirt, peeling it down over the shoulders and arms, letting it lie where it fell. Then the jeans, unbuttoning them very slowly, making the moment last. Her breasts ached and tingled, and the sensation made her restless, hungry, desperate for the ecstasy of their coupling.

Underneath his jeans, Rhys was wearing a pair of very ordinary blue cotton briefs, with nothing particularly erotic about their design. But to Melissa, at that moment, they seemed the sexiest thing she had ever seen. Rhys was achingly, yearningly hard for her and the very tip of his erect phallus had escaped from his briefs, pushing its way out from underneath the waistband, fixing her with its one lewd, glistening eye.

Peeling away the elasticated waistband, she bent to lick a dewdrop of lubricating fluid from his glans. Slowly and enticingly, she worked her tongue around the ridge between glans and shaft, making sure to tease all the hypersensitive nerve-endings on the underside, but lingering only long enough to drive him crazy, withdrawing before she risked taking him too far and making him spurt his jism.

Then she eased down his pants, watching in delight as his cock sprang out and the damp blue cotton slid tantalisingly down over the heavy twin globes of his balls. Ripe and juicy and heavy in her hand, they seemed tense with expectancy, bursting with the creamy juices she longed to have in her mouth, her sex, spattering her round, white breasts.

She stroked and kissed him, sliding to her knees to take first one, then the other testis between her lips, moistening it with her saliva, sucking and gently biting it, enclosing it within the womb-like warmth of her mouth, feeling it tense and harden . . .

Then she drew away, sliding back onto the chamomile seat and sitting facing him, with her legs wide apart.

'I can't bear it,' she whispered hoarsely. 'I have to touch myself, I have to. Would you like to watch me wank myself, Rhys?'

Rhys shivered with excitement. Somehow, ridiculous though it now seemed, Melissa had always been slightly reluctant about letting him watch her bring herself off. Even thinking about it made him hard.

Melissa licked her index finger and slid it down her belly, pulling her outer labia yet further apart to display the hard, pink rosebud of her clitoris.

'See how wet I am, Rhys, and it's all for you.'

'You're a gorgeous slut, Melissa.' Rhys took hold of his shaft and began sliding it slowly between his fingers. 'A gorgeous slut and I'm going to come all over your beautiful body . . .'

Melissa had no need to lubricate her clitoris: it was already dripping with juice. She slid her finger round and round it, following the lines of her inner sex-lips, moving in ever-smaller concentric circles until at last, she was almost – but not quite – touching it.

Reaching out on an instinctive impulse, her fingers curled around something long, hard, smooth. She picked it up. It was a small handfork, the one Simon Allbright had used for clearing the borders. He must have left it behind the last time he was here. Well, well, well . . .

'Watch me, Rhys. Watch me.'

She turned the fork round so that its handle was pointing towards her, the age-smoothened wood menacingly phallic. Then, very suddenly and very deliberately, she jabbed it into the soft wet heart of her sex.

'Aah!' she squealed as the wooden handle slid home to the hilt, the wooden surrogate prick burying itself in the depths of her tight wetness. Then she smiled at Rhys.

'Now watch me wank. Watch me wank, my darling.'

With a finger on either side of her hypersensitive love-bud, she began to rub herself, her clit too painfully aroused to be touched directly. With her other hand she manipulated the fork, pushing the handle deep inside herself then half withdrawing it, just far enough so that Rhys could see the sheen of sex-juice dripping from its length.

Rhys masturbated as he watched, from time to time reaching out to touch Melissa's bound breasts. They were so hard, so white, that they seemed almost like stone to the touch. And yet they were pulsing with a defiant inner life, pulsing and throbbing like the blood in his veiny cock-shaft.

Rhys and Melissa had ceased to be two separate individuals. Now they were a single machine, a single, smooth-running sex-machine, its engine running on high gear, throbbing and humming as it speeded up towards a sudden, devastating crescendo of power . . .

Melissa's whole body stiffened as she brought herself off, her sex muscles clenching hard about the fork shaft before releasing it in a tide of sex-juice, so that it slithered out of her onto the chamomile seat beneath her bare buttocks. Head thrown back, breasts quivering with the final effort of her pleasure, sweat trickling over her bare flesh, she moaned softly, overwhelmed by the force of ecstasy.

Rhys could feel the time upon him, very near. He got to his feet, wanking faster now, his hand gripped tight about his shaft and clear juice dripping from its tip, trickling and smearing over his fingertips.

His eyes were on Melissa's breasts, on the beautiful captive globes, on the hard pink-red nipples that jiggled on the very crests, tantalising, tantalising . . .

He spurted in a sudden, jerky onrush of sperm, his body shaking like a madman's as the opalescent droplets splashed and spattered Melissa's honey-gold skin. Great trickles of the pearly-white fluid, thick as double cream, ran down over the paler ivory of her breasts, fell in cloudy, viscous raindrops from the tips of her nipples.

Still gasping from his passion, Rhys reached out and took Melissa by the hand.

'Come with me.'

'Where?'

'Come.'

He led her across the garden, across soft grass and gravel paths, past peeping statues and heavy-scented roses, to the ornamental pool in the very centre. The water moved gently in the sunshine, sparkling as it caught the light, making patterns of sunlight and shade.

They laughed as they jumped in together, holding hands, squealing with pleasure as the cold water touched their overheated flesh. It felt icy cold after the burning afternoon heat, yet wonderfully pleasurable, cooling and soothing and exciting and arousing wherever it touched.

Rhys broke through the long rope of ivy tendrils which held Melissa's breasts captive and they sprang free, the ivy leaves floating away on the crystal water. They embraced, their hands exploring each other's bodies as if for the very first time, stroking and pinching and kneading.

Silver fishes swam about them, unperturbed by this strange and unexpected invasion. Melissa parted her thighs and a fish darted between them, nibbling at the corn-yellow tufts of her pubic hair before slithering over the rounded dome of her backside.

'Take me, Rhys,' she pleaded. 'Take me again.'

Rhys gathered her up in his arms. He no longer questioned what they were doing here or why. Anything that they chose to do in the Paradise Garden was right and natural and beautiful. Even things he had never dreamed of doing before. Melissa felt like heaven in his arms, her skin sun-dappled, the damp ends of her hair dripping rivulets of clear water down over her shoulders and breasts.

Hoisting her up, he felt her wrap her thighs tightly about his waist. He lifted her a little higher and the tip of his prick nudged into the deep crease of her pussy lips, as though it knew instinctively where to find its perfect home.

She felt like silk. Like smooth, wet, slippery silk around the hot, hard spike of his rearing cock. He lifted her up and she clutched at his shoulders, levering herself up and down, controlling the rhythm of their fucking.

The clear, brilliant sounds of birdsong filled the trees and the flowers seemed to shimmer, their colours unusually bright and fresh for such a blisteringly hot summer's day. Melissa felt elated, her body no longer a separate entity from her mind but an extension of the soul within her which ached, yearned, hungered for more and yet more, wilder sex.

The water rippled and cascaded as she moved in and out of it, brilliant droplets falling in showers from her body as she thrust down again and again on Rhys's stiff manhood. Rhys's arms were strong about her, his kisses burning on her skin wherever his lips touched.

At last they came, together this time, Rhys's seed spurting and surging into her with such power that she felt it squirt against the neck of her womb. She met his pleasure with her own, a dizzying cavalcade of sensations, tumbling, bursting, exploding in her head and making her sex drip honey-juice like nectar from some tropical orchid.

The mingled juices of their spendings dripped out of Melissa, sending little cloudy-white eddies into the clear, cool waters around them.

They did not speak. Somehow there seemed no need. In any case, they both knew what they were going to do next, where they were going to go. The gate in the garden wall stood ajar. They knew that they had not opened it, but that didn't seem important. Only sex was important now, only the warm and luxurious glow that came from making sweet

PARADISE GARDEN

love within the sheltered walls of the Paradise Garden.

Climbing out of the sunken pool, walking together hand in hand, they crossed the garden to the gate and stepped through it. Instinctively they knew where they were heading.

To the old summerhouse.

Jazz Summersdale didn't know what had got into Maudsley. He had always been rather unadventurous in the past. She had needed to coax him, show him what to do to give her pleasure – but not this afternoon.

They had come up on to the moors ostensibly because Chris needed to survey a property over Goathland way, but they had barely got two miles outside Highmoor when he'd started coming on strong.

Not that Jazz minded that. She had been waiting far too long for Maudsley to make the first move. Oh, he was a good-looking guy, nice bod, hung like a stallion, but all that hardly amounted to much when your guy was too timid to put it all to good use. She'd even been considering giving him the push, though reluctantly, because there wasn't exactly a glut of well-hung, well-heeled young guys around Highmoor. But, hell, a girl needed sexual adventure and Jazz Summersdale needed it more than most.

Up there on the moors, not far from Highmoor House, Chris had suddenly stopped the jeep and turned to her with the oddest smile she had ever seen.

'I want to shag you, Jazz,' he'd told her, and it sounded like someone else talking. 'I want to shag you right here. Right now.'

She'd thought he was kidding, well, you could never be sure with a guy like Maudsley, but he was deadly serious.

And when he'd dragged her out of the car and started ripping her clothes off, she'd actually had to tell him to be a bit careful because, you know, leather doesn't come cheap and she hadn't screwed any millionaires lately.

Anyhow, imagine her surprise when Chris took not the slightest bit of notice and just went on stripping her, clawing at her leather bustier like he'd die if he didn't get it off her, right now.

She obliged him by unhooking it at the back and he tore it off her. His eyes were fixed on her, but they didn't look like Chris's eyes, no way. They were wilder, filled with a look of the purest, most obscene, most delicious lust Jazz had ever seen.

'Oh God, Jazz, I can't stop myself . . .' he groaned. She thought she heard real pain in his voice but he was lying on top of her and his cock was iron-hard against her belly, so he had to be enjoying himself. 'I can't stop, got to have you, got to have you now . . .'

'That's all right by me,' Jazz said. And she rolled onto her side, pulling up her leather microskirt and tugging down her panties. It was a good job she hadn't worn trousers today, just the skirt and these tiny, useless panties – and the fishnet hold-up stockings under a pair of red patent-leather thigh-boots with spiky heels to die for . . . 'That's just fine by me.'

At that point she'd still thought it was a game and, really, it wasn't a game at all. There was something deadly earnest about the way they were fucking, here in the middle of this great big, open moor, with Highmoor House looming over them on the horizon. There was something compulsive in the way they were clawing and biting at each other's bodies, as though striving for release from an ecstatic torment that would never cease.

Maudsley was like an animal, wrenching apart her buttocks and buggering her without so much as a by-your-leave. In the past she hadn't even been able to persuade him to touch or kiss her, not *there* of all places. Christopher Maudsley was a nice guy, you see – polite, gentlemanly, repressed as hell. Or at least, he used to be.

Not that she wasn't enjoying it. This was one good fuck and Jazz was making the most of it. It wasn't every day that a man gave her four great orgasms in a row and they just kept on coming, coming, coming till her brain ached with the pleasure.

But at the back of her mind a worrying thought niggled at her, kept eating away at her pleasure. There was something really weird going on today, she could sense it. And in her bones she feared it might have something to do with Highmoor House.

In the public bar at the Black Lion, the landlord dried a last pint-glass and slung the towels over the taps.

Supping up the last of his ale in the empty bar, George Mainprize shifted uneasily on the bum-smoothed wooden bench.

'It's happening again, Jed,' he remarked.

'Nah then, George, don't talk daft,' replied the landlord, a little edgily. 'Just sup up and clear out, will yer?'

'Ah tell thee, it is,' insisted George. 'Tommy Gates's dogs were howling all night and his stallion's going half crazy, trying to get at the mare – and she's not even in season.'

Jed shrugged.

'It's probably the weather,' he volunteered, but he didn't sound entirely convinced. 'It does funny things to animals, you know that.' He shivered. 'Anyhow, I can feel a storm brewing up, can't you?'

George drained his glass and set it down.

'Tha knows, Jed Gibbons. Tha knows what's going on, only tha won't 'ave it said. Well ah'm sayin' it now. It's happening again.' He looked up at the clock. 'If you don't believe me, tell me what time it is.'

Jed glanced at his watch.

'It's... oh, I don't know, my watch has stopped.' He looked up at the bar-room clock. It had stopped too, the second hand poised as though the whole world were holding its breath.

'They've all stopped, Jed,' hissed George. 'An tha knows as well as ah do, they won't start again till it's over.'

The light in the old stone summerhouse, just beside the wall of the Paradise Garden, was a curious pale gold, a wash of sunlight that penetrated the ancient stone walls and made them glow, honey-gold, in the afternoon sun.

Shafts of sunlight penetrated the over-arching canopy of trees, setting dappled patterns of brilliant green dancing over the ornate stonework. Inside the summerhouse, Rhys and Melissa lay together, their bodies glowing and tingling from the last excess of passion.

How strange, thought Melissa. How strange it was that they could fuck so long and so hard and yet not tire. With each climax of ecstasy their bodies seemed to grow more eager, their desire hotter and more impossible to satisfy.

PARADISE GARDEN

Rhys swung his legs onto the ground, taking in a deep breath of summer air. It smelt of the Paradise Garden – a sunwarmed cocktail of herbs and flowers and aromatic pine and all the thousand scents of their coupling.

'We'd best get back to the house,' he said. He glanced at his watch, shook his wrist, cursed. 'Damn, my watch has stopped. The water must have got into it – and the man in the shop swore blind it was waterproof to fifty fathoms!'

They gathered up their clothes, dressed slowly and langorously and walked together through the grounds towards the house. At first all seemed as it should be but as they neared the house they noticed a few, inexplicable changes.

That door – the one by the kitchen garden. Hadn't that always been green before? Now it was sort of dark brownish red. And where was that broken-down old conservatory that he had been meaning to pull down ever since they'd arrived at Highmoor House? Now, that was just plain silly. Conservatories didn't just disappear into thin air.

None of it made sense.

More curious than afraid, they hurried to the kitchen door. It stood slightly ajar, as though welcoming them in.

'What's going on?' asked Melissa. But Rhys could not answer. He was no wiser than she.

They stepped inside the kitchen and caught their breath, staring at the scene around them. This was not the house as they remembered it. It seemed older, much, much older. Where Melissa's new gas-cooker had stood, there was an ancient, black-leaded cooking range. Rhys touched it and drew away his hand with a curse of pain. It was red hot.

Food lay on the table. A home-baked cottage loaf, just

like the one they'd found in the pantry when they arrived; wine, fruit, a joint of cooked ham . . .

'What in Heaven's name is happening?' This time it was Rhys who asked the questions and Melissa who could not answer. 'Is someone playing another practical joke on us?'

As he turned, he saw the calendar hanging on the wall beside the back door. 'July 20, 1885' it said. *Eighteen eighty-five?*

'I think we should go,' said Melissa. 'Fetch Chris and Jazz, perhaps, maybe they'd know what's going on.'

'Yes. OK. Good idea.'

Rhys turned and walked back towards the door. It was funny really, because even though he desperately wanted to leave, he desperately wanted to stay, too. There was a sweet, seductive atmosphere in here, warm, exciting, soothing, arousing . . . Like a warm hand on his heart and an even warmer caress on his prick. Like sweet music playing in his head, forbidding him to go.

He laid his hand on the door handle, twisting it to the left.

'It won't.'

'Won't what?'

'It won't open!'

'Of course it will. Here, let me try.' Melissa pushed his hand away and tried to turn the handle but it refused to budge. 'I must be doing something wrong. Look, I'll try again.'

'Maybe it's jammed?'

'Maybe.' But Melissa knew it wasn't jammed. Nor was it locked.

The door had closed itself against them by the power of its own will, keeping them here because there was something here that they must see, perhaps even something that they must learn.

She was afraid. Her whole body was quivering but not only with fear. For Rhys was here and his hands were on her body, his kisses on her lips.

Perhaps she didn't really want to leave. Perhaps she never would again.

Chapter 11

Peter Galliano looked down at the sheet of paper in his hands.

'Why do you do this to me, you hot little bitch?' he asked himself. 'Why do you do it, when you know you want me as much as I want you?'

Melissa had no idea about the photographs, of course. Galliano had paid for – and obtained – complete discretion from the photographer he had employed to capture her on film at last year's international sales conference in Brussels. He'd been pleased with the results too: a set of candid black-and-white prints showing Melissa undressing in her private bathroom at the conference hotel. It was amazing what you could do with hidden cameras.

He couldn't remember when his obsession had begun. Maybe on that very first day when Melissa had walked through the door of his office, smart and sassy and with those large, soft breasts pushing hard against her sheer white blouse. He'd vowed to have her then and sure enough he had . . . but only once. Then she'd run off to the back of beyond, leaving him with Candice Soulbury to console him and a cock that ached for Melissa's silken touch.

He glanced at the sheet of paper. The photocopier had made quite a good job of copying the prints – a little montage of half-a-dozen of the most titillating photographs from Brussels. A striptease, starting with Melissa taking off her blouse and ending with her naked, stretched out in the foaming bath-water.

That last photograph was his absolute favourite. The soap suds concealed more of Melissa than they revealed but there was something irresistibly erotic about the way they clung to her breasts, showing the dark crest of her right nipple emerging from the foamy suds like a cherry on an ice-cream sundae.

And it was quite obvious that Melissa hadn't had the faintest idea that she was being photographed. Or had she? wondered Galliano. Had she done it all just to torment him, knowing how much it would drive him mad with jealous lust to see her fingers slipping between her parted thighs, rubbing her swollen clitoris? He half hoped she had.

'Shameless slut,' he murmured to himself, stroking Melissa's picture with covetous fingers. '*Bellissima* . . . when will you admit to yourself that you are mine?'

He slid the sheet of paper, face down, into the fax machine. 'SEND READY' flashed up on the digital display. Quickly, almost feverishly, he keyed in the telephone number of Highmoor House. So that cheapskate husband of hers couldn't even run to a separate fax line. Well, once he and Melissa were together, Galliano would make sure she never wanted for anything. Especially not the thrust of his hardened cock, parting her satin-smooth pussy lips.

'SEND'. He jabbed the pink button and the display flashed up 'DIALLING'. One by one the digits scrolled across until the number was complete. 'CALLING'.

And then, inexplicably: 'NUMBER NOT VALID'.

What? Galliano looked at the entry in his address book, matched it up with the number on the display. They were identical. He'd thought about phoning Melissa so often that he knew her number off by heart. He dialled again.

'NUMBER NOT VALID. PLEASE DIAL AGAIN'.

'Stupid bloody machine!'

Galliano picked up the telephone receiver and dialled up Melissa's number. Maybe it was time he phoned her anyway, talked things out with her, stopped playing games and made her see sense.

He finished dialling and waited for the phone to ring. A long, blaring tone made him pull the receiver sharply away from his ear. He stared at it for a long time, baffled.

Number unobtainable.

It was like a dream, a crazy dream.

Melissa held on tightly to Rhys's hand as they walked along the corridor which led from the kitchen. She scarcely recognised it. It seemed so dark, so mysterious.

She glanced up. Where were the electric lights that had lined the passageway? Gas lamps hissed above her, their flames flickering in sooty glass mantles. Everywhere was dark wood, the glimmer of polished brass, the scent of beeswax and macassar oil.

What had happened to Highmoor House? Was this real? Or were they dreaming, still slumbering on the stone bench in the summerhouse or naked on the chamomile seat in the Paradise Garden? Yes. Yes, that must be it.

They hesitated before the door to the drawing room, apprehensive yet not afraid, a strange warmth surrounding them like a welcoming embrace, beckoning them in.

'Go on,' whispered Melissa. 'It'll be all right.'

Rhys looked at her and she realised how beautiful he was, how handsome that face that she had once thought ordinary. She wanted to kiss and stroke each lock of wavy brown hair, slide her hands over his body, discovering its beauty all over again.

He squeezed her hand.

'I don't understand this, but . . . here goes.'

He touched the brass beehive doorknob and it turned easily, the door moving inwards smoothly and silently. They hesitated on the threshold, uncertain, overwhelmed.

In the room beyond, a warm glow invited them in. Although it was high summer, a fire was roaring in the grate, yet it did not seem over-hot in the room, only deliciously, soothingly, excitingly warm.

But this was not the drawing room they remembered. The tatty floral curtains had gone, replaced with heavy brocade hangings drawn tightly across the windows. A dado rail ran along the wall, an elaborate embossed paper above it and a plainer one below. The furniture was massive and heavy; solid Cuban mahogany, immaculately polished and gleaming in the flickering light from the fire and the gaslight hanging above a library table of inlaid walnut.

There was hardly an empty surface in the room. Melissa remembered the drawing room being a rather empty place, only half furnished, with bare boards and a couple of lumpy armchairs in ill-fitting chintz covers. But this room was absolutely crammed with bric-à-brac: Indian brass ornaments, china knick-knacks, ivory and jade, a scrimshaw ornament made from a carved and yellowing tusk. On the table sat a huge glass dome covering a floral arrangement made entirely from shells; books; piles of sheet music; a half-finished piece of embroidery . . .

As they stepped inside, the change was instant, the transformation of mind and body and spirit complete. And all at once, they understood that they had entered another world.

The door closed softly behind them but they hardly noticed.

'Rhys!'

Melissa looked down at her clothes. Gone were the crumpled white shorts, the cotton body stained with the juices of their coupling. In their place was a late Victorian gown of burgundy-coloured moiré silk, the skirt full at the back, hanging over a bustle and layered petticoats. It was squeezed so tight at the waist that she could scarcely breathe, a boned corset lacing her so small that Rhys might almost have spanned her waist with his two hands.

Her breasts seemed fuller than ever, pushed upward by the corset, but imprisoned within the tight bodice which buttoned at the neck, finished off with a collar of Brussels lace. Full leg-of-mutton sleeves tapered to tight cuffs and, as she reached up to touch her hair, she discovered that it was piled up into intricate curls.

She scarcely recognised Rhys, his jacket of black serge tapered and long over dark trousers, stiff-collared white shirt and an embroidered waistcoat of yellow Japanese silk. His hair seemed shorter, slick and glossy with a scented pomade, and his eyes seemed to glitter with mischief in the dancing firelight.

'Where are we, Rhys? What on earth is this place?'

'Does it matter?' He kissed her, drawing her to him, crushing his lips against hers.

'Is it a dream?'

'Of course it is. It's the most beautiful dream in the world.'

They drew apart, gazing at each other. And suddenly the

questions and the uncertainties didn't seem to matter any more. It was enough to accept that this was a game, a beautiful, sensual game in which there was nothing to lose, and so much pleasure to be gained. A world in which anything at all was permitted, and the only limit to pleasure was the limit of your own fantasies.

A photograph album lay open on the library table. Rhys looked down at the pictures. They seemed ordinary enough – typical sepia prints set into oval mounts decorated with chromoliths of fruits and flowers and pouting cherubs.

'Cissy and Alexander, July 1883,' read Melissa, stroking the pictures with wondering fingertips.

The first page of photographs showed a young man and woman standing on the steps of a house. They might have been almost dreary, if not for one simple fact.

'It's here,' gasped Rhys. 'It's Highmoor House – look, there's the old conservatory, the Orangery they used to call it.'

'And look at this picture ... here, this one. That's the path that leads through the grounds to the Paradise Garden, do you see it? It looks a lot neater than it does now.' Whenever now is, thought Melissa fleetingly. But she hardly cared any more. All she wanted was for the dream to continue.

Rhys flicked over the page and his grip tightened about Melissa's waist. This time the pictures were hardly the sort you might expect to find in a typical Victorian family album.

Cissy and Alexander were pictured again, but now they were in this very drawing room. Cissy was bending forwards over the old library table, her skirts pulled up to her waist and her backside bare beneath her petticoats. She was wearing knee-length boots in shiny patent leather, the toes pointed, the heels high and narrow; and Alexander was holding a long, supple leather strap.

In the next picture, he was beating her across her bare backside, long, raised welts showing clearly against the pure, almost ghostly white of her buttocks. Melissa glanced at Rhys and saw that he, too, felt excitement, hungry for the story to unfold.

'The English vice,' murmured Rhys, his voice heavy with sex. 'That's what they used to call it. Have you ever wanted to . . . ?'

'Turn the page,' she whispered. And her fingers stroked the front of Rhys's trousers, tracing the already-swelling outline of his prick.

The next page was more arousing still. Alexander had unbuttoned his trousers and was holding a fine, stiff cock, masturbating over Cissy's upraised backside. The next frame showed him ejaculating, his semen dripping down over his lover's buttocks and into the dark crack between.

Each page revealed some new, forbidden pleasure; some secret delight captured for ever at the very height of passion.

'Look, Melissa,' whispered Rhys. 'Look – she's taking his balls into her mouth and her lips are all wet with his come.'

Melissa gazed entranced at the picture. Cissy was kneeling on the carpet before the fire, her lips parted to receive the juicy fruit of her lover's testis, her tongue already lapping at the hairy seed-purse. She was naked to the waist, wearing nothing but a pair of long bloomers, and her nipples were iron-hard with pleasure. A trail of pearly-white fluid ran down her chin and throat, just reaching the swelling mound of her right breast. Alexander was still clothed and that somehow made the scene all the more exciting, his stiff cock and seed-filled balls pale and gloriously obscene against the dark fabric of his business suit.

Excited almost beyond belief, Melissa began rubbing hard on Rhys's swollen cock, wanking him through his trousers, hungry for the touch of his stiffened flesh.

'Oh! Oh yes, Melissa. Do it to me.' Rhys guided Melissa's fingers to his fly buttons. 'Why don't you take out my cock and do it to me properly, darling?'

He slid his hand up to feel for the hard crests of Melissa's nipples. The stiff silk of her bodice imprisoned them tightly but he could feel their lust-hardened buttons pushing, demanding release. At his touch Melissa shuddered, her body tense with need.

But it was the last page of the photograph album which aroused Melissa most of all. It showed Cissy and Alexander coupling amid flowers and fruit. Amid the splendours of a beautiful walled garden . . .

'It's the Paradise Garden!' exclaimed Melissa. But it was not the garden she was looking at so intently, it was the lovers, acting out their sex games.

Cissy was sitting astride Alexander's cock, kneeling up a little with her back to the camera, so that Melissa could quite clearly make out the glistening shaft of flesh penetrating the plump flesh of Cissy's sex lips. In the next picture, taken from the side, Melissa saw Cissy's breasts hanging down as she bent over her lover, riding him to orgasm. Although her breasts were quite small, they seemed curiously pendulous and, on looking more closely, Melissa saw that they were weighted down with heavy metal clips whose jaws were clamped shut on Cissy's nipples.

She felt a rush of excitement, a gush of familiar warmth between her thighs. She turned to Rhys, wanting him so much. But she was imprisoned in this heavy dress, these tight-laced stays that held her faster than a jealous lover's embrace.

'Undress me,' she breathed, unfastening the last of Rhys's fly buttons and feeling for his cock. As she touched it, she felt a frisson of pure excitement swelling her clitoris, making it throb with longing. 'Rhys . . . oh Rhys!'

Her eyes full of covetous lust, she curled her fingers about Rhys's shaft and eased it out of his trousers.

'Oh my darling,' she murmured. 'My own darling . . .'

She fell to her knees, astounded by the beauty of Rhys's cock, so familiar and yet so new, so excitingly new. For through its plump head, just below the glistening purple dome of the glans, was a fat silver pin, passing right through the flesh.

She kissed it, stroked and caressed it with her tongue, her eyes flicking upwards from time to time to see the changing expressions on Rhys's face – astonishment, apprehension, pleasure, bliss, ecstasy . . .

'Oh my God, Melissa, I don't know what you're doing but just keep on doing it. Don't stop.'

She smiled, kissing his glans.

'Don't worry, I won't stop. I can go on doing this for ever if you want me to.'

The silver pin clinked against her teeth as she took the head of Rhys's penis into her mouth and began lapping, licking, sucking. Rhys began to moan, to whimper like a tiny child, helpless, lost in the grip of pleasure he knew not how to control.

'Melissa! Oh Melissa . . . if you only knew how this feels. It's like having two cocks, ten – a thousand. The pleasure's just so intense, oh please, please, don't stop.'

Her fingers felt for his testes and gently pulled them out, cradling the seed-sacs inside his scrotum, full of wonder that they could have grown so heavy again, so full of juicy promise.

Wriggling her tongue-tip into the tiny, weeping eye of his glans, she delighted in the salty ooze of moisture dripping from its tip and into her mouth. Her fingers worked away at the base of his shaft, stroking, squeezing, gently masturbating; and she felt it begin to stiffen to that tell-tale hardness in the last seconds before orgasm, when the whole body seems to tingle with sexual electricity.

Rhys began thrusting, pushing the full length of his cock into the deep well of Melissa's mouth so that the silver cock-pin pressed right against the back of her throat.

For a moment she could hardly breathe, she was convinced she must surely choke. But then she began to enjoy the violence of Rhys's passion. Her saliva flooded around his prick in a hot tide and her throat relaxed to accommodate his swollen shaft.

In a great, shuddering, ocean-swell of semen he came, his seed gushing and spurting into her mouth so abundantly that she could barely swallow it all and pearly runnels of it crept out from between her lips, spilling down her chin and throat, making little damp stains on the burgundy silk of her dress.

Heart thumping, Rhys drew Melissa to her feet and started

kissing his seed from her lips. He was surprised by the pleasure he derived simply from the taste of his own passion and the caress of Melissa's rustling silk skirts on his naked cock.

Hungrier than ever for her, he began undressing her. There were an impossible number of glass buttons running down the back of her dress – tiny, tiny buttons scarcely bigger than beads, each secured by a tight loop of fabric. It took an age to unfasten them, an age in which his cock swelled and ached and his balls tingled, inexplicably full to the brim again with a seething tide of hot, white seed.

Rhys kissed the back of Melissa's neck as he unbuttoned her dress with agonising slowness. As his lips touched her skin he could feel her trembling, her body in the grip of the same irresistible power which seemed to surround him, filling his mind with thoughts of Melissa's ripe and fulsome body.

The dress peeled away, displaying Melissa's bare upper back, and the intricately laced stays which nipped in her tiny waist. Half-maddened with the need of her, he wanted to tear off the silk dress, throw her to the ground and enjoy her with all the violence of the passion which engulfed him.

'Please, Rhys, hurry! Undress me quickly, Rhys, I want you so much.'

He pulled the sleeves down over Melissa's shoulders and fumbled for what seemed an age to release the row of three minute buttons at the wrists. At last the bodice fell down to her waist and all he had to do was unfasten a few more buttons ...

With a sighing swish of silk, the dress fell to the ground, forming a dark crimson pool about Melissa's ankles. She stepped out of it, and turned to embrace him. He could feel her heart thumping, her pulse racing as she tore off his jacket and waistcoat, his tie, his shirt . . .

'Take me,' she begged, covering his bare chest and belly with kisses. 'Take me now, I can't wait any longer.'

'Be patient, my darling, just a little while longer.'

'Please, please . . .'

He silenced her with kisses, passionate and fiery, hands roaming over her bare shoulders, lips and tongue and teeth tasting the matchless flesh of her breasts, plump and rosy-white as they spilled over the top of her corset, the nipples only just concealed by the trimming of coarse cream-coloured lace.

Beneath the corset she wore a pair of full white bloomers which extended to mid-calf, black stockings and black patent high-heeled boots which laced tight, hugging her slender ankles. On an impulse, Rhys ran his hands down Melissa's back, over the knotted stay-laces, the satin and lace and shaped steels which forced her figure into a voluptuous hour-glass, making her breasts and backside appear larger by contrast with her tiny waist.

As his fingers touched the swell of her rump, he noticed a curious thing – curious and stimulating. Beginning at the base of her spine, a vent ran along the crotch of her bloomers, almost entirely hidden by the voluminous folds of the crisp white linen.

He slid his fingertips inside and Melissa wriggled her hips at the sudden touch of flesh on flesh.

'Naked,' he whispered. His fingers explored the deep crevice between Melissa's rounded buttocks. 'Do you know how you excite me with your nakedness?'

PARADISE GARDEN

As his fingers reached the amber rose of her most secret, most guilty desire, he felt it open to him like a little mouth, pouting a kiss of welcome.

Melissa thrust out her backside, groaning with pleasure at Rhys's knowing touch. Never had it felt so good, never had she wanted him more. All her wildest fantasies filled her head and in some strange way it seemed to her that in this world of purest pleasure, every fantasy might come true.

To her disappointment he did not toy long with her arse but slid his hands up to her breasts, stroking the nacreous flesh, whispering to her:

'Sit on the table, Melissa.'

She did as he asked, sliding up onto the polished walnut table-top and sending the photograph album skidding away from her. Rhys held her in his arms and began to pull the pins from her hair, so that it cascaded in long, wavy ringlets over her shoulders. The corn-yellow locks glistened like molten gold in the firelight, their scent fragrant as meadow hay.

Melissa cried out as his hands dipped into the front of her corset, seizing her right breast and pulling it out. He caressed and kissed it, cradled it in his hands, making her flesh sing with ecstasy. And then he repeated the process with her left breast, freeing it from the stiff corset so that both globes hung over the top, plump and pink, their nipples defiantly erect.

Leaning back, she parted her thighs, smiling, welcoming him, and he saw the full beauty of her as the open gusset of her bloomers parted to reveal her wet and hungry sex.

The vent ran from the base of her spine to above her mount of Venus and, as it gaped, Rhys saw the fur-trimmed casket of Melissa's sex in all its seductive glory, the deep and luxuriant pink of her inner sex-lips, like a bed of wet and crumpled velvet, upon which lay the rosy jewel of her clitoris.

He had never seen such a wonderful thing before: the tiniest of gold rings, passing right through the head of Melissa's clitoris. It sparkled and glowed as it caught the light, and as he looked on Melissa moved her hand down her belly, stroking her thighs and her pubis before sliding her fingers into the haven of her vulva.

Rhys felt as if he might die of pure pleasure as he watched her twisting and turning the clit-ring, her sex oozing and trickling the sweetest, clearest honeydew whose musky fragrance made his head spin. Taking hold of her linen-clad thighs, he pressed his cock-tip against the entrance to Melissa's pleasure-haven.

She gave a gasp, a shivering sigh as the cold silver of his cock-pin breached her inner love-lips and teased the hypersensitive entrance to her vagina. His cock felt immense, the heavy silver pin adding greatly to its thickness as it pushed inside her, opening her up in a long, slow, smooth movement.

'Hold me,' she gasped. And Rhys's hands slipped around her waist, grasping her fast as they fucked, coupling now with the raw hunger of wild beasts, all their questions and fears forgotten. The only thing that existed here was the quest for more and greater pleasure.

As they fucked, the room seemed to blur in and out of focus, nothing was clear or believable any more except their own bodies. Sweat trickled over their skin as the fire burned up, intensifying the heat in the drawing room. The gas lights hissed, their flames mellowing to a sulphurous glow, casting strange, dancing shadows over the walls. And somewhere in the distance they heard music. Soft, sweet, seductive music, drifting sometimes nearer, sometimes further out of reach.

Their climax left them stunned and shaken, astonished by the power of the desire which had taken hold of them and made them its helpless prisoners. But almost before the last waves of pleasure had died away, the hunger began again, like a low ache in the belly, a warm tingling sensation over the whole body, like warm rain sprinkling down out of a summer sky.

It was unbelievable, impossible. It had to be some sort of dream.

Heads still reeling, they drew apart, Rhys helping Melissa off the table, holding her close. Their eyes met and passion rekindled, the flame as yet low but burning up, threatening to turn into a conflagration that would consume them both.

They might have begun all over again, if it had not been for the sound of the drawing room door opening.

Strange. They had not noticed that door before, the one in the wall opposite the fireplace, in the exact spot where the bookcase had stood in *their* drawing room, their world. But as they turned they saw it click open, music and light flooding into the room around the single figure standing in the doorway.

'Come,' smiled the woman, beckoning to them. 'We are ready for you now.'

She was dressed in a high-waisted gown of buttermilk-coloured muslin, the many diaphanous layers swirling about her ankles as she walked. It was cut low at the neck, exposing two small, apple-firm breasts, and about her slender, white throat she wore a choker of black ribbon, adorned with a single flashing diamond.

Her hair was jet black and worn in a Classical style, piled up in ringlets and secured by a broad velvet band. Her eyes were dark and lustrous, her mouth generous and full in her small, almost fragile face. She reminded Melissa of a porcelain doll.

'Please,' began Melissa. 'Who are you?' She realised to her surprise that she was not afraid, only curious. If this was some gloriously erotic dream, then she wanted at least to be part of something she could understand.

The young woman shook her head.

'All your questions will be answered. Come.' She stepped through the door and turned back, beckoning to them to follow.

Her voice was very soft, very persuasive. Rhys looked into those deep brown eyes and felt their sensual power. She reminded him of something, of someone ... a picture he had seen somewhere, but he couldn't find the memory in the jumble of his turbulent thoughts.

Taking hold of Melissa's hand, Rhys moved towards the open door. He could see nothing of what was beyond. He was blinded by a light which seemed blurred and distorted, a music which made him feel dizzy and disorientated.

Together, they followed the woman through the doorway and into the unknown.

There could be no going back.

Chapter 12

Christopher Maudsley parked the jeep mid-way down the lane and started walking towards Highmoor House.

He didn't know why he was doing it, but then he hadn't understood why suddenly, irresistibly, he had been overtaken by a ferocious urge to ravish Jazz in the middle of the open moor. She was still sitting in the passenger seat of the jeep, staring after him with wide, startled eyes, her leather jacket slung around her bare shoulders, covering the long red scratches on her breasts.

Walking up that lane was the hardest thing Maudsley had ever done. It was a little like being in a dream – one of those really peculiar ones where you want to run like hell but your legs feel heavy and unresponsive, like wading through warm treacle.

The house stood before him. It was a house. An ordinary thing of brick and wood and stone – so why did he feel so darned apprehensive? The thought had come to him quite suddenly, in the midst of coupling with Jazz and it had been quite specific. Go up to Highmoor House, it had said. See if you can find Rhys and Melissa. It's very important that you do.

Important? Why? He really couldn't figure it out but his head ached and his mouth was dry and, as he walked the last agonising yards to the front gate, he could hear his heart pounding in his chest, like the slow, regular thump of a bass drum.

Maudsley had lived in Highmoor long enough to know that funny things happened from time to time but he'd never believed the rumours. Only a superstitious peasant would give any credence to rubbish like that. But, as he hesitated at the head of the driveway, wondering if he really ought to go up to the house, something made him catch his breath, blink, rub his eyes in disbelief.

The image of the house before him, the solid, reassuring bulk of brick and stone, seemed to be shifting in and out of focus. One minute it was the way he remembered it from his last visit to Rhys and Melissa; the next, it was changing, its shape altering, the gardens around it changing too.

It all happened so quickly that there was scarcely time to make sense of the images alternating before his eyes with the unsteadying, nauseating swiftness of stroboscopic lights. But Christopher Maudsley had seen enough to know that something wasn't right. It was as if there were two houses, one superimposed on top of the other; the modern and the ancient together, co-existing, conflicting, battling for supremacy.

'Are you all right, Chris? What's up? You look like you've seen a ghost.'

He swung round and saw Jazz getting out of the jeep, walking towards him.

'Can't you see it?'

'See what?'

'The house. It's . . .'

Jazz laughed and kissed him, drawing away in suprise at the sudden chill of his lips.

'I'm not blind,' she said. 'I know a house when I see it.'

'But you don't see anything . . . different about it?'

Jazz shrugged.

'What is there to see? It's still the same smelly old heap it was when you took me to that dinner party . . . Chris!' Realising Maudsley was no longer listening to her, she grabbed him by the shoulder. 'Are you going to explain this to me, or am I going to have to suck the truth out of your cock?'

Her fingers moved skilfully over her lover's crotch, using every ounce of her seductive power on him, but Maudsley remained unresponsive, just staring in front of him, his eyes wide and the colour draining from his cheeks.

'I saw it . . .' he kept repeating, over and over again. 'I saw it, I swear I did. But now it's gone . . .'

The room was filled with music and light, and for a long time Rhys and Melissa stood stock still in the doorway, their senses unable to cope with this new and sudden transformation.

They were standing in a room which Melissa vaguely recognised as the music room at Highmoor House. It had stood almost derelict for many years but now – incredibly – she was seeing it as it must have looked almost two hundred years before.

It was a perfect Regency music room. The walls were hung with tapestries depicting the nine Muses, and the parquet floor was adorned with sumptuous Afghan rugs. In the far corner of the room, half concealed by an ebony and ivory japanned screen, sat four musicians in powdered wigs and knee-breeches, playing string quartets to which a group of six young men and women were dancing.

But it was not the dancers who drew Melissa's eyes.

Before the fireplace stood a tall man of perhaps thirty-five, his wavy black hair drawn back into a short ponytail tied with a black velvet ribbon. His smooth, creamy-gold skin contrasted most attractively with the embroidered black satin of his waistcoat and breeches.

No-one seemed to be paying the slightest attention to the two newcomers – and certainly not the handsome, black-clad young man, for his attentions were entirely devoted to a red-haired woman in a filmy green dress. Her back was to him and she was leaning against the ornate fireplace, her hands grasping the edge of the mantelshelf and her cheek laid against the white marble. Melissa saw tears glistening at the corner of her eyes and her lips were parted, letting out soft whimpering sounds – of fear or of pleasure? Melissa had no way of knowing.

The young woman, although richly dressed in fine materials and jewellery, was almost naked from the waist down. Her dress and petticoats had been pulled up and kilted about her waist with a girdle of golden cord. Underneath, she wore nothing but white silk stockings, held up with garters of white lace interlaced with green satin ribbon. These reached only to mid-thigh, leaving her upper thighs, buttocks and lower back completely bare.

The man in black contemplated this sight with obvious appreciation. Melissa could see the way his tight black satin breeches clung to the contours of his firm, well-muscled body and could not suppress a warm rush of pleasurable lust. His thighs and buttocks were tight and firm, their muscles tensing and relaxing beneath the sheer black fabric as he moved with a fluid, almost feline grace.

As Melissa watched, he unbuttoned his lace-trimmed

cuffs and rolled up his shirt sleeves. The flesh of his forearms was the same creamy-gold colour, giving him the appearance of some wonderfully sculpted statue, brought to life. The diamond signet ring on his right hand flashed fire as he snapped his fingers and a liveried footman stepped forward, bearing a cushion of purple velvet.

Melissa held her breath, watching the man reach out and take something from the cushion. Something long and thin; something whose suppleness he tested between thumb and forefinger, bending it into a broad, curving arc then letting go of it so that it sprang back with a light swish.

As he raised it above his right shoulder, Melissa saw that what he held was a riding-crop. But it was no ordinary riding-crop. This was an exquisite creation, almost an *objet d'art*. It was the very riding-crop that she and Rhys had found in the old oaken chest . . .

The crop was made from tightly plaited black leather, amongst which had been woven strands of silver wire. The handle of the crop was also fashioned from silver, in the form of a woman's body, her breasts bare, her back arched and her head thrown back, hair flowing in long, gleaming tresses.

The woman in the green dress wept silently, her knuckles white as she clutched at the mantelpiece. Her buttocks were ivory-white, a little fleshy but well-formed – soft and rounded and inviting as two juicy peaches.

The young man stretched out the riding-crop and ran its tip lightly over the young woman's backside, making sure that it slipped into the crease between her buttocks, running down towards the deep valley of her sex. It emerged glistening with moisture.

'You have a passable arse, Lady Darnleigh,' commented the young man, his face registering little expression though Melissa could see how his cock strained beneath his tight breeches. 'And I have decided to accept your husband's proposition.'

The young woman shivered visibly but Melissa thought she saw a tiny trickle of moisture escaping from her sex, glistening in the candlelight as it ran down her inner thigh.

'Yes, Lady Darnleigh. Offering me the use of your body in perpetuity is an unorthodox way to repay your husband's gambling debts but, as you know, I was ever a charitable man.' The smooth, honeyed voice was full of irony but deeply sensual. Melissa sensed that he would thoroughly enjoy fulfilling his part of the bargain.

'I pray you, Lord Highmoor. Have pity on me, be gentle . . .'

Highmoor laughed, his whole body shaking with mirth, dark eyes flashing in the orange glow from hundreds of candles.

'Upon my word, Lord Darnleigh, what a sweet, innocent child your wife is. But she must learn that a bargain is a bargain.'

The young man's friends stood in a silent circle as he lifted the riding-crop. Lady Darnleigh trembled, her body tensing, her thighs slightly apart.

The first stroke fell with a sudden swish as it cut through the air, striking across Lady Darnleigh's full white buttocks. She let out a yelp of pain, her fingers scrabbling for a tighter hold on the mantelpiece.

'Silence!' Highmoor snapped, his voice full of lecherous hunger. 'Discipline is the first rule of our little society of libertines, did your husband not tell you that? Or has he not told you of the pretty whores he has whipped and depraved, and the high-born ladies who have done as much to him?' Once again he ran the tip of the crop over her buttocks, marked now with a reddening welt where the first blow had struck home. 'No matter how hard I strike you, Lady Darnleigh, no matter how great the pain, you must keep silence.'

'But Lord Highmoor, oh please . . .'

A light swipe of the riding-crop made her buttocks leap and quiver, the flesh trembling violently as the supple leather smacked against it, criss-crossing it with a second stripe.

'I have told you to keep your silence and you *will* obey me. Or would you prefer that I take Darnleigh Hall from you, as I took your cousin's estate from him?'

'No, please, not that. Would you ruin us utterly?'

Highmoor chuckled.

'No, my dear lady. That is not my intention at all. In fact it is my intention to please you. But first, you must learn the arts of self-control. Only through the power of endurance will you understand how the sharpest pain may become the most piquant of pleasures.'

'My lord . . . aaah!'

Lady Darnleigh's entreaties rose to a high squeal of pain as Highmoor struck her, not lightly this time but with all the force of his powerful body. Melissa shivered and trembled as she watched, feeling Rhys's hand tighten about hers. Such a thing as this, she had never seen in her whole life. And the most terrifying thing about it all was the warm glow of excitement which was running through her body, making her breasts grow firmer and her nipples stiffer beneath the tight bodice of her white, high-waisted dress. Could such terrors really provoke not pain, but pleasure? Could the cut and swish of a silver-handled riding-crop really awaken ecstasy with the same power as it reddened flesh?

Swish, cut. Swish, cut. The riding-crop fell again and again onto Lady Darnleigh's bare rump. Lord Highmoor was beating her with an almost mechanical efficiency now, establishing the rhythm of the punishment she must receive for her husband's unfulfilled obligations. Melissa wondered how any man could sell his wife to a man like Highmoor . . . Or had Darnleigh known that through the bargain his wife would discover pathways to the purest, most secret pleasure?

'Feel it.' Highmoor's voice was a demonic hiss, accompanying the swish of the riding-crop. 'Feel it, my lady. The cut and the burn as I mortify your flesh.'

Melissa could not take her eyes off Lady Darnleigh's bare buttocks – no longer a creamy-white but now patterned with a lurid latticework of scarlet stripes. In places, the silver wire had cut through Lady Darnleigh's skin and crimson beads of blood were standing out against the martyred flesh.

'Oh, oh, oh.' Lady Darnleigh's cries had muted now, to little more than quiet moans of torment. Tears still sparkled in her eyes but there seemed a new intensity in her gaze, an expression no longer of simple fear but of astonished anticipation. 'Oh, my Lord Highmoor . . .'

'Pleasure – can you feel it? I'll wager you can, my sweet doxy. For that is what you are, my dear Lady Darnleigh. Nothing but a pretty whore, who likes nothing better than the rod across her bare backside and a pego between her lips.'

Suddenly, a thought seemed to enter Lord Highmoor's

head, and he stopped beating his victim. She seemed not pleased but more distressed than ever, her eyes rolling and her hips thrusting rhythmically in and out, as though begging for the return of the pain which she had learned to crave.

Highmoor ran the riding-crop over Lady Darnleigh's inner thighs, moving it slowly and tantalisingly higher until it was touching the russet fringe of her pussy lips.

She let out a sharp cry as he slid the riding-crop back and forth with a sawing motion, rubbing the silver-woven leather over the delicate flesh of her vulva.

'Oh, oh, oh, yes, yes, YES!'

She screamed her pleasure now, fingers clawing at the marble fireplace, propping herself up on her arms so that she was gazing into the mirror above the fireplace, seeing not only her own face, startled by her body's pleasure, but Highmoor's face too, his expression of perfect satisfaction as, little by little, he forced her closer to the point of no return.

'Do you wish to spend, Lady Darnleigh?' he asked her, reducing the movements of the riding-crop to a slow, light movement, scarcely more than a tickle.

'Please, please do not ask me that . . .'

'Come, come, my lady – wherefore so coy? Have I not seen your pretty quim and arse and all the secrets of your body? If you wish to spend, you must tell me.'

'Y-yes. Please . . .'

'Tell me.'

'I wish to spend, I need to. *Make* me spend, oh please, please.'

'Very well, perhaps I shall. Or shall I make you do it to yourself?'

Aurelia Clifford

'No, no, I could not!'

'Ah yes.' Highmoor smiled to himself, a smug, sardonic smile which both repelled and excited Melissa. She was beginning to realise that there were many sensual pleasures which she had scarcely even dreamed about, so many as yet undiscovered and untried. 'Ah yes, my dear lady, that would be an excellent exercise in obedience. Part your legs.'

Lady Darnleigh obeyed, sliding her feet a little further apart on the polished parquet floor.

'Good. Your obedience does you credit. You shall yet be a worthy neophyte for our society of libertines. Now, finger yourself.'

'No, my lord, I cannot!'

'You can very well and by my life, you shall!' Highmoor's eyes blazed with anger. 'Remember, Lady Darnleigh – you are mine now, and I can do with you exactly as I choose. Or would you prefer that I take my pleasure by ruining you and your husband for ever?'

Taking hold of Lady Darnleigh's hand, he forced her to let go of the mantelpiece and drew her fingers down to her pubis, pushing them between her thighs until her fingertips met the warm lake of her desire.

'Now – caress yourself.'

This time, Lady Darnleigh did not defy her master. She knew that he would carry out his threats. But Melissa could see that there was more to her compliance than simple fear. Lady Darnleigh was neither helpless nor unintelligent. There was something in those green eyes. Something far more akin to ecstasy than torment.

As Lady Darnleigh's fingers worked over the hardened nubbin of her love-bud, Melissa saw Lord Highmoor's grip tighten about the handle of the riding-crop. Without warning, he jabbed its tip between Lady Darnleigh's buttocks, seeking out the tight, warm seat of pleasure which had until now been a secret shared only with her husband.

'My Lord Highmoor! No. No, you must not . . .'

'On the contrary, I must, my lady. I must, for there is much that you must learn about pleasure.'

In a single, brutal rapier-thrust, the riding-crop entered her, penetrating the secret pleasure-garden of her arse with such great ease that Lady Darnleigh's cheeks burned with shameful delight.

Her fingers worked away at her clitoris, her eyes closed now, unable to bear the shameful spectacle of her own delight. The riding-crop thrust in and out of her, the roughness of silver wire and leather tormenting and stimulating the entrance to her arse. Lord Highmoor was a practised libertine; he knew exactly how to take a woman to the brink of ecstasy and beyond. How to take agony and transform it into unbearable pleasure, in the blinking of an eye.

Subtly and slowly, he began twisting and turning the riding-crop inside Lady Darnleigh's arse, making its flexible tip push and twist against the elastic walls of her rectum, making them stretch and distort, forcing his victim to abandon all self-control.

'Oh, oh, it is too much, I cannot bear it!'

'You can and will, my lady.'

'Have mercy, my lord.'

'There shall be no mercy for you until you submit to the tyranny of your own desire.'

'I cannot, oh, I cannot. I . . .!'

With that, she came, her back arching and her eyes opening very wide in utter astonishment. Melissa saw no such astonishment on the face of Lord Highmoor, only a smile of self-satisfied pleasure as he watched the clear, sweet liquid gush from between Lady Darnleigh's pussy lips and down her slender white thighs, soaking the tops of her white silk stockings.

Strange to tell, Melissa realised that she too was sharing in Lady Darnleigh's orgasm. It was as though their minds and bodies had fused for a few brief seconds and all that Highmoor's victim felt, Melissa felt too. How powerful it was – the burning of bruised and reddened buttocks, the deep, dark pleasure of the riding-crop, buried deep inside forbidden flesh, the tension as orgasm approached, and then the long, luxurious sigh of release as the waiting was over and there was nothing left but the pure white light of total, liberating ecstasy.

As the last waves of pleasure ebbed away, it seemed that all the strength had left Lady Darnleigh's body and she slumped to the floor in front of the fire, limp and faint with exhaustion. Highmoor regarded her with a knowing smile.

'Give her Rhenish wine,' he commanded one of the footmen, handing him a small green glass bottle. 'And be sure it contains four drops of this elixir, no more. In excess, it may be dangerous to the neophyte.'

It was at that moment that Rhys and Melissa realised that Lord Highmoor was turning to face them. Up to that point, they had seemed to be no more than spectators at this bizarre soirée, watching and feeling but disregarded by the others in the room. Now all eyes were upon them. Melissa shrank from the heat of their gaze.

The young woman in the yellow dress led them forward. Rhys could not help noticing how diaphanous her dress was against the fierce blaze of candlelight, clearly displaying the beauty of her fragile form beneath layer upon layer of thin muslin.

She knelt before Lord Highmoor and he gave her his hand to kiss but his eyes never left Rhys and Melissa.

'Your guests have arrived, my lord,' the young woman announced.

Highmoor smiled. His smile was like ice and fire, sending hot and cold shivers through Melissa's body; his dark eyes like black diamonds, burning into her soul.

'You are most welcome,' he told them, beckoning them into the inner circle of his company. Somewhere behind them, the music of the string quartet went on and on, the dancers whirling tirelessly, their innocent pleasure an incongruous counterpoint to Lord Highmoor's far more sophisticated tastes.

Rhys stepped forward, suddenly emboldened, a question surfacing through the confusion of sensual warmth that had numbed his brain and made him long only for more and greater pleasure.

'Why . . . why have you brought us here?'

Highmoor snapped his fingers and the footman returned with a silver salver, containing two glasses of wine and the green glass bottle Melissa had seen earlier.

'Why?' He laughed. 'To learn . . . to enjoy. Why else? Why else would anyone come to my little *musical* evenings at Highmoor House?' He took the green glass bottle from the tray, removed the stopper and let four drops of apple-green liquid fall into each of the glasses. Stoppering the bottle, he set it back down on the tray. 'Please,' he gestured towards the glasses. 'Please refresh yourselves.'

Rhys found himself reaching out for one of the glasses. He knew it was pure idiocy. Whatever that green stuff was that Highmoor had just put into the champagne, you could bet it wasn't crème-de-menthe. But something compelled him, like an unheard voice whispering at the back of his mind that everything would be all right, that all he had to do was lift the glass to his lips and drink – and wait for the pleasure to begin.

Melissa laid a hand on his arm.

'Rhys, do you think we should?'

Highmoor's voice compelled her attention, his eyes drawing hers.

'Drink,' he said quietly. And her fingers slipped around the stem of the glass.

The wine tasted cool and fresh and sharp. You couldn't even notice that there was anything in it, unless you held it up to the light and saw the faint, greenish tinge.

But seconds after he had swallowed the last drop, Rhys began to feel an incredible warmth spreading through his body, a languourous, lazy feeling like swimming in a tropical sea. He looked at Melissa, and knew instantly that she felt it too.

Care seemed to melt away, fear and resistance transformed into far-distant chimeras that had no place in this extraordinary world of rarefied pleasures. Rhys heard someone laughing, and realised that it was himself. He looked at Highmoor. He was still smiling.

'My dear Rhys,' said Highmoor. 'Allow me to introduce you to my excellent friend, Madame de Carcassonne. She was obliged to leave Paris when her husband was guillotined by that upstart Napoleon, but she has found great favour among the English nobility.'

Madame de Carcassonne stepped forward. Rhys had never seen a more strikingly attractive woman. There was a fire in those violet eyes and her high-cheekboned face was both aristocratic and sublimely cruel.

'I like to think that I have certain . . . abilities,' she said in her soft, sultry voice. 'Certain talents which enable me to give great pleasure to those who choose to offer themselves to be my pupils.'

'Madame de Carcassonne is the greatest of teachers,' Highmoor assured Rhys. 'She has taught me much about the use of the whip and the discipline of pain.'

At this, Rhys felt a distant ache of alarm. He did not wish to feel pain, not even at the hands of this delicious Gallic tormentress. But her hands were already caressing him, unfastening the loose cotton shirt and the front flap of his tight woollen breeches. He could not have resisted if he had wanted to, and as her fingers touched him, stroking the bare pink spike of his penis, he began to realise that resisting was the last thing he wanted to do.

Through eyes that refused to focus, Rhys saw to his surprise that his cock was no longer pierced. So his clothes were not the only part of him to have undergone a transformation . . .

'He is not quite ready for the lash,' announced Madame de Carcassonne. 'He requires a little persuasion.'

Lord Highmoor nodded to one of the serving-lads, who stepped forward. Melissa looked at him with appreciative eyes. She too could feel the effects of the elixir, making her head swim and removing every inhibition she had ever had. She scarcely realised that it was Lord Highmoor's hands that were slipping down the front of her white, high-waisted dress, pulling out the firm, heavy globes of her breasts, but she welcomed his caresses. She would have welcomed any caress which might relieve the desperate yearnings surging through her helpless body.

The serving-lad must have been around seventeen or eighteen years old. He was blond, boyish, slightly built, with a face like an angel and eyes of the softest dusky-blue. His lips were full, cherry-red as a young girl's, and his hands were soft and feminine.

'Prepare him,' said Lord Highmoor. 'And be sure that you give him pleasure, or you shall pay a harsh forfeit indeed.'

Rhys scarcely realised what was happening to him until the young boy was kneeling at his feet, cradling his swollen dick in those slender, butterfly-soft hands.

'No ... please,' he protested, but his protests were faint and feeble. His mind reeled, the last vestiges of his resistance rekindled by the curiously stimulating sight of another man kneeling at his feet, caressing his cock.

'You have no cause to fear, my dear Rhys,' Lord Highmoor assured him. 'I'll wager sweet Gennaro will please you. And surely it is not the first time you have had a man's lips upon your pego ... ?'

Rhys closed his eyes as the pleasure began but he could not rid his mind of the tormenting, tantalising images which swam around and around behind his closed lids. It was many, many years since he had let another man touch his prick, not since he was at school, but even now the memory lingered. It had been one of those games, that was all. Horseplay in the changing rooms after rugby. All the fifth-form boys had been in on it, experimenting, finding ways of relieving their frustrations when there were no girls around to do it for them.

They had formed a circle on the tiled floor of the changing room, he and Danny and Kurt and Andy and all the rest. Each took hold of his neighbour's prick and started wanking it – a circle jerk, that's what they called it in America or that's what Danny said. It had been fun, sure, just harmless fun . . . but nothing like this.

This felt like heaven.

Melissa watched, entranced, as Gennaro sucked Rhys's prick. Strange, she'd always thought she would go crazy with jealousy if he even thought of going with another man, but watching him now just made her feel incredibly excited.

Lord Highmoor had taken her breasts out and was standing behind her, stroking and pinching the nipples as he kissed her throat, whispering the most seductive obscenities into her ear.

'He has a fine cock, Melissa, but mine is finer. Do you not care to feel how fine?'

He took hold of her hand and drew it back until she felt the smooth satin of his breeches.

'Feel it, Melissa. Touch it, do not be afraid. I shall take it out for you and you shall hold it in your pretty hand.'

Highmoor's seductive gentleness was in sharp contrast to the brutal pleasure he had forced from Lady Darnleigh's body just a few moments before. But she could still sense the darkness within him, the strength that must possess, to pleasure or destroy.

His cock was firm and smooth, not larger than Rhys's but somehow more potent, more menacingly sexual. Such a cock might be not only the instrument of pleasure but the instrument of torment.

'He is ready now,' announced Madame de Carcassonne and to Rhys's immense disappointment Gennaro let his prick slip from between those cherry-red lips. He gave a deep bow and withdrew, losing himself in the crowd.

'Clear the table and tie him onto it,' instructed Madame de Carcassonne. Footmen glided forward, carrying away silver dishes and vases of blood-red roses.

Rhys had not one ounce of strength to resist. The pleasure within him was all-consuming, all-demanding. It was the only reality left to him, annihilating all rational thought. Gennaro's gentle ministrations had left his cock swollen and aching, keeping him for what seemed an eternity on the very brink of far greater pleasure. Gennaro was skilful and he knew how dearly his master's displeasure would cost him if he were to spoil the game.

Strong arms carried Rhys across to the table and, the next thing he knew, he was sprawled on his back on the white damask cloth, his arms and legs bound to the table legs by silken cords. Directly above him, hundreds of tiny candles blazed in a crystal chandelier, their dancing lights confusing his senses, turning the figures standing around the edges of the table into mere moving shadows, dark and sinister.

'I shall teach you, *mon cher*, about the power of pain,' whispered Madame de Carcassonne, selecting a red leather bullwhip from the cushion. It lay coiled there like a sleeping serpent, beautiful but deadly. As she picked it up it uncoiled, glossy and sinuous, until it fell in a single, shimmering rope from her upraised hand.

She ran her fingers along its length, as though it really were some beast, that loved to be petted and stroked into obedience. Certainly it seemed to Melissa that there was a darkly sensual life within it, a desire that burned and snarled for release.

The first flick of the Frenchwoman's wrist sent the whip snaking through the air with a crack as loud as a pistol shot. Unable to see his tormentress, Rhys flinched, but this time the whip's tip merely skated over the surface of his skin.

The second stroke came as a terrible, undreamed-of pain and the savage bite of leather marked him diagonally across his body, from thigh to shoulder. Again and again she struck him and he writhed on the table top, at first crying out with pain and then with a subtler, indefinable torment which began as suffering and would end in ecstasy.

On her hands and knees on the carpet beside the fire, Melissa heard but could not see her lover. She had a new lover now, the sardonically handsome Lord Highmoor. His hands were on her bare thighs and her dress thrown up over her head, so that the white skirt cascaded down over her face like a bridal veil.

He beat her with the flat of his hand, slap after slap on her bare buttocks, making them quiver and shake. At first all she could think about was escaping from the discomfort, the dreadful inferno burning her flesh. But Highmoor had been right. There was a secret, shameful enjoyment in pain – an insidious pleasure that crept up almost unsuspected in its slyness.

Little by little, the burning began to change, the pain

lessening and then a new warmth sweeping over her. It was at that moment that Highmoor's cock entered her, parting her plump, sex-swollen labia so smoothly that it might have been dripping with scented oil.

Rhys lay in torment, his body straining under the whip, its kisses stinging, biting, arousing... He could bear it no longer and then the very tip of the whip began stinging his lower belly, his thighs, moving closer and closer to the very pleasure-centre of his being...

'No, no, no, please!'

It was no use. Madame de Carcassonne was not listening. And besides, she knew very well that Rhys would rather have died than have her stop now. Two strokes more of the whip, maybe three at most, and he would have learned the lesson she had set out to teach him: that pleasure and pain are very close together, sometimes inextricably close.

'Oh, oh, I can feel it, I can feel it coming...'

With a skilful flick of her wrist, the Frenchwoman wrapped the very tip of the whip around the shaft of Rhys's penis. This last, savagely burning kiss, proved more than he could bear and with a roar of agonised ecstasy he felt his seed gush out of him, his prick jerking, spitting its own creamy venom.

Melissa felt his pleasure and his pain, felt every touch of the whip, every burning kiss as Lord Highmoor possessed her. In her imagination she was no longer corporeal, her whole being transformed into a fiery spirit, turbulent and wild, crackling with sexual energy. And Highmoor was her demon lover, the force that gave her existence through the creating power of pure pleasure.

She could feel Highmoor holding back, waiting for the

moment when he knew she was ready for him. *Slowly now, slowly, don't rush it,* whispered the voice in her head. *Make the pleasure last, here it comes, here it comes, here it COMES.*

With a squeal of delight, she met the onrush of Highmoor's seed, pushing back hard onto his shaft, greedily taking its full length inside her. She wanted every drop of his sexual essence, wanted to feel the tip of his cock pushing hard against her womb, possessing, pleasuring, liberating.

He withdrew from her and she slumped to the ground, her shoulders heaving, her corn-gold hair escaping from its pins and the flowers from her corsage scattered all over the carpet.

'Cut him free.' Madame de Carcassonne watched with a half-smile as the footmen slit through the ropes holding Rhys to the table. He slid to the ground, his clothes ripped and torn, his flesh bruised and bloody beneath the dampened rags of his former finery.

Lord Highmoor took Melissa's hand and drew her to her feet, kissed her and placed her hand in Rhys's.

'You have learned your lessons well. And now, my dear friends, it is time for you to dance.'

'Dance?' Melissa exchanged puzzled looks with Rhys. 'But we can't ... we don't know how ...'

'Dance.' This time, Highmoor's voice was firmer, more commanding. Melissa saw the dark flash of his eyes and knew that they must not disobey.

Highmoor took Lady Darnleigh by the hand and led her into the midst of the dancing couples. Melissa and Rhys followed behind, feeling clumsy and confused.

They did not speak, but held each other tightly, looking

into each other's eyes, sharing every thought, every feeling. Slowly they began to dance, discovering to their astonishment that they knew the steps, and moved together with surprising grace.

As the dance speeded up, the room seemed to blur around them, a change coming over them, the world slowly spinning and transforming . . . into what?

'Is it over now? Is it going to end?' asked Melissa. 'Will we wake up and find it was all a dream?'

Rhys stroked the hair back from her face.

'I'm with you,' he replied. 'I don't care if I never wake up again.'

Chapter 13

It felt good to be in control at last.

Candice Soulbury slid slender, stockinged thighs out of the car and began walking towards Peter Galliano's exclusive apartment building. She took slow, confident steps, glancing neither to left nor right, yet aware constantly of the eyes on her as she turned the corner into New Bond Street. Men, women, they couldn't take their eyes off her, following her with stares that wanted to devour her, undressing her in the secret silence of their imagination.

That thought excited her so, so much. Some people might call her a control freak, but Candice preferred to think of herself as a sensual woman who was excited by the discipline and responsibilities of power. Like the power which, little by little, she was beginning to exert on her lover.

Power over her own body, too. These last few months, Candice had submitted herself to a complete sensual re-education, visiting places she had been told about in hushed whispers. Backstreet shops where exotic confections in PVC and rubber hung alongside leather whips and harnesses. Private clubs and exclusive bordellos where a woman might learn all she needed to know to give a man the most sublime pleasure And Candice had learned – fast.

The secret between her thighs filled the deep well of her sex with a warm, liquid anticipation. No-one knew it was there, only Candice. She had chosen it in the women-only sex shop she had discovered in the West End, enchanted by the little trinket's prettiness and the astonishing effects of its kisses upon her flesh.

It was called a butterfly, the saleswoman had told her. And at first glance that was exactly what it looked like: a pink butterfly moulded from the softest material imaginable, which must have been some sort of rubber but which felt almost as soft and warm as living flesh. Its wings were decorated with splashes of colour – vivid lapis and scarlet and yellow giving it the appearance of a jewel rather than a toy.

But turn it over and you saw the secret within. The underside was decorated with flexible spikes in the same pink rubbery material, the spikes of different lengths according to their positions on the flat, slightly curved disc, but a little longer than the rest at the centre.

At the four corners of the butterfly, piercing its wings, hung straps of white satin, with buckles which allowed the butterfly to be fixed between the thighs, the pink flexible spines pressed hard against the soft pink vulval flesh.

Candice had fallen in love with the butterfly the moment she touched it, cradling its seductively warm softness in the palm of her hand. She wondered now why she had hesitated, even for a second, before buying it.

'Won't you try it?' the saleswoman had urged. 'It will give you such pleasure.'

And as soon as Candice had felt its kisses between her thighs she knew that she had made the right choice.

With each step she took, the soft spikes of rubber tickled and teased the fleshy interior of her vulva, whilst the longer spikes pushed back the hood of her clitoris, gently rubbing it in a dozen different ways.

The sensations were exquisite and irresistible. It took all the self-control Candice could muster to avoid betraying her mounting excitement. As it was, her eyes sparkled and she could feel a smile twitching the corners of her mouth. It both excited and amused her to be so very much in control of her own pleasure. To think that here she was, walking through an elegant London street with the butterfly massager strapped between her vulval lips, and not one single person had the slightest inkling of what she was doing.

She was masturbating; masturbating at her own pace – walking slowly, setting the rhythm, determined not to hurry herself towards a climax. The climax would be later, in the apartment, when she undressed and Galliano saw what a resourceful young woman she really was. She might be crazy about Peter Galliano but she didn't want him to suspect, even for a moment, that she needed him. Well, she certainly didn't need him to give her pleasure . . .

Heads turned as she crossed the street, cutting a striking figure in her green Armani suit, cut high in the leg and with a flimsy white silk blouse underneath the jacket. She knew that whenever the jacket fell open passersby could see the luscious hills and valleys of her breasts, their pink crests dancing unfettered under the gauzy fabric. She didn't give a damn. No matter what they could see on the outside, none of them could see her secret pleasure.

This was it, the sumptuous apartment block in which Galliano had rented the penthouse suite. Things had been going exceptionally well for her lover lately, what with Candice to make sure he always made the best of every opportunity. His success was hers and she didn't mind one bit. When Galliano made it to Chairman of Jupiter Products International, she would be there at his side, basking in his glory.

There was no need for identification. The security guard gave a respectful nod as Candice walked across the foyer to the lift and pressed the button.

Waiting was agony. Standing stock-still was a torment she had not been prepared for. In order to keep the sensations flowing and building in her sex, she must keep moving, keep the butterfly kisses rippling across her vulval lips, the pulsing head of her clitoris.

A terrible shivering, burning feeling filled her, making her feel as though her love bud were on fire. Rather than damping down the sensations, her immobility seemed to intensify them, as though her clitoris deeply resented this lack of attention to its pleasure and was trying to force her to be less dilatory.

She shifted a little from one foot to the other and a huge rush of relief passed through her body, swiftly followed by the dull ache of frustration as she stopped moving again. But she couldn't keep walking about, could she? She took a few steps to the left, pretending to admire one of the paintings on the wall of the reception area, turned, then walked back the other way.

'Anything the matter, Miss Soulbury?' enquired the security guard.

'What?' Candice spun round, momentarily thrown by this unexpected variable.

'Are you all right? You look a bit edgy.'

If only you knew *how* edgy, thought Candice with a secret smile. And why!

'I'm fine,' she replied. 'This lift takes a long time to arrive, doesn't it?'

'I expect it's coming down from the top, Miss,' commented the guard.

'I suppose so.'

Where is it, where is it? The question kept thundering through Candice's fevered brain as her body fought to rebel against her, trying to force her to give it the sensations it demanded. But she kept very still, refusing to give in to the impulses which were seeking to overwhelm her resistance.

At last the lift arrived, with a clanking of gears and a tinkling of piped musak as the doors slid open. She stepped in with an audible sigh of relief, pressed 'Penthouse and viewing gallery', and turned to face the closing doors.

As the lift slid upwards towards the twenty-fifth floor, she admired herself in the full-length mirror set into one side of the carpeted wall. Her hips swayed slightly in the tight green skirt, slit from mid-calf to high above the knee, as her instincts began to obey the need for pleasure. She ran her hand through her short hair, normally dark brown, but now dyed a deep, glossy plum colour which gleamed like polished glass as she tilted her head in the golden glow from the wall-lights.

Mmm, yes, she was looking good. Good enough to eat. And did she feel good? She almost laughed out loud. The discovery of this infinite sexuality within her had been the ultimate liberating experience. And now that that sly bitch Melissa Montagu was out of the way, she felt good all of the time. What a lucky boy Peter Galliano was to be getting the full benefit of all this unleashed sensuality.

The lift reached the top floor and she stepped out on her four-inch heels, setting off along the corridor. On one side the wall was almost entirely made of glass from floor to ceiling, so that it was like stepping out into mid-air, or walking a tightrope hundreds of feet above the teeming metropolis below.

If she hurried, she would get there before him. She knew he'd had a meeting at Jupiter's HQ this afternoon. Well, she'd prepare him a drink or two, maybe take a bath, take a long look at some of those Persian erotic paintings Galliano had bought for the bedroom. 'An investment,' he'd told her, perfectly straight-faced. An investment in their mutual sexual pleasure, maybe . . .

She rummaged in her bag for the key and slid it into the lock. It turned easily and she stepped inside. Breathtaking. White marble floors and pillars, furniture in simple modern styles, interspersed with antiques and *objets d'art* so rare and so exquisite that it seemed impossible that they could be real. But Candice knew they were – Galliano's family had never been short of money.

'Peter?' She paused. 'Peter, darling . . . ?'

No reply. Good. She liked to be there first, waiting for him, ready to soothe all the tiredness from his body and replace it with another, far more welcome, kind of tension.

As she walked across the living room towards the bathroom, she glanced through the door of Galliano's home office and noticed the fax machine. There was paper spewing out of it in a long white coil, so many pages of it that they had formed an untidy mess on the floor behind his desk.

The PA in her took over and she decided to clear it up. As she bent to gather up the pages, she noticed a sheet of paper lying beside the machine, a scrawl in Galliano's handwriting:

'It's no use running away, Melissa. You know I'll find you in the end.'

Underneath was a crude montage of pictures – pictures of Melissa Montagu in various stages of undress. Anger reared up in Candice's throat, the bitterness of bile filling her mouth. So, he'd been faxing pictures to Melissa, had he? The bitch had obviously been leading him on, tormenting him, wouldn't leave him alone. Candice picked up the sheet of paper, tore it neatly in two and dropped it into the wastepaper bin, a grim smile spreading across her face.

Well, Peter needn't worry. Candice would make sure Melissa didn't get her filthy claws into him ever again.

Dismissing Melissa from her mind, she bent to haul the long white snake of fax paper onto the desk. There were pages and pages of it. She most probably wouldn't have bothered looking at them very closely, if she hadn't seen her name on the first sheet. And it wasn't just typed once – it was typed over and over again, hundreds of times, the single word 'Candice' covering sheet after sheet of paper like some intricate embroidery.

After the tenth page, the pictures began. Line drawings, quite well executed – or at least, well enough for it to be obvious that they were pictures of her.

Images of Candice giving head; Candice bending forward over an office desk, her skirts around her waist, her backside bare and striped with the marks of a rattan cane, brought swishing down by an unseen hand; Candice stripped naked and lying on a bed, her thighs wide apart, her fingers probing the depths of her sex with a huge, penis-shaped dildo which distended her flesh . . .

She could feel herself trembling as she looked for the

sender's name, the sender's number, anything to give her a clue as to where these pictures had come from. Nothing. Nothing at all. What was going on?

Her eyes moved to the last picture of all. It made no more sense than the others. All it showed was Candice Soulbury, walking barefoot and naked along a path towards the open gate of a walled garden. There was nothing especially significant in that, nothing at all – so why did she feel this overwhelming excitement building up inside her as her eyes moved greedily over the picture, somehow inexorably drawn by it? And they were drawn by her own image in particular, the clean, curvaceous lines of her womanly body, the grace of her rounded hips and slim thighs.

The mystery that she sensed lay just a fraction further on if only she could see it, beyond the walls of the garden, frustratingly veiled from sight.

As though in a dream, she put down the sheet of paper and stretched out her hand for the receiver of the fax machine. She picked it up, and the faint sound of the dialling tone purred out of it, like a cat pleased to be stroked.

She cradled it in her hand for a few moments, feeling its weight, its smoothness, the thickness of its girth, the heaviness of its bulbous head. Then she began running her fingers up and down it, very slowly, savouring the silky feel of the matt plastic.

Hungry. So desperately, desperately hungry. It was wicked and depraved but she couldn't resist, she just couldn't.

Lifting up her skirts she pulled down her panties and stepped out of them. The butterfly pressed hard against her sex for an instant and she shivered with excitement, then swiftly released the small buckles which held the straps taut against her body.

Laying the butterfly on Galliano's desk, she sat down on his chair, facing the fax machine. The receiver was bleeping its protest in her hand, but she scarcely noticed. All she was aware of was the overwhelming need for a brutal, sudden pleasure.

With a long, agonised groan of need, she thrust the receiver between her thighs and into the waiting heart of her womanhood. Juice dripped from her, lubricating it, making the penetration easier, but the receiver still felt immense as it stretched open her sex lips to a wide and willing O of need.

She had forgotten everything – even Galliano. And when, a little while later, he arrived back at his apartment, he was astonished and aroused to find his mistress fucking herself with the fax receiver, whilst the carpet about her feet was inexplicably strewn with dewy-fresh, damask roses.

They danced so hard and so fast that the world was reduced to a blur of light and colour and sound.

Melissa felt Rhys's arm tightly gripping her waist, the warmth of his body reassuringly constant against hers, but there seemed nothing beneath her feet but empty air, nothing to stop them falling together into a fathomless abyss beyond time and space and sanity.

At last, the music seemed to slow and fade, the dizzying whirl turning to a slow spin which reduced in speed and intensity as the world came back into focus. A voice. There was a voice in her head, someone speaking to her – at first it seemed a very long way off, but it grew louder and more distinct as though that too were beginning to sharpen its focus.

'Sirrah, allow me to present to you the lovely Melissa.'

She opened her eyes and found herself looking into the face of a man with a powdered wig and a small, heart-shaped beauty-patch, stuck in the middle of his right cheek. He was dressed in a highly ornate frock-coat and breeches of blue silk brocade, and full lace cuffs hung from his coat-sleeves and over his silk-stockinged calves. He wore high-heeled buckled shoes and was peering at her through a gold-handled spyglass.

'Gad, sir, she is a tasty morsel indeed.'

Melissa stammered out a response and curtseyed as the man took hold of her hand and pressed it to his lips. The voice which spoke was hers and yet not hers – the words phrased in ways which sounded curious and quaint.

'I . . . you are most gracious, kind sir.'

'I'll wager she's a spirited filly,' commented a lady in dazzling white satin, her heavy skirts billowed out with hooped petticoats and her full breasts half-exposed by the low, square-cut neckline. 'Is she not an actress? One hears such tales of their roistering in the London stews.'

'Aye, and a fine one,' cut in a second man, younger than the first and more handsome. 'She comes new to our company and hath still her mark to make upon the stage, but already I swear she hath set her mark upon my heart.' He gave an exaggerated bow, provoking a flurry of laughter and applause.

'I've a mind to take her to my bed tonight,' commented the first gentleman thoughtfully. 'Milady Kate has lost her appetite for the pleasures of the flesh since she was brought to bed and 'tis too long since I enjoyed a maid such as this one.'

'No maid, alas,' laughed the young actor-manager. His eyes met Melissa's and she felt herself blushing. She already felt extremely conspicuous, for the dress she was now wearing was cut very low at the front and her large, soft breasts were pushed up by a stiff corset of pasteboard and wood, making them seem huger than ever.

'Then you had best hope she hath not the pox!' remarked the fine lady.

Suddenly realising that Rhys was no longer at her side, Melissa looked around her in alarm. She saw that she was still in the old music room at Highmoor House, that much it was possible to discern, but the scene had changed greatly from the room in which she and Rhys had danced at the command of Lord Highmoor.

This room was also finely decorated, though less ostentatiously; and instead of the dancers and musicians who had filled the room before, there was now a small improvised stage at one end, a heavy velvet curtain cordoning off about one third of the room.

As she looked around at the chattering throng, dressed in all the foppish finery of the 1680s, she caught sight of Rhys. Like her, he was dressed in the costume of the period: brocade breeches trimmed with lace, a full-sleeved shirt and flowing cravat beneath an embroidered waistcoat which clung to him like a second skin.

The style suited him so well that she felt a surge of lustful jealousy ... for he was talking with a very beautiful young woman, dressed in the costume of a young lady of quality. She was clearly enjoying his company, her hands on her hips, her eyes sparkling, her laughter floating across the room. And Rhys's eyes were on her, following each sinuous movement of her voluptuous body, his lust speaking every word that his lips would not.

'Thy company enchants me, Melissa.' The older man who had first spoken to her unlaced a soft leather purse which hung at his belt and took out a golden sovereign. He held it up to the light for a moment, letting it glow and sparkle. 'This could be thine, my little doxy, a whole golden sovereign.'

'Indeed?' Melissa licked her lips nervously, trying to smile. She knew instantly what this lecherous old rogue was proposing: that she should let him have her, give her body to him for a single golden sovereign. What a curious dream this was, it seemed so real. Even her lust felt real, incredibly so. It fizzed and bubbled inside her like the finest champagne, and suddenly the idea of selling herself to this man seemed the most exciting in the whole world. Here, in this dream-world, nothing was forbidden. Such freedom. She could do anything, ANYTHING she wanted . . .

'Indeed, sweet Melissa.' The man pulled her to him suddenly, crushing his lips against hers. 'Be not afeared. Sir Roderick Carlyle will never do harm to any lady.' His lip curled into something between a smile and a sneer. 'Although, begad, thou'rt no lady, my sweet. Thou hast the devil in those sweet lips . . .'

His hand fumbled with the folds of her skirt, feeling for the plump mound of Venus, rubbing it hard through the stiff petticoats. Melissa was astonished at how powerful the sensations were, realising all at once that she was wearing no bloomers beneath her dress, nothing but her thigh-length cotton stockings and her smooth, bare skin . . .

'You would have me pleasure you, sir?' she asked him sweetly, still surprised at her own boldness, though already this dream had taken her into realms of unashamed adventure which she had scarcely even fantasised about before.

Yes, that was it. This was a fantasy come true.

'I would have thee pleasure me all night long,' he replied. 'Wilt thou accept my bargain?'

She smiled, no longer afraid, only excited.

'Sir, I accept it with gladness.'

'No matter what I demand of thee, thou shalt not say me nay?'

She looked deep into his eyes.

'I shall do as you command.'

Sir Roderick held the gold sovereign between his finger and thumb, then ran it over the swell of her breasts, half-spilling out of the low-cut bodice. It felt cool and made her flesh tingle. With a self-satisfied grunt, he pushed the coin between her breasts, right down so that it disappeared into the deep, dark, tight-pressed cleft and was quite hidden from sight.

'Pleasure me well, sweet doxy.' The libidinous aristocrat took hold of her hand and touched it briefly to his lips. 'Close thy pretty lips about my manhood and tomorrow morn there shall be another sovereign for thee.'

Melissa was about to reply when she felt a hand on her bare shoulder. She turned round to see the young actor-manager standing behind her.

'We must prepare, Melissa. Our play is about to begin, and thou art our brightest star.'

Melissa's heart beat faster. Her eyes searched the room for a sight of Rhys and she saw him walking towards the makeshift stage with the young woman he had been talking with earlier.

'Greville, thou'rt as welcome as a dose of the clap,' growled Sir Roderick, clapping the young actor on the shoulder goodnaturedly. 'Be sure to bring her back to me. She and I have struck a bargain.'

Greville walked with Melissa towards the stage. A gaggle of actors and actresses were talking and laughing in the wings, their clothes gaudy and the women's faces heavily painted with white lead, in the fashionable style of the time. Melissa wondered what on earth was going to happen to her. Was she really being asked to step onto that stage, to play a part in a play which she knew nothing about? In desperation she turned to Greville.

'I cannot . . . I cannot do it.'

His sharp features softened into a smile.

'My dear Melissa, such foolish words! Thou canst and shall do thy part.'

'But, Greville . . . I have forgotten everything, every word. What am I to do?'

His eyes searched hers out and she felt a shiver of electricity pass between them.

'Have no fear, Melissa. When the time comes, the words will come to thee. Only listen to thine own desire.'

No longer understanding anything at all, Melissa followed Greville into the wings. In front of the curtain stood a flamboyant dandy of a man, resplendent in powdered wig and a suit of scarlet satin.

'This is a tale of love betrayed,' he chanted in a sing-song voice. 'Of Cupid's dart and of the sweet defilement of a fair young maid...'

The curtain drew back to reveal a painted backdrop representing a walled garden. Although the scenery was primitive, Melissa recognised the scene instantly – it was the Paradise Garden! But she had little time to question why or how... for seconds later she saw Rhys step onto the stage, accompanied by the beautiful young woman in the dove-grey dress.

Rhys had caught sight of Melissa across the crowded music room. He knew that she was watching him and that knowledge brought the warmth of excitement to his already-aroused body.

He did not question why he was here, or how he could possibly know which words to speak, which moves to make. This was a dream, a warm and sensual dream in which all things were possible and in which he was about to undress a beautiful young woman in front of dozens of strangers.

By some miracle he knew his part perfectly. He was Monsieur Garonne, the dancing-master, and the beautiful young actress with the flame-coloured hair was Cordelia, daughter of the master of Highmoor House.

'Ah, Monsieur.' Sinking down onto a bench beneath a painted rose-bower, Cordelia looked up at him through the long, dark sweep of her eyelashes. 'Monsieur, why hast thou brought me here?'

He sank onto one knee before her, taking her hand and kissing the white, translucent flesh. She was as beautiful as a classical statue, as hot and lustful as a she-wolf. He could feel her racing pulse, heard her rapid, shallow breathing.

Cordelia might be a consummate actress, but this display of desire was not feigned.

'I have brought thee here, sweet maid, to perfect thine education in the gentle arts of womanhood,' Rhys replied. He had almost forgotten the watching eyes of the audience, conscious only of Melissa, watching him from the wings, the actor-manager Greville stroking her breast as they stood beside the stage. He drew Cordelia's face down to his and their lips met, her breath hot and sweet and dry.

'I always strive to learn my lessons well, Monsieur,' simpered Cordelia. She looked so modest and so very young in that grey silk dress, quite high in the neck with a lace fichu which veiled the creamy swell of her small, budding breasts.

He sat down on the bench beside her and, reaching out, plucked a single grape from a bunch hanging in the bower. He took it between his teeth and then kissed Cordelia again, so that when their lips met the fruit was between their mouths. He bit into it as they kissed and the purplish juice flowed like nectar, dripping over their lips and chins.

He pushed the rest of the grape into Cordelia's mouth with his tongue and flesh met flesh, the sweetness of the grape juice mingling with the saltiness of abundant saliva.

Withdrawing, he kissed the last of the sweet juice from her lips.

'Now thou shalt do the same,' he instructed her, plucking a second fruit and giving it to Cordelia.

She had indeed learned her lesson well and, as the fruit crushed its sticky-sweet juice over Rhys's lips, her tongue pushed into his mouth, like a moist penis thrusting into a virgin's maidenhead. He found himself surprised by her passion, for in truth the girl looked too young and too pure to have much experience of the world.

'Since thou'rt so willing and so eager to learn...' he began.

'Oh, I am, Monsieur,' she assured him. 'Upon my word I am.'

'Then turn and I shall unlace thy dress.'

'But, Monsieur... what if my father should see? Or my cousin Melissa? They are so jealous of my maidenhead...'

'No-one will see us, Cordelia. But if thou'rt too afraid...'

'No, no, Monsieur.' Her eyes glistened with eager desire. 'I am sixteen years old. I fear nothing.'

She half-turned on the bench so that her back was facing him, with its long row of laces running from the neck to the waist of her grey silk dress. Rhys unlaced them slowly, tantalisingly, resisting the surging excitement which had already swelled his cock, pushing its aching, burning head against the inside of his breeches.

Beneath, Cordelia was wearing no corset, only a white linen chemise which hung loosely over her young and delectable form, making her look still more girlish and undefiled. Rhys slipped her dress down over her shoulders and loosened the threaded ribbon at the neck of her chemise, so that it too slipped down, bearing her snowy back and shoulders.

'Turn to face me, Cordelia.'

'Yes, Monsieur.'

She turned slowly round, not only to face Rhys but to face the audience, and a sigh of approval ran around the assembly. Her skin was a perfect, snowy white; so smooth and so flawless that it seemed sculpted from the finest alabaster. A network of tiny, bluish veins showed through the flesh of her small, pointed breasts, making her skin seem almost transparent.

Her breasts were barely more than buds, pouting kisses of flesh which swelled into bright pink crests, small and hard and inviting. Rhys stroked his gloved hand down the side of her cheek, her throat, her shoulder, and down the side of her flank; only then returning, with painful slowness, to stroke the side of her breast.

'Ah! Ah, Monsieur...' sighed Cordelia, her breath escaping in a long, shuddering sigh.

'Thy breasts are passing comely,' Rhys told her. 'Take care always to keep their skin soft and supple.'

'My mother bids me bind them so they grow not too large,' Cordelia told him. 'She believes large breasts too immodest.'

'Fie, sweet child!' Rhys pinched Cordelia's nipple between his gloved fingers and was rewarded with a tiny squeal of astonished pleasure. 'Thou shalt let them blossom unfettered and they will be beautiful and will give thee great joy. Thee and thy lovers.'

'Every night, rub your breasts with a lotion of olive and ginger oil, blended with fresh rosewater,' he instructed her, reaching into his waistcoat pocket and taking out a small glass phial. 'This will keep thy bubbies soft and supple and increase the sensations of pleasure.' He slipped off his gloves, folded them and put them into his pocket. 'Allow me to instruct thee in its proper application.'

He took the glass stopper from the phial and emptied a little of the clear, pinkish liquid into his palm, warming it by rubbing his hands together. Then he laid his hands gently on Cordelia's breasts and began massaging them with long, slow, circular movements, beginning at the outer margins of her breasts and working gradually inwards, towards the very apex of her desire.

Cordelia's expression turned to one of the most angelic pleasure as Rhys massaged her breasts. He could feel her quivering at his touch, and pushing her flesh against his hands, as though willing him to be less gentle and more demanding, forcing pleasure from her body and releasing her from the torment of the desire he had awakened within her.

The warm oil glistened on her skin, lending it the sheen of polished silk, rose-pink and soft. Little trickles of the spicy, warming oil ran down her breasts from throat to nipple, falling from the very tip in fat, viscous droplets. Other runnels of warm liquid ran down her belly, soaking into the plain grey silk of her bodice, which now hung from her skirt, baring her beautiful young body to the waist.

When at last he began pinching and kneading Cordelia's nipples, the violence of her reaction astonished him. Her hands clutched at him, her whole body rearing as pleasure surged and tingled through her.

'Oh Monsieur, Monsieur, whatever ails me?' she gasped, and Rhys thought that he saw genuine astonishment in her pale grey eyes.

'It is only pleasure, my dear,' replied Rhys. 'All pleasure is good, that is a lesson which thou needs must learn if thou art to grow from a comely girl into a beautiful woman.'

'Oh Monsieur, Monsieur, show me what I must do! These feelings, these torments . . . they are more than I can bear . . .'

He took his hands from her breasts and moved them down

over her rustling skirts, feeling the firmness of her body beneath that silk and starched lace petticoats.

'Pull up your skirts for me, Cordelia.'

Hesitantly, Cordelia took hold of the skirt of her dress, and pulled it up a little way, revealing the hem of her petticoat. Rhys squeezed her breast and she shuddered, once again overtaken by need.

'Higher, Cordelia – petticoat *and* skirt. I must see you naked.'

'But, Monsieur . . . my mother . . .'

Rhys feigned impatience, removing his hands from Cordelia's trembling body though he yearned simply to throw her onto her back and take her there and then; anything to ease the terrible ache of need in his painfully swollen prick.

'I am your teacher, Cordelia, not she. Either obey me or dismiss me, but thou shalt not say me nay.'

'I . . . will do as I am bidden, Monsieur.'

He could hear the tremble in her voice as she bent to ruche up her skirts, seizing great drifts of silk and starched cotton lace, hitching them up, baring slender stockinged ankles and calves and thighs . . .

Rhys could scarcely bear the suspense as he watched Cordelia baring herself, inch by agonising inch, each new delight more beautiful and more exciting than the last. He wondered, in the haze of his sensual need, if Melissa could feel it too, this irresistible sexual heat which made all other thoughts, all other sensations, utterly irrelevant.

'Is my nakedness pleasing to the eye, Monsieur?'

Cordelia's voice was almost childlike in its pleading. Rhys looked at her: the long, slim legs, so shapely in their stockings

PARADISE GARDEN

of knitted ivory silk; the white satin garters; the embroidered stocking-tops leading to inches of bare, smooth thigh only slightly darker than the pure ivory of her stockings.

But most beautiful of all was the nakedness between those bare thighs. The mound of Venus, almost bare save for a fuzz of gingery down. Her vulval lips, peachy-pink and soft, the inner lips quite concealed by their plump lobes.

Rhys bent and – to Cordelia's embarrassed delight – planted a kiss between her thighs.

'Thy beauty is a great delight to me.' He paused. 'And now, perhaps, my own nakedness shall please thee.'

He felt for the unfamiliar flap which took the place of flies on his breeches. It was held closed by two hartshorn buttons which took an age to yield. Cordelia, her skirts kilted about her waist and her sex perfectly bare, watched him with round eyes and moist, parted lips as he unfastened the flap and reached inside for the hard branch of his penis.

'Oh . . . Monsieur!'

'Thou has never seen a man naked before?'

'Never! No, never, Monsieur, I swear it.' Her fingers stretched out fleetingly, as though tempted to touch Rhys's prick, but drew back, timorous and trembling.

'Hast thou a fancy to touch my cock, Cordelia?' Rhys asked her. He held it out to her, presenting it to her as though it were a gift, matchlessly beautiful and costly beyond price.

'Monsieur . . . I could not. I must not.'

'Touch it, my sweet. Feel its smoothness between thy pretty fingers.'

With a sigh of delicious capitulation, Cordelia accepted the gift of Rhys's prick, touching it at first with just the very tips of her fingers.

'It is so hard! And yet the skin is so soft, so smooth.' She ran her fingers over its domed head, feeling the slippery wetness oozing from the tip, dripping from it slowly and luxuriously like the warm oil dripping from her breasts. 'Such wetness...'

'Shall I permit thee to taste it?'

'May I...?'

'Taste it, Cordelia. Take a little of the juice upon thy fingers and taste it.'

Hesitantly, Cordelia put her finger to her lips and licked Rhys's sex juice from it with her questing tongue.

'That is the taste of my thirst for thee,' Rhys told her. 'Canst thou taste how strong it is? How strong is thy thirst for me...?'

His fingers stroked their way up Cordelia's inner thighs, moving inexorably towards the secret heart of her sex. Suddenly a little afraid, she tried to close her thighs, but Rhys's determined kisses made her surrender to him, parting her legs yet wider as he reached the object of his quest.

As her legs spread wide, Cordelia's sex lips parted, releasing the sweet, musky odour of her desire. Rhys's heart was racing, his blood boiling and surging in his veins. Her scent was so potent that he almost believed he might ejaculate there and then, so aroused was he by the heady perfume wafting from between Cordelia's thighs.

Her inner sex lips were small compared to the plump and sensual peach of her outer labia. Deep pink and dripping with the clear elixir of her need, they resembled a delicate rose, its frilled petals wet with dew, its fragrance warm and intoxicating. Her clitoris was surprisingly long, a turgid pink stamen rising from the heart of the fleshy petals, begging to be kissed.

He bent to take it between his lips, to tease it with his tongue-tip, to bear her away with him into a world of unending ecstasy . . .

'So, sir! This is the way thou teachest my cousin Cordelia to dance?'

Melissa's voice rang in his ears – proud, sweet, full of a feigned anger which could not quite mask the heavy, husky lilt of sexual arousal. She was walking towards him across the stage, her long primrose-yellow skirts swishing on the ground as she crossed the painted garden, her lips pouting and her large breasts mobile within their tight corsage.

Rhys knew his part and played it to perfection, getting hastily to his feet.

'Madame, I fear I am misunderstood . . .'

'Misunderstood!' snapped Melissa, her blue eyes flashing. 'Others would call it an outrage, Monsieur . . . defiling my virgin cousin's sacred modesty, seducing her into thy lustful debauch . . .'

'I beg of you, Melissa, dear, sweet coz, be not angry,' pleaded Cordelia, getting to her feet and embracing Melissa; but Melissa pushed her away.

'Wretched girl! Wilt thou keep silence?' Melissa turned to Rhys, her voice much softer now, her eyes speaking her desire to him, telling him of the delectable games which they could share with young Cordelia. 'Now, Monsieur, thy explanation for this outrage against decency!'

Rhys bowed, kissing her hand.

'I am your humble servant in all things, Madame. Your humble and most devoted servant. Mademoiselle Cordelia's education is my utmost concern. I was seeking only to enlighten her, to teach her some of the mysteries of the womanhood that buds within her . . .'

'Indeed.' Melissa's expression softened. 'Is this so, Cordelia?'

'It is, sweet coz.'

'And thou hast a mind to learn the mysteries of pleasure?'

'Oh yes, Melissa!'

Melissa held Cordelia's hands very tightly, looking straight into her eyes.

'Lie down on the grass, my dear. Monsieur and I shall fuck thee.'

Cordelia obeyed, sinking down onto the soft green carpet which had been laid across the stage. The audience was hushed, watchful, excited.

Rhys was in heaven. It must be heaven, this ethereal paradise where every desire came true. Cordelia lay stretched out on the stage before him, her skirts thrown up and her breasts bare and glistening with oil. Reality and fantasy were now inseparable in his mind. What world was this — what time, what universe? The universe of dreams?

He knew that Cordelia was an actress, a practised dissembler, and yet, as he lay between her thighs and pushed his cock-tip against her soft pussy mound, he was utterly convinced by the sixteen-year-old virgin lying before him, her body quivering with ecstatic anticipation. Was she real or just a fantasy girl, conjured up by the all-creating power of his desires? He could almost believe that he was making love to her not in the music room at Highmoor House but in the Paradise Garden — and that the year was 1683.

Melissa too was living the dream, rejoicing in its every

second, for soon, surely, they would awake and all this would be gone. It would live on only as a half-forgotten fantasy in the half-light of memory. As she hitched up the skirts of her dress, the embroidered yellow brocade shimmered gold in the smoky lamplight. Her eye caught Sir Roderick's for a fleeting moment and she smiled at him, the gold sovereign still tucked safely away between her breasts; a token of her complete and shameless sexual abandon.

It excited her to know that Sir Roderick was watching as she pulled up her dress, baring creamy thighs and bare, rounded buttocks. It pleased her to know that he was rubbing his cock through his breeches as she knelt over Cordelia's face, her pubis just inches from her eager lips.

There they were now, Rhys and Melissa, face to face across the body of this willing, helpless conquest. And as Rhys pushed into Cordelia's tight vagina and Melissa lowered herself to receive Cordelia's hungry kisses, it seemed that it was not Cordelia that they were seducing, but each other.

'Oh yes, dear coz, suck me harder, harder,' panted Melissa, pulling open her vulval lips so that Cordelia's tongue could penetrate more deeply into her eager haven. 'Make me spend...'

She felt Cordelia's body go rigid as Rhys forced himself into her in a last, hard thrust which took him deep inside. How strange – it felt as though Cordelia really were a blushing young virgin, her body fleetingly rebelling against this brutal invasion before surrendering to the great ocean-deep swell of ecstasy. And it was something that all three lovers felt, their bodies locked together in a curious symbiosis, each feeling the others' sensations, so that the pleasure was threefold and yet still more, so much more . . .

It was then that Melissa really understood. It didn't matter one jot what things *seemed* to be. Because here, in this world of dreams where all desires were fulfilled, everything would always be exactly as she wanted it to be.

Chapter 14

It was quiet on the mountain road above Highmoor – perhaps a little too quiet.

Hardly a blade of grass stirred in the brassy noonday heat. The sun baked down out of a blistering sky, cloudless and unforgiving as burnished metal. A heat haze shimmered over the heather, with just the occasional bumble-bee wandering from stalk to stalk, the drone of its song adding to the timeless monotony of this unchanging scene.

Christopher Maudsley got back into the jeep, trying to jab the key into the ignition with shaking fingers.

Jazz looked at him, concerned. Touching his arm, she felt the tension turning his muscles to bundles of steel wire.

'What's the matter, Chris?'

He looked at her with haunted eyes.

'I saw . . . oh God, I don't know what I saw. Something, nothing.'

Jazz smiled. It was a soothing smile, calming, warm like a caressing hand.

'You're just tired. They'll be in later, you wait and see.'

Maudsley passed his hand over his forehead. It was damp with sweat.

'I wish I understood. All of this is beyond me. Maybe all those stories were right. I have to find some way . . .'

Jazz shook her head, stroking Maudsley's shoulder.

'Some things are best left alone.'

'But, Jazz...'

'Leave it, Chris.' This time her voice carried an authority which forced him to listen. Gently she switched off the ignition and took the keys from his hand, dropping them onto the dashboard. 'Maybe we're not meant to understand. Maybe we're just meant to do what we feel.'

Her hands knew a thousand ways to reawaken desire, stroking his flesh through the leg of his denim jeans. It was burning hot outside but he felt cold, shivery, deeply uneasy. He could feel the tension crackling in the air, the suspense turning an ordinary summer's day into something eerie and unnatural.

Only Jazz's caresses could take that unease away. Earlier, it had been Maudsley who had taken the initiative, obeying a desire so violent and impetuous that he had scarcely recognised himself. Now, Jazz was the strong one and he had become almost childlike in his vulnerability, silently pleading with her for the caresses which would silence his fears.

She looked like a beautiful demon, with her tousled hair and her tanned flesh showing through the tears in her tattered clothes. Had he really done that to her? Had he really left those deep-red scratches all over her breasts in the heat of his passion?

'Don't worry,' she said softly, her voice as smooth as double cream. 'Don't worry. Everything will be fine. There's nothing we can do about it ... just relax.'

She was right, of course. He wondered why he'd never realised before just how sensible Jazz was. Even if the old stories were right, even if something weird really *was* happening to Rhys and Melissa, what the hell could he and

Jazz do about it? Far better just to let things ride, drift with the warm undertow of blissful hunger that was still there within them, waiting to be released.

'Mmm. Yes, oh yes, Jazz. Where did you learn to do that . . . ?'

Her fingers were still on the outside of his jeans, fingering him lightly around the throbbing swell of his balls, teasing him through the rough material. After they'd fucked out on the moor, he hadn't bothered to put his boxer-shorts back on and each light caress was intensified tenfold by the sensation of rough denim and metal rubbing against the naked flesh beneath.

His cock did not become erect immediately. Had it done so, he would probably have spurted instantly into her hand, so skilful and light and seductive was her touch. No, she kept his desire in abeyance for what seemed an eternity, stimulating him so that his penis swelled just a little, but remained only semi-erect, tormenting him with desires and sensations to which he could not yet respond.

It was the sweetest torment, designed to drive any man out of his mind with lust. Lascivious images tormented Maudsley's mind – strange, inexplicable images of days gone by, men and women in period costume stripping each other, fucking like beasts . . .

'Harder,' he gasped, laying his hand on top of Jazz's and trying to make her grip him more tightly. But she resisted him with gentle insistence.

'I want you to be really ready for me,' she told him.

'I *am* . . . I want you . . . oh Jazz, for pity's sake . . .!'

'Just be patient. I know what I'm doing, believe me I do.'

Maudsley didn't doubt it for a moment. He wouldn't call himself inexperienced but he had never had such practised fingers on his cock before. Without even touching bare flesh, without even making him erect, Jazz was giving him more pleasure than most women had given him with all the divine wetness of their sex.

When at last she did unbutton his jeans, he could have cried out for pure joy. The sensations in his poor, tormented manhood were so intense and so turbulent that he wondered if he would be able to bear the touch of her fingers on his flesh.

That touch was very nearly magical. At the very first contact, his cock reared in an electric tingle of pleasure, the flesh growing, swelling, hardening; the rich blue veins on the underside standing proud beneath the silky-smooth pink skin. Her fingers skated lightly and lovingly over the flesh, forming a loose ring about its girth, sliding up and down, skimming and brushing the flesh and making it ache for a more brutal, but less cruel, form of stimulation.

He wanted to reciprocate with caresses of his own, wanted to undress her and take her, the way he had done out on the moor. But now the positions had been reversed and instead of being the lust-crazed beast, he had become the trembling adolescent, the neophyte rendered utterly helpless by the power of his own desire.

Jazz drew back for a moment, taking her fingers from his cock. He let out a quiet sob of loss, reaching out and seizing her by the wrist, his eyes pleading with her.

'No, Jazz, please don't stop. You don't know what you're doing to me.'

Extricating herself from his grasp, she wriggled out of

her leather jacket and slung it over the back of the seat. Her bustier was practically in tatters, her breasts showing through the soft, torn leather, but she took that off too, unhooking it and dropping it on the floor. Maudsley looked in an agony of frustration at her small breasts, standing proud, their nipples pert and hard and almost menacing in their aggressive display of appetite.

He moved to undress but she shook her head.

'No need.'

A kind of voluptuous warmth bathed his body as she bent over him, her breath forming a moist, hot cloud about his bare flesh. For an age she did nothing but take the tip of his cock into her mouth, her lips not even touching it, but forming a wide O about it, and her breath adding to the moisture which already flooded from its tip.

The torrid noonday heat was as nothing compared to the burning in Maudsley's loins, the inferno of desire crying out for gratification. And when Jazz began licking his cocktip, Maudsley felt tears rising to his eyes. How many years was it since he had wept? More than he cared to remember. But now the tears were spilling out, running down his cheeks, the symbol of a joyful agony.

He was so aroused that he might have expected to come almost instantaneously but Jazz Summersdale knew better than to let her lovers spurt before she wanted them to. Besides, today she was inspired . . .

Up and down his shaft ran her tongue, leaving a thin, cooling trail of saliva which only served to intensify his desire. There was no release, no relief from this sensual servitude.

He clutched at her cropped hair, twisting and turning the

strands around his fingers. If it was painful, she did not seem to mind. Jazz too was lost, completely absorbed in this game of sensual torment. Her lips and tongue worked at his erect cock, licking, sucking, teasing with an infinite lightness which augmented but never satisfied his desire.

Just when he thought he could take no more, she withdrew from him, sliding his cock out from the tight sheath of her lips with a suddenness which left her bereft.

She smiled up at his crestfallen face.

'Don't worry. Everything's all right. Just you wait . . .'

She was holding her breasts, one in either hand, kneading and stroking them.

'Aren't they beautiful, Chris? You love them, don't you? You love to suck and bite my nipples.'

'Beautiful,' murmured Maudsley, letting his fingers play over the small, firm globes. 'Just so beautiful.'

'How would you like to feel them wrapped around your dick?'

He did not reply in words, his only reply a great shuddering sigh as Jazz bent over him and slid his cock-shaft into the valley between her breasts.

They were not large breasts but their firm and juicy flesh formed a perfect haven for his manhood, pressing tightly against it as she squeezed them together, forming a narrow tunnel lubricated with her sweat and with his own sex-juice.

She talked to him as she fucked him with her breasts, talked his desire to bursting-point and kept it there, refusing to offer him any release.

'You like it, don't you, Chris? You like having my tits wrapped round your dick?'

Maudsley moaned wordlessly, twisting and turning in his

seat, utterly subjected to the desire which was ravaging his body and his soul.

'I know you like it, Chris, 'cause I can feel you getting harder, did you know that? You have such a nice firm cock. Lovely and long and it fits so perfectly between my nice firm tits.'

'Jazz, you're driving me crazy. I swear if you don't make me come, I'll go mad . . .'

He watched the way her tits changed shape as she slid them over and around his cock, bulging into fat globes as she pushed them down and his cock-tip emerged, purplish and slippery with wetness; then sliding back up to cover his sex completely, imprisoning it within her soft and covetous flesh.

Then she made his torment even worse, sticking out her tongue and lapping at his glans each time it emerged from between her breasts. He couldn't stand it much longer, he really couldn't. But on the other hand, he wanted this whole episode to go on for ever. He wondered how it would be to spend his whole life fucking – eternity even – just to be here, bathed in the warmth of a massive orgasm which was building up inside his belly, his balls, the base of his shaft.

'Lovely, isn't it, Chris? It's lovely having my slippery-wet tits sliding all over your cock.'

'Jazz, for crying out loud, make me come, I can't stand it much longer!'

'Lovely,' repeated Jazz, putting out her tongue and winding it about the very tip of her lover's erect cock. 'Lovely and salty your cock is, Chris. I could drink down every drop of your spunk.'

Maudsley could do little to bring himself off but he began

moving his hips, thrusting hard so that Jazz was forced to wank him faster. The tunnel of love between her breasts was silky-smooth and warm, every bit as wonderful as the tightness of her dripping sex. In some respects it was even better, because when they fucked this way, he could see *everything*: his cock sliding between her breasts, the way her breast-flesh quivered and distorted into a hundred different, breathtakingly beautiful shapes, the swollen head of his cock, emerging from between her tits, each time a little closer to the apotheosis.

Jazz's words were scarcely more than a whisper now, but they entered his very soul, seemed to stroke his flesh like a lover's shameless fingers.

'If I let you come all over my breasts, Chris, will you take me in the arse? Will you, Chris? Say you will . . .'

He groaned in sudden distress, the pain of pleasure too great, the burning torrent of semen at last pouring forth from him in long, abundant spurts.

The creamy-white fluid gushed and spattered out of him and still Jazz held him tight between her breasts, laughing and sighing with delight as the thick, pearly droplets landed on breasts and face and throat and hair, trickling down over her bare flesh like melted ice-cream.

'Fuck me in the arse, Chris,' she whispered, putting out her long cat's-tongue and licking semen off her own breast.

And Christopher Maudsley knew, in that very instant, that he would do whatever Jazz wanted him to.

Rhys and Melissa left the noisy festivities of the music room behind them as they stepped through the door and found themselves back in the kitchen.

But this was neither the kitchen they were familiar with, nor the kitchen they had seen before, with its calendar proclaiming '1885'. This was something much, much older – older even than the last room they had visited.

'We must have moved back in time again,' gasped Melissa, looking down at the heavy clothes she was wearing. Both she and Rhys were dressed in a dun-coloured woollen fabric – Melissa in a heavy-skirted dress over a coarse linen camisole, with a white cap over her hair, and Rhys in a sort of jerkin and leggings.

They gazed around the kitchen. It was deserted, but in the huge open hearth an entire pig was hanging on a spit over an immense log fire, filling the room with the richly aromatic scent of sizzling, spitting pork. On the long wooden table were arranged great piles and platters and baskets of food: fruit, meat, fish, poultry, bread – everything laid out as if for some great feast.

Quite suddenly and unexpectedly, Melissa began to laugh.

'It's *our* dream,' she said, holding Rhys very close. 'All ours!'

He put his strong arms around her.

'So . . . ?'

'So we can do anything we like. *Anything* – understand?'

'Ah.' Rhys pulled down one shoulder of Melissa's camisole and gently nipped the flesh between his teeth. 'And what have you in mind, my hot little vixen?'

Melissa turned round, surveying the vast array of food set out on the long oak kitchen table. Some of it had been cooked and arranged on wooden or metal dishes, other items of food seemed in the midst of being prepared. On impulse, she picked up a heavy earthenware jug of rough, sweet cider.

Raising it to her lips, she took a long draught of the powerful brew, then lifted it, very deliberately, a little higher, so that the contents of the jug spilled over the side and went trickling and gushing down over her face, her throat, the front of her dress.

Rhys felt more than a flicker of interest as he watched the coarse fabric of Melissa's dress turn a deeper brown and cling to the curves of her body. How it excited him to see how the wet woollen stuff caressed the stiff points of her nipples, the generous domes of her full and heavy breasts.

Excited beyond belief, he seized another jug – this time filled with mulled red wine – and emptied it over the front of Melissa's dress. Now the whole of the front of her dress was soaked through, and rivulets of cold cider and warm wine were trickling down over her arms, her breasts, into the deep valley of her cleavage, adding the sweet aromas of apples and musky cinnamon to the fragrance of the roasting meat.

Her bodice was laced at the front and it was an easy task to slit the laces with a rusty old kitchen knife. Then it was a matter of seconds to pull down her loose white camisole, exposing her breasts.

Shrieking with laughter, Melissa spun round and ran away from him, her wet breasts glistening in the firelight. Reaching the end of the table, she found a huge bowl of soft curd cheese and, seizing great handfuls of it, she started flinging them at Rhys. He ducked but she caught him on the face and hair with the second handful, then on the jerkin and breeches.

'Just wait till I catch you!' he laughed, his ribs aching with mirth. 'I'll . . .'

'Ah, but you'll have to catch me first!'

She dodged out of his way, knocking over a pail of warm milk which spread out across the rush-covered floor in a large, white pool. A chicken scuttled away, then a rat, bolting for cover as a thin tabby-cat set off in pursuit of it, disappearing into the shadows. Then Melissa caught her foot and stumbled, reaching out to catch hold of the table.

'Got you!'

Rhys caught hold of her and wrestled her into submission, their eyes meeting and a powerful surge of desire passing between them.

'So what *are* you going to do to me, then?' Melissa demanded defiantly.

'I'm going to make you pay for your insolence, you shameless hussy!'

Rhys spied a bowl of ripe and juicy peaches lying within arm's reach and picked one up. It was so ripe that it yielded instantly to the touch, the flesh soft and squishy. With a predatory growl, he crushed it against Melissa's bare white breast. She squealed in protest, wriggling and kicking, but he was not going to be deterred by her struggles . . . in fact, they only excited him more, inciting him to further liberties.

Another peach. Squeeze, crush; watch those gobbets of juicy flesh dripping down over her breasts, flesh and juice mingling, the sweet stickiness seasoned by the salty trickle of her sweat.

One by one, he crushed the fruits over Melissa's breasts, massaging the soft, sticky flesh and delighting in the luxurious softness of flesh on juicy flesh.

'Peaches for a peach,' he murmured, and all of a sudden he grabbed hold of Melissa, lifting her up and practically throwing her onto the kitchen table. Pots and pans and dishes scattered and clattered in all directions, a pitcher of ale tipping over and soaking Melissa's white cap as she lay kicking and shrieking with laughter on her belly on the table-top.

'Beast!' she screeched.

'Hussy!'

Rhys pulled up her skirts without further ado and exposed the round full moons of her backside. My, but she was irresistible, even dressed in these coarse woollen rags. She wore no petticoat, no knickers, nothing but her own bare skin, white and unblemished underneath the rough serving wench's dress.

Picking up the largest and juiciest of all the peaches, Rhys crushed it on Melissa's bum cheeks, the sweet flesh soothing and the grittiness of the stone abrading her delicate skin. He pulled apart her buttocks and saw the secret heart of her desire, concealed within the dark valley between the fleshy globes. But there were no secrets from him. Taking up the last of the peaches, he squeezed and squashed it right into the crack of her backside, making sure that it was full to the brim with juice and crushed fruit-flesh.

The feel of the peach stone rubbing along the crease of her backside had the effect of reawakening Melissa's desire. Despite the indignity of her position, she found herself striving to open herself still further to her lover, longing for more intimate caresses. At the touch of his fingertip on her secret gate it opened wide, begging him to enter in, forgetting all its coy resistance.

Cream. There was a jug brim-full of thick, country cream on the table, just within reach of Rhys's right hand. He was quite sure it hadn't been there before – but then, that was the thing about this most superior of erotic dreams. Whatever you wished for, whatever your heart or your body might desire, all you had to do was imagine it and there it was, at your command.

He picked it up and inverted it over Melissa's backside. The cool cream fell in a white waterfall over her buttocks and into the valley between, soothing, awakening, arousing.

'Oh Rhys, Rhys, whatever are you doing!' cried Melissa, trying in vain to skew her head round.

'Peaches . . . and cream,' whispered Rhys, dribbling the very last of the cream onto his lover's welcoming flesh.

'Rhys. Oh, that feels so . . . strange, yet so good . . .'

'I bet they taste good too,' commented Rhys, the huskiness of sensual excitement in his voice.

In this dream, you could do anything, Rhys told himself. Anything at all. Even things you wouldn't normally dream of doing.

He bent to kiss Melissa's backside, lapping at the mingled cream and peach juice covering her skin. But he did not stop there, hungry to sup at the secret well of her sex.

Her arse had turned to a little lake of creamy fluid, marbled with the pale gold of peach juice. Rhys began to lick at it, touching sometimes only the cream, more often the flesh beneath, receptive and sensitive, twitching and tensing at his touch.

As he drank away the cream and the peach juice, he discovered the beauty of the secret glade beneath, the deep valley leading in one direction to the well-spring of Melissa's vagina but, just above him, to the matchless beauty of her perfect arse.

Aurelia Clifford

He could not resist. His desire drove him beyond endurance. He thrust his tongue into the very heart of Melissa's amber rose, penetrating her with deep sword-thrusts which set her crying and writhing with pleasure. His hands clutched tightly at her buttocks, holding them far apart whilst he buried his face between them, alternately lapping and thrusting with his tongue.

How could anything taste so good? How could he possibly have missed this glorious pleasure, this forbidden yet exquisite delight? He could scarcely believe the excitement he was deriving from licking her out, his cock hard and ready in his pants, his head reeling with the divinely mingled scents of his lover's most secret intimacy.

Anything. They could do anything they wanted, anything they dreamed . . .

'Rhys. Oh Rhys, won't you put your dick inside me? Won't you take me in the arse?'

Melissa's voice was soft and quavery, her body yielding now. She had long since ceased to struggle. He could smell the sweet honeydew oozing from her sex, the sweat trickling over her body as the heat from the fire flared up and the desire boiled and crackled within her.

He felt for his cock, pulling it from his leggings, sliding on top of her on the table, amid the mess of cream and crushed fruit and spilt ale. But he did not notice the chaos around them, only the beauty of Melissa's body and her voice purring mellifluously to him:

'Please, Rhys. Do it to me. Do it to me now . . .'

'Yes. YES!' He speared her flesh with his cock-spike, the heavy table creaking and rattling beneath them as he pushed his hardness deep inside her, right up to the hilt.

What remained of the cream and the peach juice added to the lubrication dripping from his prick and made their coupling silken-smooth and so, so blissful that he might have been fucking some warm, soft cloud.

Melissa's flesh closed about him, caressing tenderly, almost timorously, like a virgin's lips. His cock felt immensely swollen, with twice its normal sensitivity, and each thrust brought some new wave of sensation, some desperate pleasure which threatened to push him over the edge of his self-control.

Beneath him, Melissa squirmed and wriggled and moaned, each movement of her buttocks or hips provoking a turmoil of excitement in his loins, each low, whimpering cry from her pouting lips arousing him almost to the point of no return. Her hair was bedraggled from the spilt ale and cream, white creamy gobbets trickling down the tangled yellow strands, like freshly cooling sperm. He wondered, as they fucked, how it would feel to fuck her hair; to wrap long tendrils of that corn-gold mane about his dick and thrust into it until the semen rose up his shaft, spitting like snake venom into the warm and fragrant mass of hair.

'Oh darling, rub my clit, please . . . I can't bear it . . .'

Melissa's voice was a sob of desperate need and that desperation itself hardened his member to the smooth stiffness of carved ivory. Propping herself up on her arms, she raised her buttocks a little off the table, and he succeeded in slipping his hand underneath her.

Her maidenhair was damp with a mixture of her own pleasure juices and the wine which had soaked through her dress. He stroked her as he might stroke a pet cat, smoothly and sensually, making her arch her back and sigh with pleasure. Then he pushed his fingers through the outer lobes of her sex and felt the full force of her passion as her wetness gushed from her, soaking his fingers.

The flower stalk of Melissa's clitoris was slippery with juice, and almost eluded his attempts to capture it between his fingers – made still more difficult by the jerky movements of her hips as she pushed herself against his groin, filling herself up with his stiff lingam.

At last the prize was his and his efforts were rewarded with a sob of agonised pleasure as he began gently wanking Melissa's hard, smooth nubbin.

'Ah. Ah yes. Yes, yes, please don't stop . . .'

'I won't ever stop,' gasped Rhys. 'Not until you're screaming for mercy and I'm filling your beautiful backside with my jism . . .'

'Tell me again. Tell me what you're doing to me.' Melissa's whole body reared off the table as she forced herself back onto the hardened spike of Rhys's penis.

'I'm buggering you, my darling. My dick is in your arse and I'm fucking you. Oh, do you know how good it feels? Like a wet silk glove about my dick. How does it feel to have me inside you?'

'It feels . . . oh, oh! It feels . . . like paradise.'

The last word escaped from her in an almost imperceptible sigh as, very suddenly, her body tensed then relaxed, massive spasms of ecstasy overwhelming her as her womanhood flooded with juice and the muscles of her arse tensed in sympathy with her orgasm.

That slight tensing of her arse was all that was needed to turn Rhys's intense pleasure into a sublime ecstasy which left him speechless, helpless, the puppet of his own body's tyrannical need. He spurted into her, his hands clawing at her bare flesh as he drowned in pleasure and the whole world drowned with him.

At last he slid off her, his dick still hard but his desperate need temporarily sated. Melissa rolled sideways, pressing her mouth against his, wrapping her bare thighs about him.

When Rhys opened his eyes, he saw that they were no longer alone in the kitchen. Two figures were standing just inside the doorway, side by side. They were a man and a woman, naked and masked, but as Rhys sat up, bidding Melissa to do the same, they uncovered their faces, smiling, stretching out their arms in an embrace of welcome.

'Maia . . . ?' gasped Melissa.

'Jim – is it really you? No, it can't be . . .'

Rhys gripped her hand tightly and they got up off the table.

'Remember, Melissa, it's just a dream. Isn't that so, Maia? Just a dream . . .'

The woman was beckoning to them.

'Come with us.' It was Maia's voice, no doubt about it – that same, syrupy, sexy drawl which had lovers throwing themselves at her feet.

'Don't be afraid,' said Jim. 'Come on, it's all right.'

'I . . . OK.' Rhys stepped forward. 'Why not?' But Melissa hung back.

'What's going on, Rhys?'

He kissed her.

'I told you, darling. It's just a dream. A wonderful dream where we can do whatever we choose. Come on, let's follow them. I want to see what happens next.'

They followed Maia and Jim through the doorway and

out into a passageway lit with flickering candles. Before them, a dark spiral staircase wound up into the darkness.

'Up there? You want us to go up there?' Rhys looked questioningly at Jim. Maia handed him a candle, then gave one to Melissa.

'We must leave you now. But we will meet again.' Maia kissed first Melissa, then Rhys, her lips fiery-hot in the cool darkness of the stairwell. 'We will be waiting for you.'

Seconds later, she and Jim had vanished, and Rhys and Melissa found themselves climbing the stone staircase into the darkness.

Chapter 15

They stepped through the door at the top of the stairs and into the room beyond.

It was almost a disappointment.

'It's our own bedroom!' exclaimed Melissa, standing in the middle of the room and gazing at the familiar furnishings – the Chinese rug she had blown two months' wages on, the horrible porcelain statuette they had been given as a housewarming present, the Deco vase of roses, freshly cut that very morning from the Paradise Garden. And in the very centre of it all, the ancient oak four-poster, looking very inviting and just a little exotic in the candlelight.

'I told you it was a dream,' Rhys reassured her. 'Look – even the old clothes have gone.'

They were dressed as they had been that morning, in the garden. White shorts, cotton body, scuffed denims . . . it all seemed so normal, mundane even, after the sexual adventures they had lived out in their imagination.

'Let's go to bed,' Rhys suggested, unzipping Melissa's shorts as they sank down onto the soft velvet bedspread together. 'There are a few things I dreamed of doing that I'd like to do to you again.'

'Rhys . . .'

'Mmm?' He left off kissing Melissa's neck for a few moments to gaze deep into her eyes.

'If this is a dream . . .'

'Which it is.'

'... whose dream is it – yours or mine?'

The thought silenced Rhys for a split second, then he smiled.

'I'm yours and you're mine.'

'But Rhys, that doesn't make sense...'

He gently stripped the cotton body down over her shoulders, exposing the fullness of Melissa's breasts.

'Does it really matter? Relax, Melissa. Just relax and enjoy what I'm going to do to you.'

And really, Melissa told herself, Rhys was right. What did it matter? Maybe Rhys was just a part of her dream, a sensual fantasy conjured up by her subconscious to give her body greater pleasure.

And what pleasure! As they lay together on the bed, not even bothering to slide under the sheets, the same delicious desire crept over her again, as it had done countless times since the dream began. That was perhaps the surest proof that this *was* a dream: for desire just wasn't like that in real life. An appetite, once satisfied, was stilled. But not here, not now. Here, in the warmth of this perfect dream, they could fuck and go on fucking for ever – and it need never stop until the moment when she woke.

It was daylight when Melissa awoke with sunlight pouring through the curtains, caressing her bare, golden skin.

She lay where she had fallen asleep, her head on Rhys's chest, his arm curled about her shoulders. The room seemed filled with fragrance: the spicy, musky aroma of their mingled sex, the dewy freshness of the morning air, the heady perfume of roses, surrounding them like a cloud of sweetness.

Smoothing her hand down Rhys's belly, she felt him stir, and heard him murmur his pleasure at her caress.

'Oh, Melissa, you're a witch.' He passed his hand over his eyes, rubbing away the sleep. 'Did I dream all that . . . ?'

'If you did, so did I.'

'The Regency bucks . . . fucking some woman in the middle of a play . . . the kitchen . . .'

'The peaches and cream,' added Melissa with a knowing smile.

'You? You remember it too? But that's crazy. How can two people dream the same dream?'

'That's what I said, remember?'

'Yes.' Rhys's voice was a wondering whisper. 'Yes, I do remember.'

He sat up and was just about to get off the bed and draw the curtains when sounds began to fill the room. Birdsong, clear and sweet; music, light as a zephyr and so, so sensual that it made him want to gather Melissa up in his arms and possess her body, again, again, again.

Rhys and Melissa exchanged looks, no longer understanding, lost in the sudden eroticism of the moment. Their hands reached out to caress each other's bodies, touching bare flesh as though for the very first time, discovering, delighting, rejoicing.

'Come. It is time now.'

The woman's voice, though sweet and low, filled the room, surrounded them with its coaxing warmth.

'What?' Startled, Rhys looked around for the source of the voice but they were still alone.

'You must come now. Don't be afraid. We have been waiting for you for so long.'

Melissa turned towards the sound of the voice and saw the bedroom door begin to open, very slowly, very mysteriously.

'Who . . . who is it? Who's there?'

'Come, Rhys. Come, Melissa. Do not delay. We are waiting, waiting, waiting.'

Suddenly, in a flood of the brightest golden light, the door swung inwards. They found themselves drawn towards the light, although they could scarcely make out anything in the fierce glare, only a few moving shadows.

Melissa's hand was in Rhys's and she pressed herself against him, her heart pounding and her body singing with exhilaration as though in anticipation of something unknown but utterly, unbelievably beautiful.

They scarcely noticed the moment at which the room they had just left dissolved and disappeared. They were aware only of what lay before and around them, the fierce sun-glow which began to fade to a mellower gold, revealing wonders beyond their understanding.

They found themselves standing in the Paradise Garden. But it was not as they remembered it, hemmed in by high walls. The walls had disappeared and the garden seemed to stretch on for ever, its trees and knots and flowers fading into far-distant hills, its verdant beauty ordered, yet untamed.

Huge butterflies danced among flowers of brilliant blue and softest pink, the span of their wings broader than a man's outstretched hand. As they paused to sip nectar from the trumpet-shaped flowers of tropical orchids, Melissa saw how their colours shimmered through a spectrum of iridescent hues.

Exotic fruits hung from espaliers and vines: mango and

papaya and passion fruit adding their fragrance and colour to the purple of succulent grapes and the soft hues of peach and nectarine and quince.

Scents filled the garden – the spicy, warm fragrance of bay and sage, thyme and lemon verbena; a thousand natural perfumes rising from the sun-warmed leaves of the many knot-gardens arranged between and among the winding alleyways and shady, leafy nooks where lovers might share and explore their passion in perfect seclusion.

Tree-lined avenues led into the distance, beyond the familiar shape of the summerhouse and past a wonderful fountain where a naked girl was washing herself, letting the cooling water trickle down over her upturned face.

There were other shapes too, moving out of the shadows and into the sunlight. Some were strangers, others . . . others they remembered from their dream. Lord Highmoor, Cissy and Alexander, Lady Darnleigh, Sir Roderick and the beautiful Cordelia . . . even the two lovers they had glimpsed that night, long ago, at the Black Lion Inn.

Rhys stepped back, suddenly afraid. For he had recognised other faces from the newspaper articles he had read at the library. Blurred and yellowed the old photographs may have been, but there could be no mistaking the faces of the two young teachers who had disappeared from Highmoor just over a year ago . . .

They were smiling, walking towards Rhys and Melissa, their hands outstretched.

'Welcome.'

To her surprise, Melissa found herself responding, accepting the touch of their hands, joining with them in their sweet laughter.

'Melissa, are you sure . . . ?'

She turned and beckoned to Rhys.

'It's all right, don't you see? This is all part of the dream. Isn't it the most beautiful thing you've ever seen? Doesn't it make you feel . . . as if you could fuck and fuck and never stop?'

Rhys joined Melissa and together they were led along a tree-lined path, their bare feet cushioned by crimson flowers which released their heady scent like wafting incense.

Yes, he felt it too. How could he not? Sex was in the very air he breathed, in the soft flowers and grasses whose leaves and petals brushed against his bare skin, sending frissons of pleasure running through his body. His cock was hard, harder than he could believe possible, his mind filled with thoughts and images of sensual beauty . . . but none so intoxicating as the sight of Melissa, walking naked through the Paradise Garden.

At the end of the tree-lined pathway, two figures stepped out to greet them.

'We've been waiting for you,' smiled Maia, taking Rhys by the hand. He made no protest, for his body ached with a delicious need. Melissa felt Jim's arm snake around her waist and she felt the old desire return – the feeling that had all but overwhelmed her at the dinner party, that night when Maia and Jim had so mysteriously walked out of their lives. Only this time, Melissa realised that all her guilt and all her resistance had gone, leaving only the desire.

'Waiting for such a long time.' Jim kissed Melissa's throat and ran his fingers over her breasts, his touch erecting the nipples into crests of almost painful longing. 'We were beginning to wonder if you would ever come. But you're here now...'

'... And you're going to be so happy here. So happy, just like we are.' Maia led Rhys towards the summerhouse, and Melissa and Jim followed.

'Where are you taking us?' asked Melissa.

'To meet someone. Someone who will help you understand what all of this is about.'

There were two people in the summerhouse. Rhys and Melissa had never met either of them before but they recognised them both instantly. It was impossible... but what did that matter? This was a dream and, in a dream, everything is within the scope of your desires.

The man was tall, dark and broad-shouldered, magnificent in his black velvet doublet, embroidered with silver thread. He took Melissa's hand and kissed it, graciously, seductively. As he looked into her astonished face his dark eyes seemed to search and possess her very soul.

'Welcome, Melissa,' he said, smiling. 'Welcome to the Paradise Garden.'

'But...' Melissa felt her face draining of colour. 'Fairfax... Reuben Fairfax?'

Quite unperturbed by Melissa's astonishment, Fairfax drew his lady forward, smiling at her as she presented herself to them with a deep curtsey. She was far more beautiful than she had appeared in her portrait – her raven-black hair glossy and abundant, her creamy skin flawless and her lips full and sensual.

'Perdita...' gasped Rhys, overcome by the beauty of the young woman before him. This woman who did not, who *could* not, exist.

'You are surprised?' Fairfax did not wait for their reply. 'Of course you are. But your fears will soon turn to pleasure . . . if you remain here with us.'

'Remain here?' Rhys looked puzzled. 'In a dream?'

Fairfax chuckled, his fine dark eyes sparkling.

'This is no dream, my dear Rhys. It is no idle phantasm, fragile and fleeting. The Paradise Garden exists and it shall exist for as long as there are lovers at Highmoor House.'

'But this garden . . .' began Rhys. 'It can't be the Paradise Garden, it looks so different . . .'

'Let me explain. More than four hundred years ago, my mistress and I came to Highmoor, where I built the house as a love-gift to her. The Paradise Garden I created as a symbol of our union and a haven from the world, where our pleasure might be enacted in the most perfect seclusion.

'But the world is cold and cruel, Rhys. There was great hatred and suspicion of us in Highmoor, for I was an alchemist and sorcerer, and there were rumours of witchcraft and the black arts.

'In time, we sought a more perfect escape from the world. But it was only by chance that I discovered the way . . . the way to create another Paradise Garden, a magical place, perfect in every respect, beyond the reach of the material world. A realm where pleasure might reign for ever.'

Melissa turned and gazed at the garden, its beauty indeed perfect beneath a cornflower-blue sky.

'Seasons never change here, Melissa. Our bodies never age, our beauty never fades. Only our pleasures change. Eternity is a long, long time to explore pleasure, Melissa. And now we have others to explore it with us. Now we have you.'

She turned back and looked at Fairfax.

'Is this real, or is it a dream?'

'It is no dream. But it is beyond reality, a mirror image, if you wish. In this realm there is no care but pleasure.'

'Why have you brought us here?' asked Rhys.

'We drew you to Highmoor House because we saw the sensual power within you. We knew that you would rediscover the Paradise Garden and begin restoring it to its former beauty. It was inevitable that, through the sorcery of your own sensual power, you would discover the gateway to this true garden and come to us to become our sensual companions. You have discovered the gateway to Paradise and passed through its many tests and trials to win the right to remain here.'

Rhys looked out over the shimmering beauty of the garden, stretching as far as the eye could see – at the couples embracing naked in the sunshine and bathing together in the sunken pools.

'For ever? You're trying to tell us that this will last for ever?'

'For as long as the garden at Highmoor House continues to exist,' replied Perdita. 'For our own paradise is focused upon it, deriving its power from the spell cast within its walls.'

'To live forever in perfect pleasure,' said Fairfax. 'That is your choice, my dear friends. You may return to your own lives, to the toil and disappointment of your former existences, or you may elect to remain here with us, in the Paradise Garden. But understand this, my children: once your choice is made, you may never leave.'

Rhys and Melissa looked at each other. They did not need

to speak. The pleasure within them was so strong that it needed no expression but the language of kisses and caresses. Their desire had already made its choice.

EPILOGUE

Peter Galliano followed the estate agent out of the dining room and back into the hallway.

'You didn't say why the owners were selling,' he remarked.

'They... er, moved away quite suddenly,' replied Maudsley, slightly jittery about being back at Highmoor House. He still hadn't got over that day, six months ago, when he'd come up to the house to try and find Rhys and Melissa. They hadn't been there that day – or the next, or the one after that.

'So where did they go?'

'I'm sorry, sir, I haven't a clue. They just sort of... went.'

In fact, they'd never come back at all. Now Maudsley's agency had been instructed to sell the property and he didn't even know who by.

'It's cold in here, Peter,' complained Candice, following Galliano out into the hallway.

'It won't be, not when I've had the underfloor heating installed. Don't you worry, Candice, you won't recognise this place once it's been converted into a management-training centre.'

Since Melissa's sudden disappearance, six months ago to the day, Galliano had gradually lost interest in taking over Jupiter International. It had been quite a shock to the system, being forced to acknowledge how much that girl had bewitched him, and he'd realised that what he needed now was a new challenge.

So he'd decided to set up his own sales training consultancy. It would be a big success – everything he ever did was a success... if you didn't count his attempts to make Melissa Montagu his mistress. Even in this new venture, he hadn't been able to get her out of his mind. He'd tried everything to track her down – even employed a private detective to find her, but nothing.

When he'd seen Melissa's old house in North Yorkshire advertised in the Saturday paper, he'd at first dismissed the idea as romantic nonsense. Let's face it, you didn't buy a house just because someone you had the hots for had once lived there. But the more he'd thought about it, the more sensible it had seemed. It would be cheap, so he'd get a good deal. It was somewhere attractive and had plenty of land to build sports facilities and the like. Yeah, it might just work.

But that wasn't the real reason why he was going to buy it. The minute he'd stepped inside the house he'd felt as though Melissa were just a whisper away, as though her blue eyes were watching him, catlike, from the shadows. Almost as if he might just turn round and see her smiling at him, stripping off her blouse, offering her bare breasts for him to kiss...

'It'll need a lot of work doing on it,' remarked Galliano, beginning the spiel he had prepared to beat Maudsley down to a decent price.

'Yes, I suppose it will,' Maudsley agreed. 'The west wing needs a new roof and there's a bit of dry rot in the library.' Galliano could scarcely believe what he was hearing. Where was all that 'bijou residence' crap so beloved of estate agents?

'I won't beat about the bush. The price is too high.'

Maudsley shrugged.

'Fair enough. Apparently the client is prepared to be very flexible for a quick sale. How about ten thousand less?'

Galliano blinked in astonishment.

'*Ten* thousand?'

'Or more . . . if it's a problem.'

Galliano swallowed hard.

'My lawyers will be in touch to negotiate a mutually acceptable figure.' He paused, his head spinning, trying to remember what he'd meant to say. 'Ah yes, Mr Maudsley – planning permission. I take it there won't be any problem about my building one or two leisure facilities in the grounds?'

'Shouldn't be. As you know, one of the previous owners was a hotel group which planned quite extensive works.'

'Good. That tatty old walled garden will have to go, for a start.' Galliano did not notice Maudsley's eyebrows twitch almost to his hairline. 'It's been let go, these last six months – and the site would make a great place for the swimming pool.'

'No, Peter, don't do that.' Galliano was surprised to feel Candice slipping her arm through his, hugging him to her so that he felt the hard points of her breasts through her suit. Spiritually speaking, there was sod all between him and Candice, but physically . . . 'Mr Maudsley was telling me it's a real Elizabethan garden. Why don't you let me take charge of it? We could get people in to help restore it to the way it was.'

'Well, I suppose . . .'

'Oh, go on, Peter. It would be a real attraction for visitors. And just think of the parties we could hold there.' She treated Maudsley to a flirty smile. 'Let's have a huge housewarming party there in the summer, when it's all finished. We could invite lots of people. What do you say, Mr Maudsley? Will you come?'

A Message from the Publisher

Headline Liaison is a new concept in erotic fiction: a list of books designed for the reading pleasure of both men and women, to be read alone – or together with your lover. As such, we would be most interested to hear from our readers.

Did you read the book with your partner? Did it fire your imagination? Did it turn you on – or off? Did you like the story, the characters, the setting? What did you think of the cover presentation? In short, what's your opinion? If you care to offer it, please write to:

> The Editor
> Headline Liaison
> 338 Euston Road
> London NW1 3BH

Or maybe you think you could do better if you wrote an erotic novel yourself. We are always on the lookout for new authors. If you'd like to try your hand at writing a book for possible inclusion in the Liaison list, here are our basic guidelines: We are looking for novels of approximately 80,000 words in which the erotic content should aim to please both men and women and should not describe illegal sexual activity (pedophilia, for example). The novel should contain sympathetic and interesting characters, pace, atmosphere and an intriguing plotline.

If you'd like to have a go, please submit to the Editor a sample of at least 10,000 words, clearly typed on one side of the paper only, together with a short resumé of the storyline. Should you wish your material returned to you please include a stamped addressed envelope. If we like it sufficiently, we will offer you a contract for publication.

Also available from LIAISON, the intoxicating new erotic imprint for lovers everywhere

SLEEPLESS NIGHTS

Tom Crewe & Amber Wells

While trying to capture the evening light in a Cotswold field, photographer Emma Hadleigh is intrigued to discover she has an audience. And David Casserley is the kind of audience any smart young woman might be intrigued by – he's charming, he's attractive and he's sensational when it comes to making love in a cornfield. What's more, like her, he's single. But single doesn't necessarily mean unattached. And, as they are both about to discover, former lovers and present intrigues can cast a long shadow over future happiness . . .

0 7472 5055 3

THE JOURNAL

James Allen

Before she married Hugo, Gina used to let her hair down – especially in the bedroom. And though she loves her husband, sometimes Gina wishes he wasn't quite so straitlaced. Then she discovers that there is a way of breathing a little spice into their love life. Like telling him stories of what she used to get up to in her uninhibited past. The result is the Journal – the diary of sexual self-analysis that Hugo writes and which Gina reads. When she tells her best friend Samantha what it contains, the journey of sensual exploration really begins . . .

0 7472 5092 8

Adult Fiction for Lovers from Headline LIAISON

SLEEPLESS NIGHTS	Tom Crewe & Amber Wells	£4.99
THE JOURNAL	James Allen	£4.99
THE PARADISE GARDEN	Aurelia Clifford	£4.99
APHRODISIA	Rebecca Ambrose	£4.99
DANGEROUS DESIRES	J. J. Duke	£4.99
PRIVATE LESSONS	Cheryl Mildenhall	£4.99
LOVE LETTERS	James Allen	£4.99

All Headline Liaison books are available at your local bookshop or newsagent, or can be ordered direct from the publisher. Just tick the titles you want and fill in the form below. Prices and availability subject to change without notice.

Headline Book Publishing, Cash Sales Department, Bookpoint, 39 Milton Park, Abingdon, OXON, OX14 4TD, UK. If you have a credit card you may order by telephone – 01235 400400.

Please enclose a cheque or postal order made payable to Bookpoint Ltd to the value of the cover price and allow the following for postage and packing: UK & BFPO: £1.00 for the first book, 50p for the second book and 30p for each additional book ordered up to a maximum charge of £3.00.
OVERSEAS & EIRE: £2.00 for the first book, £1.00 for the second book and 50p for each additional book.

Name ....

Address ....

....

....

If you would prefer to pay by credit card, please complete:
Please debit my Visa/Access/Diner's Card/American Express (Delete as applicable) card no:

Signature .... Expiry Date ....